NIGHT OF
THE AVENGING
BLOWFISH

Also by John Welter

Begin to Exit Here: A Novel of the Wayward Press

JOHN WELTER

NIGHT

OF THE

AVENGING

BLOWFISH

A NOVEL OF COVERT OPERATIONS,
LOVE, AND LUNCHEON MEAT

1994
ALGONQUIN BOOKS OF CHAPEL HILL

Published by
ALGONQUIN BOOKS OF CHAPEL HILL
Post Office Box 2225
Chapel Hill, North Carolina 27515-2225

a division of
WORKMAN PUBLISHING COMPANY, INC.
708 Broadway
New York, New York 10003

LIBRARY OF CONGRESS CATALOGING-IN-PUBLICATION DATA
Welter, John, 1951–
    Night of the Avenging Blowfish : A Novel of the Secret
Service / John Welter.
        p.   cm.
    ISBN 1–56512-050-7
    1. Secret Service—United States—Fiction. 2. Man–
Woman Relationships—United States—Fiction. I. Title.
PS3573.E4963N5   1994
813'.54—dc20   93–42846
                                                        CIP

10 9 8 7 6 5 4 3 2 1
First Edition

*To some woman
I haven't met yet*

NIGHT OF
THE AVENGING
BLOWFISH

1

You wouldn't know, by looking at us in our sunglasses, our somber dark suits, and carrying our concealed pistols and compact machine guns —meant to rapidly and coarsely dismantle the flesh of anyone threatening the life of the president—that we were sitting in the privileged sanctum of the White House planning a clandestine baseball game. We weren't supposed to be planning one. Agent-in-Charge Doltmeer was opposed to it, but that only meant we wouldn't let him play.

Without explanation, which frequently was how our lives progressed, someone put this flyer on the bulletin board at work:

First Annual Baseball Game
between
the CIA and the Secret Service.

Date: July 14
Time: Classified
Location: Classified

It was decided by senior members of the Service and
the CIA that the rivalry between the two agencies
could be furthered and settled in an annual baseball
game.

It has been agreed that the game should be played
covertly. The game will be played at night, without
lights, to avoid letting the opposing team know where
the game is.

Clues will be provided, to allow team members to
locate the playing field and the game time. If only one
team shows up, it wins. The winning team will be
given a spookball trophy.

Sign up now, if you can find the sign-up sheet.

It seemed juvenile and a little stupid, so most of us liked it
immediately. A few of the agents regarded it as nothing more
than an excessively ludicrous joke, which maybe it was, but
those of us who still had spontaneous glee in our hearts for
no sensible reason badly wanted to play that game.

Anyone at all could have printed the flyer, meaning its
authenticity was thoroughly unknown, but that was precisely
the nature of what we and the CIA were all about: confronting
the unknown. And, in some cases, inventing the unknown.

Doltmeer didn't think any of it was funny.

"Who put this crap up here?" he asked, as he looked at the
flyer.

"I'll start an investigation immediately. Plus we'll need
some uniforms and gloves," I said.

Doltmeer looked annoyed, but he usually looked annoyed,
so I couldn't tell if he was annoyed by me or by the ordinary

course of his life. He took the flyer from the bulletin board and folded it up, as if that would prevent us from remembering what it said.

"I'm not going to have my agents screwing around wasting time looking for a phantom baseball game," he said.

"We won't. We'll look for a real one," Widdiker said.

"What should we call our team?" Pascal asked.

"Jesus Christ," Doltmeer said wearily.

"That's not a good name for a team," Widdiker said.

"There's not going to be a team," Doltmeer said, with authority we didn't care about.

"Where's the sign-up sheet?" someone asked.

"We'll make our own."

"Isn't that cheating?"

"I think that's how you're supposed to play this game," Widdiker said.

"How can you see a ball at night without lights?" Pascal wondered.

"We could use phosphorus grenades," someone suggested.

"I think it would delay the game too much if you killed everyone in the infield."

"We'll need team jerseys," DeMarco said. "Should we have our names printed on them?"

"Of course not. We don't want the CIA to know who we are. We'll have *fictitious* names printed on our jerseys," Widdiker said. "They could be, like, the names of famous characters from books, like Tom Huck and Finn Sawyer."

"Good idea."

"Excellent."

"Goddamn it. This is an asinine waste of time," Doltmeer said.

"To you, perhaps. But to the rest of us it's a splendid waste of time," Widdiker said.

He seemed to be right. We could either waste our time huddled around the president, guarding him against the various assassins who routinely weren't there, or we could waste our time preparing for a baseball game that might not exist. There was no reason to choose one over the other. We could waste our time doing both.

2

Ideally, our highest professional and moral obligation was to concentrate solely on preventing assassins from killing the president or someone. Those were the two categories of people whose lives we were assigned to watch out for: A) the president; or B) someone. But most of the time no one had any interest in killing the president. Or someone. Hardly a day went by that dozens of people in all nations of the world secretly made no plans to kill the president. Uncounted millions of dollars were spent each year on the most lavish and extensive measures to guard the president from the myriad threats that weren't being made. So I think we had time for a baseball game.

Nine agents showed up Saturday for the covert spookball practice at an abandoned pasture in Maryland. The pasture wasn't abandoned at first. A farmer was there. We were wearing our new baseball jerseys and we told the farmer we were with the Secret Service.

"Why should I believe you?" the farmer said with polite suspicion.

"Offhand, there's no reason at all to believe us. But here's my U.S. Treasury ID," I said, showing him the ID in my wallet.

"Do you want to see one of our machine guns?" Yamato asked, like a boy willing to show someone his new bike.

"No," the farmer said.

"We'd just like to practice some baseball for a couple of hours, and this looks like a good field," Widdiker said.

"I didn't know the Secret Service played baseball," the farmer said.

"We do it all," Pascal said. "Protect the president and drive in runs."

We rented the pasture for twenty dollars. The farmer drove off on his tractor, thinking he now had something to do with national security.

We picked the remote pasture to prevent the CIA from finding us, although there was no reason to believe the CIA was looking for us. It still hadn't been proven that a baseball game was scheduled for July 14th, Bastille Day, but no one cared. It was strangely exhilarating to prepare for a game that might not be played. It was like religion. In both cases— religion and the spookball game—people were exuberant about the fantastic approach of something that might not be approaching. In religion, people awaited the afterlife. In spookball, we awaited the joy of being hit in the head by a baseball in the dark. So if it didn't happen, we faced less disappointment.

DeMarco, Oxler, and Yamato brought lawnmowers to get rid of the weeds and grass and small trees so we could practice. Everyone had guns. It was the only baseball team I knew of that could prevent or carry out assassinations. All of us had gone to sporting-goods stores or specialty shops to buy jerseys, none of which matched, and all of which had fictional names silk-screened on them. Widdiker's jersey had "Beowulf" on it.

"Who the fuck is Bee-o-wolf?" Deek asked.

"It's Bay-o-wolf, asshole," Widdiker said. "You guys don't know anything about world literature, do you? Beowulf was an eighth-century baseball player."

Deek's jersey said "Cervantes."

"Cervantes isn't a fictional name, dickhead," Pascal said. "Cervantes was a real person." And everyone began laughing at Deek.

"But the CIA probably hasn't heard of Cervantes, so that's all right, Deek," I said. "Besides, Cervantes is a wonderful name for a spookball player. Cervantes is famous for writing about people who looked for things that didn't exist."

On Pascal's jersey was the name "Bovary."

"Madame Bovary?" DeMarco said. "You're a woman?"

"Show 'im your dick," Widdiker advised.

"I don't want to see his dick," said DeMarco, on whose jersey was the name "Smerdyakov."

This puzzled everyone.

"Who the fuck is that?" Yamato wondered.

"Is it one of the Smurfs?" Oxler asked.

"Smerdyakov is some character from *The Brothers Karamazov*. But I don't know which character. I didn't read that book," DeMarco said.

"It's good to have Russian names. The CIA'll think we have players from the KGB," Widdiker said.

Oxler's jersey said "Caulfield," which he said came from a book by J. D. Salinger.

"Okay. You'll be the catcher, then," Horner said.

The name on Horner's jersey was a long one: "Miss Ophelia St. Clare." And, of course, we were mystified by it.

Pleased that we didn't know who it was, Horner said, "That's some old woman in *Uncle Tom's Cabin*."

"Now we've got two women on the team: Madame Bovary and Miss Ophelia St. Clare," Widdiker complained.

"What's wrong with having women on the team?" Horner said threateningly, as if, having taken a woman's name, he was now going to defend all women everywhere.

"We've got *three* women on the team," Yamato said happily, turning around so everyone could read the name on his jersey: "Dilsey."

"Who's Dilsey?" Widdiker asked.

"She's the Negro cook in William Faulkner's novel, *The Sound and the Fury*," Yamato said.

It was Jessup's turn to show off his silk-screened name: "Earwicker."

"And who, may I ask, the fuck is Earwicker?" Pascal said.

"I don't think you have to know," Jessup said haughtily. "This is a covert game."

"Oh come on. Who is it?"

"I'm not saying."

"We won't let you play if you don't tell us who you are," Oxler warned.

"All right. Earwicker is a character in *Finnegan's Wake*." This didn't help.

"What's Finnegan's wake?"

"It's a wake they held for Finnegan."

"Jesus Christ, you guys are ignorant."

"*Finnegan's Wake* is this extremely long and difficult novel that practically no one understands. It's one of the most famous books in history that no one reads," Yamato said.

"So," Widdiker said, "you're named after a character that no one's heard of in a book no one reads. Impressive."

And then everybody looked at me to see what bizarre or obscure name I'd chosen for my jersey. I turned around to let them read my back.

"K?" several of them asked, with simultaneous puzzlement.

"I wanted a name that was easy to spell," I said.

"But K's not a name, goddamn it," DeMarco said.

"Yes, it is. K is the name of the main character in *The Trial*, by Franz Kafka," I said.

It seemed like everybody was pretty satisfied with our fictional names, and we began our practice by drinking cold beer. Widdiker, who arbitrarily decided he was the player-manager, tried to impose order and discipline.

"Okay. Everybody do wind sprints for five minutes," he said.

"Fuck you."

"Eat me."

Modifying his plans, Widdiker began drawing up roster assignments, which he wrote on a clipboard for everyone to look at:

Catcher: Caulfield.
Pitcher: Beowulf.
1st base: K.
2nd base: Madame Bovary.
Shortstop: Smerdyakov.
3rd base: Miss Ophelia St. Clare.
4th base . . .

He did that just for fun, then he crossed 4th base out.

Right field: Earwicker.
Center field: Dilsey.
Left field: Cervantes.

Now that the roster was set and everyone had had at least one beer, it was necessary to look at the playing field, and we realized no one had brought any chalk to mark the base paths. And there were no bases.

"Are we playing baseless ball?" Yamato asked.

"Gentlemen, this is spookball," Widdiker said. "We don't necessarily need base paths or bases. That way, when an opposing batter hits the ball, he won't know where to run."

"And we won't know where we're supposed to be on the field either, dumbshit," Oxler said.

Yamato and Horner and I went looking for rocks and things to use for the bases and the pitcher's plate. In the woods near a rutted dirt road, we found a discarded General Electric oven.

"Somebody help us carry this oven to first base!" I yelled. From back on the playing field we heard people saying "What?" and "Kiss my ass."

A little while later, Yamato yelled happily, "Look! Here's a sixty-foot cedar tree we can use for second base!"

"Will you guys quit screwing around?" someone yelled.

Next to a dried-up stream, Horner spotted something.

"Would it be okay if we used this dead raccoon for third base?" he asked. "No. Wait. I'm the third baseman. Never mind."

For several minutes we searched the woods, finding nothing that looked like bases or pitcher's plates.

"It makes you wonder how the prehistoric Indians played baseball," I said.

Tired of looking for stuff, we began grabbing whatever was nearby and walked back to the playing field with some substantial pieces of rotting trees.

"Those are our bases?" Widdiker said with contempt.

"Bases don't occur in nature. This is rotten wood," Yamato

said, smiling as he and Horner and I positioned the wood in the approximate locations of the bases and the pitcher's plate.

"There," I said with satisfaction. "Is that stupid enough for everyone? Good."

With the field ready, everyone got another bottle of beer. Then we put our gloves on and walked out to our positions, almost as if by instinct or genetic predisposition—just naturally walked out into the field to precise, imaginary spots, making each of us feel remarkably peculiar for doing so after we got there. We were quiet and reflective, meditatively drinking our beer amid the generous sprawl of nature.

"Hey! I found a dinosaur bone!" Deek yelled from left field.

"Shut up," Widdiker instructed him from the pitcher's mound.

"What kind of dinosaur?" I yelled.

"Well, I'm not a philanthropist. I don't know."

"You mean a paleontologist."

"I'm not one of those, either."

"Shut up."

We remained standing at our positions in the field, sipping our beers bucolically and looking at each other expectantly. Widdiker held the ball at the pitcher's plate, staring at Oxler, the catcher. It seemed likely that everyone was sharing a group insight—an important realization that grew and matured in the silence. I wondered who was going to say it first.

"Hey Beowulf," Horner called out from third base.

"Yes, Miss Ophelia?" Widdiker said.

"We don't have a batter."

"Thank you, Miss Ophelia."

No one else spoke; we remained at our positions, wiping

sweat from our faces and drinking beer as we looked at each other wonderingly.

"How're we gonna practice without a batter?" Cervantes asked, and not as if he expected an answer.

"This is Zen baseball. We envision the batter," Dilsey said in center field.

"Envision my ass," Earwicker said.

"Envision my dick," Dilsey said.

"Hey. This is supposed to be a family game. Genitals aren't allowed."

"We could play Hindu baseball, and say we had a batter in one of our former lives," Madame Bovary said at second base.

"Time out," I called. "I think we need a conference on the pitcher's mound. And remember to scratch your crotch. Everyone, scratch your balls, except for Miss Ophelia and Madame Bovary and Dilsey."

We huddled around Widdiker at the pitcher's mound, which actually was a slight depression, since the field wasn't level.

"If this was a real game, someone would spit," Jessup said.

Deek spat. Then Horner and Pascal spat.

"Quit it," Widdiker said.

DeMarco burped.

"Now someone should fart," Oxler said. "Who's the designated farter?"

"We don't do that in this league."

"I hafta piss," Deek said.

"Not on the pitcher's mound," Widdiker objected.

"This isn't a mound. This is a depression."

"Well, I didn't design the goddamn field now, did I?"

"Why'd you call time out, Doyle?" Pascal asked.

"I think we need a batter. I'll be the batter," I said.

"Then who'll cover first base?"

"I'll cover first base *and* be the batter," I said. "If I get a hit, I'll run to first base and tag myself out. Then I get to be the batter again."

"That's cheating," Pascal said.

"I think we agreed at the start that cheating was going to be our basic approach," Widdiker said. "The rule is: anyone who isn't caught cheating will be ejected from the game."

WHEN THE practice was over and a few of us went to the Nevermore Bar & Grill in our new baseball jerseys, hoping that women we'd never met before would be attracted to men wearing shirts that said Beowulf and Dilsey and Miss Ophelia St. Clare and K, one woman at the bar asked us what team we played for.

"Ours," Yamato said.

"Well, does your team have a name?" the woman asked.

"Not that we're aware of," I said.

"We're an expansion team," Horner said. "The front office hasn't given us a name yet."

"Do you play with a recreational league?" another woman asked.

"We haven't found our league yet. We're still looking for it," Widdiker said, which I think was the final disquieting remark that drove the two women away, right as Lou Benador of the CIA saw us at the bar and, with a suspicious smile, walked up to us and stared at our jerseys.

"Where'd you get those?" Benador asked.

"The store, Lou. They sell them in sporting goods," Widdiker said, because we had no intention of telling him anything that mattered.

"Who the fuck," Benador said as he turned to look at the back of Horner's jersey, "is Miss Ophelia St. Clare?"

"You guys in the CIA don't know shit," Yamato said.

"How can you call yourself an intelligence organization if you've never heard of Miss Ophelia St. Clare?" Horner asked incredulously, although now that he'd had four or five beers, Horner probably didn't remember who Miss Ophelia St. Clare was, either.

"Is this for the spookball game?" Benador asked.

"Pardon me? I don't know what the fuck you're talking about," Widdiker said.

Horner whispered in my ear, "Who's Miss Ophelia St. Clare? I forget."

"Are you guys taking this seriously?" Benador said, squinting at us with disbelief. "Have you already formed a *team*?"

"These are our bowling shirts," Yamato said.

"How come you have grass stains on a bowling shirt?" Benador said, looking at Yamato's jersey.

"We bowl outdoors," I said.

"What makes you think there's even going to be a spookball game? That's just bullshit. No one believes it," Benador said.

"We'll kick your ass," Horner said.

"So you really formed a team?" Benador persisted.

"Bowling," Yamato said.

"Don't play dumb with me," Benador said.

"He's not. He really is dumb," Widdiker said, staring at Benador. "So have you guys formed a team?"

"No. But our jerseys are better than yours," Benador said.

"I doubt it. You assholes in the CIA can't even spell," I said. "That's why you abbreviate the name CIA."

"Where do you guys practice?" Benador said.

"North America," Widdiker said. "Come by and watch us sometime."

"It's useless talking to you guys," Benador said.

"Well, we're always willing to be of no help to you," Yamato said.

"See you at the game," Benador said.

"No you won't. We're not going to tell you where it is," I said, although it was equally possible that we wouldn't be able to locate the game either. As Yamato said later in the evening, under the mystical effects of alcohol, "It's not whether you win or lose. It's whether you find the game."

"Who said that? Ralph Waldo Emerson?" Widdiker asked.

"Why?" Horner said. "Is Emerson on our team?"

"He's dead," Yamato said.

"We'll have to put him on the injured-reserve list," I said. It occurred to me, and not with any understandable reason, that even if we didn't find the game, it was going to be played anyway—an insight that was either Zen or Michelob Dry.

3

Americans liked to believe
that the White House was a center of power and wisdom,
but I favored the idea that the White House was like Disneyland with machine guns. Like Disneyland, the White House
had its famous and fabled characters, instantly recognizable,
known primarily for a few exaggerated qualities, who came
into and out of the public's lives in thoroughly controlled rit-
uals. Just as people went on pilgrimages to Disneyland to see
Mickey Mouse and Goofy, they came to the White House to
see the president or other stray eminences. There was no
Goofy at the White House, but you could soundly argue that
the public always elected one, and he went by a different
name. The White House didn't have any rides, unless you
figured that since the president controlled intercontinental
ballistic missiles with multiple nuclear warheads that could

transform hundreds of foreign cities into gigantic clouds of radioactive dust, it was sort of the world's scariest ride that no one had taken yet.

Disneyland didn't have machine guns, but we did, which was one of the strangest things I never got over—how we were required to be groomed immaculately, with short hair precisely combed, wearing neatly tailored suits and neckties so we'd project a handsome, civilized presence during our protection assignments as we looked warily through every gleeful and obsequious crowd, ready in an instant to shoot someone to death with complete civility and grace. I thought that, if this ever happened, if at an elegant state dinner amid all the stray eminences someone's life was threatened and I had to shoot someone, I'd stand over the body and say, "Excuse me."

I tried one time—I think when I was at a bar with Widdiker and Yamato—inventing lines I'd say to someone I'd just shot during an assassination attempt, and what I thought of was, "I hope your death isn't an inconvenience to you."

This was at the Nevermore Bar & Grill, which seemed to have gotten its name from a poem by Edgar Allan Poe that we hadn't read, although we sometimes enjoyed sitting around at the bar getting slightly drunk and trying to show off our erudition to strangers by saying we could quote Edgar Allan Poe by heart. And if someone asked us to do so, one of us would stand up, pause significantly, and say: "Nevermore."

It seemed appropriate for Secret Service agents to hang out at a bar associated with Poe, because Poe was grim and morbid, and so was the Service, to which all of life was an imminent death. This put us in the same brooding category as soldiers, police officers, and medical examiners. The only reason we existed was that we expected the worst. We were always trying to think up new mottoes for the Service, such as "When in doubt, pull the trigger." Yamato said the Secret Service motto should be something concise and lyrical: "Aim for the head."

"Shooting someone in the head isn't lyrical," I told him.

"But it's concise," he said, smiling that night toward three young women nearby, none of which he was likely to meet and fall in love with. We were expected to be very careful about who we met and who even knew we existed, since it was our obligation to remain as secret and anonymous and unknown as possible, never telling anyone who we worked for, except to describe our employer as "the government," which almost always caused people to assume we worked for the CIA or the Secret Service. At this point, if any of us had talked with anyone long enough to mysteriously announce that we worked for the government, they'd say, "You mean you're spies?" To which we frequently responded by saying, "Yes, but we're not supposed to tell anyone." One night, a woman who assumed Widdiker and I were spies said, "Do you work for our government?" And I said, "I don't know. Which government is yours?"

It was a bad thing, going into a bar after work, wanting to meet some woman you couldn't really talk with because, if she wanted to get to know you, you had to make sure she didn't. Although usually I never met any women anyway. It's not as if every time we went to the Nevermore there was a handy supply of unmarried women eager to meet whatever strange man entered their field of vision. Usually, nobody met anybody, and being alone in the world awhile longer was still painfully certain. Most of the agents were married, so they didn't hang out with us in bars (which was somewhat discouraged anyway, since drunk or hungover agents were professional liabilities). Still, bars were where Yamato and Widdiker and I often gathered to drink immoderately and look with wonder at all the women we'd probably never know. Even if you did finally meet a woman—and I think that was partly why I existed, to finally meet a woman—there was very little you could tell her. One night I met an agonizingly cute woman named Marcia, who sat next to me at the bar, periodically bumping her knee against my thigh, either because she was attracted to me or because she had bad coordination. She told me freely about herself, that she was a Senate staffer, and described the legislation that she was working on. Then she asked what I did.

"Things," I said.

"Things?" she asked. "Could you be more specific?"

"Yes. I do things and stuff."

"And for whom do you do things and stuff, or is that too personal?"

"It couldn't be personal. I work for the government."

"Which branch?"

"It's not a branch. It's more like a concealed root."

"You're being awfully secretive. Are you a spook?" she asked, looking a little bit amused and uncertain.

"No. I'm real. Touch me."

She laughed, and put her fingers on my wrist, saying, "I don't doubt that you're real. I just want to know who you work for. Is it the CIA or the NSC? Am I getting warm?"

I put my hand on her forehead and said, "You're a little warm, but it seems normal."

"Are you with the Secret Service?"

"No. I'm with you."

"I'll bet I've seen you on the TV news before, standing behind the president with your sunglasses on. Why do Secret Service agents always wear sunglasses?"

"I think they like Ray Charles."

"Do you protect the president when he sleeps?"

"I've never slept with the president. I think his wife does that."

"Wow. You really aren't going to tell me anything about your job, are you?"

"I'd like to, but I'm not supposed to."

"You mean you can't even say who you work for?"

"Oh, I can say that. I work for the government."

"Well, maybe I'd like to get to know you, Doyle, but how am I supposed to do that if you won't tell me anything about yourself?" she said with exasperation.

"It puzzles the hell out of me, too."

"Are you married?"

"No."

"Do you have a girlfriend?"

"No."

"Well, who do you talk to at the end of the day?"

"I'm allowed to talk to myself, as long as I don't reveal very much."

"You must be lonely," she said, putting her hand briefly on my shoulder.

"My employer doesn't restrict that. We can be as lonely as we want to be. It gives us something to do when there's no one else around."

ACTUALLY, Agent-in-Charge Doltmeer approved of male agents being married, since he believed men were more emotionally stable when they had a woman to share their lives with. But he also preferred us to be single, so we wouldn't be distracted by marital problems. I got the impression from Doltmeer that the best male agents (and the majority of us, by far, were male) were men with wives and children to live for, while the equally ideal agent was an unmarried man who couldn't be interfered with by a woman. And I thought of Natelle, the one woman in the world I always wished would interfere with me. Sometimes in a meeting when we were being briefed on the most critical details of protecting the president or some visiting benign tyrant friendly to the United States, Natelle spontaneously came into my mind, as if she'd always been there and always would be. Natelle was a fundamental truth to me, like air. She was the one person I loved more than I could recall love ever involving before. And when I thought of death, or the afterlife, I didn't imagine rushing joyously toward the embrace of God, but toward Natelle—who might be available in the afterlife, but not now. She was married. And one day, when my emotions were ready for something that my reason didn't know anything about, I fell in love with her. That was a violation of a commandment, the one saying thou shalt not covet thy neighbor's wife. But Natelle wasn't married to my neighbor. She lived across town. Perhaps there should have been a commandment saying thou shalt not covet someone's wife even if she lives across town. But I didn't really covet her. I secretly, wistfully, loved her, which maybe was the same thing as coveting, but it sounded better.

And of course I never told her. It was hard to be in love with a woman and not tell her, but it seemed like a kindness I owed her. Maybe it was because I had morals. Possibly I was born with those morals, because I didn't remember adopting them. There were times when I wanted Natelle, and I couldn't tell her, and I felt so moral that all I could do was crumple in my heart and cry. That was my secret life. Everyone had a secret life. Everyone waited to find the one person they could tell it to. I found her. I just wasn't supposed to tell her so.

Psychiatrists call that neurosis. Most people call it love. Both sides are probably right.

One day at the end of work as Yamato and Widdiker and I were getting ready to go out drinking, Doltmeer told us we should try to meet some nice women, as long as we didn't talk with them. No one understood Doltmeer, and we didn't particularly try. What he asked of his agents was that they give the Service 110 percent, the same kind of routinely stupid exhortation that coaches gave their athletes. Whenever he did this in a meeting—asked everyone again to give 110 percent—someone would always say, "I think 109 percent's enough," or someone might say, "I'm a little tired today. I'm only giving 102 percent."

Of course there were people like Sandlin and Ardink and Yegg, utterly somber and obedient career agents who would never annoy or contradict Doltmeer and who regarded people like me with pious distaste. Ardink in particular was proud of giving 110 percent and tried to politely scold any of us who wouldn't. He said, after one meeting where some of us had pissed off Doltmeer again, that, at least for the morale of everyone, if for no other reason, we should shut up and stop taunting everyone who was willing to give 110 percent.

I said, "Ardink. Do you know how much 110 percent is? It's 10 percent more than exists."

"I'm not stupid," he said.

"Oh, don't be modest," Widdiker said.

"If you guys don't like the Service, why don't you just quit?" Ardink suggested.

"If we quit, you might have to give 120 percent," Oxler said. "You'd go into a meeting one day, and Doltmeer'd say he needs everyone to give 160 percent. And then you'd die."

"You guys aren't nearly as amusing as you think you are,"

Ardink said. "If you can't show a simple sense of profession-alism, why don't you consider resigning?"

"Resign? This is the only job in the world where you can dress up like you're going to church and carry a machine gun. It's too neat to resign," Yamato said.

"I can't stand here jabbering. I've got to go now and give 101 percent," I said.

We didn't invite Ardink or any of the bothersomely seri-ous guys to join our covert spookball team, partly because they didn't want to join it and partly because we thought they were pricks. Which was also what they thought we were. A troubling fact I figured out years earlier when I was in my twenties was that for every five people you could name as pricks, they could also name at least five, one of whom was probably you. So I thought that, at least once in their lives, and probably a lot more than that, everyone in the world was a prick, or they'd at least been called one.

4

Yamato frequently didn't want to protect the president because he hadn't voted for him. Naturally, we'd all been meticulously screened for loyalty and psychological suitability for the Service, with great emphasis on our supposed moral character and sanity, although I was never convinced it was provably sane to have a job where you carried pistols and machine guns and were willing to shoot any human in the world to protect a politician you didn't vote for and maybe didn't even like.

Usually, when I was assigned with Yamato to protect the president from the various crowds that invariably had no interest in killing the president, Yamato would say to me privately, "I'm not going to protect him. He's a Democrat."

This didn't matter. Of the approximately 260,000,000 people who lived in the United States, not including the fifteen or twenty million people the U.S. Census Bureau didn't count because they didn't feel like it and said so, almost nobody wanted to kill the president. Possibly a few thousand people at any given time wanted to slug the president, maybe even knock the wind out of him. But these weren't enemies of the state. These were voters. If the Secret Service had an accurate list of all the Americans who ever said threatening things about the president, we'd have needed a new federal prison just to hold them for questioning, and some of the people being questioned would be senators, representatives, and members of the White House staff. A president might be beloved by many, but he's endured by the rest.

Including Yamato, who always seemed willing to turn the other cheek and let someone slug the president just once.

"I've been practicing my timing," Yamato said to me quietly as we stood in our vigilant poses at the edge of a grandstand where the president was making a few tedious and self-serving remarks at a lower-income housing project in Houston, Texas. We looked in the crowd for assassins. Assassins were allowed to look like anybody, so, unfortunately, the Secret Service had often relied on a proven method of identifying assassins:

Boom! Boom!

Aha!

I glanced at Yamato and asked, "What timing?"

"If someone lunges at the president," he said.

"You mean your timing to stop them?"

"No. I mean my timing to valiantly get there after they've hit him at least once."

Yamato almost always had a kind and cheerful expression, as if he possessed some inscrutable spiritual tranquility that would make him do whatever seemed best for anyone, but this could easily have been a genetic disguise, a deceiving accident of the way facial features appear on people regardless of their real emotions and desires. Despite Yamato's soothing countenance, he could be just as moody and sullen and hostile as any normal person, so it was always a little astonishing and funny to look at his kind and cheerful face as he said, "I wouldn't mind it if someone hit the president with a board."

I wanted, for sentimental and probably irrational reasons, to think that the people hired by the Service represented the full mix of cultures and nationalities that made America as expansive as it was, but it hired mostly white men. How Yamato, who was Japanese, got in, I didn't know. He told me his father owned a carpentry shop in California and was an American citizen before Pearl Harbor was bombed. Not long after that, Yamato's mother and father were put in one of the prison camps for Japanese that we weren't taught about in school because the revisionists who wrote American textbooks wanted all American children to believe that America was incapable of the kinds of crimes that the textbooks routinely reported in other nations.

"Imagine me, growing up in America in the 1950s, when all the white kids I went to school with assumed my father bombed Pearl Harbor," Yamato told me once.

"Just one guy bombed Pearl Harbor? I thought it was more than that," I said.

"And then when I told them that my parents were put in a prison camp in California by the American government, they called me a liar and tried to start fights with me. They said I couldn't be American because I was Japanese."

"Ignorant buttholes. Do you remember any of their names? We can look them up in the computer and have them killed."

"I've thought of that. But two wrongs don't make a right."

"Well how many wrongs *do* make a right? We need to find out."

That same night, while Yamato and I were drinking beer at Nevermore, I asked him how he got his first name.

"The story I've been told, which seems reasonably true, or at least somewhat believable, is that my father, after he got out of prison and somehow wasn't very bitter, wanted his first child to have an American name, or something that sounded American. He was always watching movies on TV and he saw some gangster movie one night where the main American gangster was named Dutch, so he named me Dutch Yamato. Of course it backfired. In school, people not only accused my father of bombing Pearl Harbor, they said a Japanese boy couldn't be named Dutch. At first I hated my name."

"Dutch?" I asked.

"No. Yamato. Anything that sounded Japanese was always associated with World War II. And so my peers, these naive schoolchildren, these young, innocent bastards, were actually teaching me to despise my own heritage, as if anything that was Japanese was innately evil. I think when I was six or seven I asked my mother which one of our Japanese ancestors was named Dutch. I said I wanted the rest of his name, too, so I wouldn't have a Japanese name and people wouldn't hurt me anymore. I imagined that one of my grandfathers in Japan was named Dutch O'Flannery or something, but of course I knew this was stupid, and what I was, was this strange boy who was part Japanese, by blood, and part American, by citizenship. I gradually began to figure out from what we were taught in history class that, goddamn it, even the people who called themselves Americans weren't really American, because mostly it was a bunch of organized thugs from Spain and England and France who came over here on ships and basically stole the country from Indians. And then I began to wonder, which was worse? Bombing Pearl Harbor, or stealing the whole country from Indians?"

"Well, Dutch, as an American citizen, you're not supposed to say we stole this country. Didn't you learn in school that, in American history, stealing is a synonym for discovery? That's why the Indians were always saying 'Help! Help! I'm being discovered!' This made us realize that once the Europeans began settling North America, the leading cause of death among Indians was discovery. They were almost annihilated by discovery. And then we named some baseball teams after them."

"And where's the justice, then?" Yamato asked.

"It's in the movies, Dutch, where you got your name."

As Yamato and I, on our side of the grandstand, watched for assassins while the president droned on to the poor people in the crowd about self-reliance and self-esteem, hurling enough platitudes at them to encourage self-delusion, a man in a black suit and a yellow necktie pushed his way through the crowd nearest us and approached the side of the grandstand, waving a black Bible at us. I tensed, ready to knock him on his ass, having no idea if he was a danger but assuming he was. I stared at him malevolently, the way a hawk stares at a bunny.

"Do you know Jesus?" the man asked, either to the president or to me or to no one in particular, as I walked toward him so he couldn't advance.

"Get out of here," I said, watching his hands, looking for a weapon, as three cops behind him moved quickly along the edge of the crowd to come get the man. I pushed him back with my hand, not even trying to be polite, but just wanting the son of a bitch to leave.

"Do you know Jesus?" he asked again, as if I simply must answer the question.

"You can't come up here. Get back," I said, steadily pushing him backward even though he was a lot bigger than me.

"The Lord's coming," he said.

"He can't come up here, either," I said, pushing the man back into the arms of two of the cops.

I felt a little bad about that later, being so rude to an ordinary zealot. But it was true. Without the proper clearance, we wouldn't even allow the Lord to approach the president. There were rules.

5

Flies were in the White House most of the day Tuesday, landing on everyone without regard to rank or social standing. When they weren't landing on famous paintings or eminent guests, they rested upside down on the historic ceilings, or flitted, buzzed, and careened with reckless impunity through confidential meetings, because flies just don't care.

Chief of Staff Gardenaul called the flies a breach of security.

"Where'd all these goddamn flies come from?" he asked me peevishly in one of the hallways.

"Outside."

The idea that I could piss off the chief of staff never particularly worried me, since I worked for the Treasury and wasn't a member of his staff. He couldn't fire me. Certainly he could *recommend* that I be fired, but not just because I announced that the most likely origin of flies was outside. Gardenaul flung his hands upward in the direction of some flies zigzagging nearby and said, "Well, what's the goddamn Secret Service doing about it?"

"I don't think we're responsible for flies. That might be the General Services Administration," I said, as we both seemed to be looking at flies here and there. People in the hallway seemed amused as they swatted their hands at passing flies, not as if there was a plague of flies, but just enough of them to be conspicuous.

"So you're not going to do anything?" Gardenaul said in a slightly accusing tone.

"I don't think the president's being endangered by flies."

"Are you taunting me?"

"I'm not authorized to taunt you."

"Get out of my way," he said, although I wasn't in his way, and he walked angrily down the hall on an imperious mission to find some subordinates to browbeat about the flies.

"Eat me," I said quietly, wondering how many days I'd spend in jail if I kicked Gardenaul in the back of his head. I wouldn't really do that. The front of his head, maybe.

As I stood idly in the hallway, looking at a fly crawl across the face of my wristwatch, a sudden and incomprehensible sense of panic seemed to surge through my entire body, tingling in my head and washing instantly across my skin in a cold sweat. I felt suddenly lonesome and lost, which had happened before in recent months, as if all of my normal sensibilities and emotions instantly vanished and were replaced by some horrifying tangle of repressed, lethal sadness, leaving me with the sense that all my life I'd been lost, and I had no idea where I was supposed to be, or whose face I needed to look at and ask to hold me, because there was supposed to be someone, and there wasn't. I felt this way now, that somehow I was living the wrong life, and that the sequence of all the ordinary hundreds or thousands of decisions I'd made to get me here in life was a horrifying mistake, and that whoever I desperately needed to hold—as if there were such a person—was nowhere in the world, and I had just now realized it.

My vision blurred a little bit. Things went out of focus and I was dizzy, as if this sadness I couldn't explain or stop was damaging my eyes. Then I realized that things were blurry because I'd started to cry, just standing there staring at a fly on my watch, because I had no idea why I was supposed to be anywhere in the world. It felt like some secret part of my mind was telling me the only truth that mattered, that all my life had been taking me nowhere, and now I was finally there. And the only one to greet me nowhere was me.

I breathed in deeply to quit crying, to try shaking off the panic that still trembled through me, knowing someone might see me and think I was mentally ill, which maybe I was. I was looking at the fly on my watch while down the hall I heard Widdiker saying, "Raid kills bugs dead." He was talking to Gardenaul, which I didn't care about, because I was so thoroughly sad and in a panic, suddenly wanting to live my life well and find whoever in the world was supposed to want me, with no proof that such a person existed. I thought of Natelle, but she was married. I tried to stand up straight, and casually, so, if anyone looked at me in the hallway standing oddly alone, they wouldn't think there was something wrong with me, which there was. It wouldn't go away. I felt exhausted and frighteningly alone, this being only the truth, the way in an instant of insanity you at last see something true.

I couldn't decide if I should step left or step right, or step anywhere at all. To step from nowhere to somewhere required a reason I didn't have. It seemed like I should go down the hallway to Natelle's office, although Natelle didn't know this was happening to me. How do you suddenly tell that to someone, even Natelle? *I think I'm having a nervous breakdown. I've had these before, but I politely kept them to myself, so that my horror was graciously kept private. Or maybe it's not a nervous breakdown since I don't know what that is. Maybe I've just lived my life wrong all these years and I feel utterly, hopelessly lost and I've learned to repress all that every instant of my life. But sometimes it won't be repressed anymore and it breaks free and swarms all through me and I'm reminded in an intense and cruel panic that I'm alone and I'm the only one who knows it. I'd like to hold somebody without having to ask permission. And I remember that there is nobody to hold. And no wonder I hurt so much. No wonder I should go crazy at last, knowing then that the only time someone will hold me is if they come to carry me away.* How do you say that?

I stared at the fly on my watch. I knew I'd be fired if someone thought I was crazy. You could be fired for sadness. And so I stood there pretending I was okay. Widdiker came up to me, seeing nothing in my eyes, the way men sometimes willfully see no emotions in other men's eyes because they want to pretend nothing's there, just like I pretended there wasn't.

"Gardenaul thinks we're responsible for flies," Widdiker said.

I didn't say anything.

"There must be hundreds of goddamn flies in here," Widdiker said, impressed with the success of the flies. "What're we supposed to do? Detain them?"

"All right," I said, still not knowing if I should step left or right.

"I told Gardenaul to call the Smithsonian and ask for the director of flies."

I nodded my head, and a fly flew off of it.

"Maybe we should go outside, where there aren't any flies," Widdiker said.

I was going to pray something, but I couldn't think of what, as if my prayers were sinking inside me and couldn't escape.

"Are you okay?" Widdiker finally said, staring at me seriously.

"I'm pretending like I am," I said.

"What's wrong?" he said.

"I'm depressed."

"About what?"

"Eventually I'll die. I'll be better by then."

"Of course you will. Is there something wrong?"

"There's always something wrong. That's how the world works."

"You look exhausted or something."

"I am."

"Did something happen?"

"Yeah. I'm forty-one years old, and when I go home at night, no one in the world wonders where I am."

"You mean a woman?"

"That's who I want to wonder where I am. Yes."

"So then you're depressed because you don't have a woman? I don't have a woman and *I'm* not depressed."

"That's because you're too stupid to know how awful you should feel."

"Do you know how long it's been since I've had sex?"

"I don't want to know."

"It's been nine or ten months."

"That's trivial. I haven't had a girlfriend in five years."

"Five years? Goddamn. What's wrong with you?" Widdiker said, glancing down the hall as if he didn't want anyone to hear two Secret Service agents telling secrets. "Five *years*? Frankly, I'm a little concerned that your dick might fall off."

"I have some electrical tape in the car," I said.

Widdiker waved some flies away from us and said, "So that's why you look as if your brain just blew up. Maybe we should go out looking for women tonight. You still have your dick, don't you?"

"Probably just for sentimental reasons," I said.

6

Of course, when we went out looking for women, Widdiker and Yamato and I dressed in jeans and T-shirts instead of our stupid suits—three reasonably good-looking men on a secret mission too ordinary to suppose it was really secret. The mission was to search randomly in the world for a woman who'd care about us and whom we could care about, which in a way reminded me of tadpoles in a pond searching for food. You took whatever was there. This was sad.

I used to believe, and still had a strong sense of it that I couldn't evict from myself, that somehow in whatever part of the world you were in, willingly or unwillingly, you could find a woman you should be with, as if on one day that you didn't know about, a girl had been born and had lived her whole childhood and teenage years and early adult life without even knowing you existed, but then, by some grand accident or by providence (providence was the word you used when you needed to explain something and had no idea what it really was), you finally met this blessed woman, as if this was fate. If this were true, that you had to spend most of your life waiting in frustration and emptiness for the one person you should meet, fate was a pretty shoddy force. Also, there were probably thousands of women you could get along with and love, and thousands of men they could love, and so why you ever met anybody didn't seem so much like providence as it seemed like an accident. You were just waiting for the right accident.

It was no more romantic than wildebeests mating on a nature documentary. I didn't believe that. I just enjoyed hurting my feelings by imagining it. I wondered why the National Geographic Society didn't set up cameras in the bar we were in, filming all of us and our glances and stares and comical, urgent attempts to meet that one person whom, from the distant beginnings of eternity, we were going to meet by accident. The National Geographic narrator would say on the soundtrack that these were the diverse mating behaviors of North American *Homo sapiens*, who tried to meet and form intimate relationships by drinking enough alcohol to disable their judgment. "However," the narrator would say, "they will not actually copulate in the drinking establishment."

Such films had been made, but they were usually called pornography. Humans regarded themselves as the only animals on Earth whose mating was obscene, even though nearly all of them hoped to do it repeatedly.

Being in the bar was depressing. Not being in the bar

would have been depressing, too, so we sat in the bar drinking our depressants, which was how I ordered drinks when we sat down.

"Could we have depressants, please?"

"We're here to find someone to mate with. Whom would you recommend?" Widdiker asked the bartender.

"I think you should go slow on your first date," she said.

"You mean mate slow? That's good advice," Yamato said.

Naturally, we didn't meet any women. This was because when women saw three men together at a bar, they assumed that the only reason they were there without women was to *find* women. So women wouldn't look at those men and avoided them, as if the kind of man they wanted was a man who wasn't looking for a woman. We figured this out to the point of incomprehension.

"If a woman thinks you're looking for her, then that's predatory and she doesn't want you," Yamato said.

"That's right. And if she thinks you're not looking for her, it's just a trick and you really are looking for her, so she still doesn't want you," Widdiker explained.

"I know. And if you're really not looking for her and show absolutely no interest in her, then she'll like you because she'll never have to meet you," I said.

"True," Yamato said, glancing at some women who weren't glancing at him.

Another reason we didn't meet any women, we thought, was that even if a group of two or more women came to the bar to talk about the men they didn't have in their lives, they didn't want to be interrupted by men—as if there *might* be good men in the world, but certainly not at that bar.

"Or else maybe they want to meet a man, who of course happens to be a stranger, but they assume that if a strange man wants to meet them, there's something wrong with him for wanting to talk with a woman he doesn't know. Am I making any sense?" Yamato asked.

"In a way I don't understand," I said. "Or maybe they really do want to meet us, but they'd rather know us before they meet us."

"You mean they only want to meet people they already know?"

"What are we talking about?"

"I can't tell."

"Why're we doing this?"

"Because we're stupid."

"The one thing you can't do is be honest," I said.

"About what?" Yamato said.

"About anything. People say they want honesty, but they don't, usually. See that brunette over there? In the green blouse with the symmetrical breasts right beside each other? I'll bet she insists on honesty and says it's one of the most important things in life. But just think what would happen if you walked over to her and said, 'Excuse me. Even though I have no idea who you are and I've only seen you for a few minutes, I get an erection when I look at you.' "

"I think that's too honest," Widdiker said, nodding.

"I know. The truth is usually too upsetting. That's why you seldom find out what it is."

"Well, don't start walking around here telling women they give you an erection," Widdiker said.

"Now isn't that an interesting expression? *Women give you an erection.* If they give it to you, don't they want you to use it?"

"I think most of them want you to keep it."

"And then it goes away."

"It wasn't a very good gift, then."

"And sometimes when women give you an erection, they mean to give it to someone else."

"You mean you can get somebody else's erection? Sex is too complex for me."

"We better be quiet, or they'll throw us out."

"No they won't. We have guns."

What we did, then, was not meet all the women who were there, which at least didn't take very long. And even though I made jokes and was ironic and pretended to be cheerful, I was just sad, as if that was the only emotion I had left. At least I had hope, I told myself abstractly, wondering what hope was, and if I really had any. Hope was when you had nothing at all but you acted like whatever you needed was on its way, even though you had no reason to believe it was. This only confused me, so now I had two emotions—sadness and confusion. I decided it must mean I was starting to feel better.

7

I was still in the doldrums the next day, full of a kind of anxious indifference to everything, because nothing in my world worked but I was expected to go on anyway since people are always pretending life is fine, when in fact it's wretched. I wandered into the White House kitchen to eat whatever free food was lying around, and I saw Abbas Amal, the Jordanian chef, opening cans of Spam. One by one, he plopped the pink globs of nearly rectangular meat onto a wooden cutting board.

"What's that for?" I asked Abbas, who looked unhappy and sullen.

"For eating," he said.

"Are you fixing that for the president's dinner tonight?"

"If you have to bother me, could you go bother me somewhere else?"

"I think bothering you here is convenient. What're you doing with Spam?"

"I'm wiping the scum off of it. Then I'm going to cook it."

"Really? For the state dinner tonight? You're serving Spam to the president and the prime minister of England?"

"And cat food," Abbas said in a quiet and resentful voice. "There are certain kinds of cat food, made from chicken, that look and smell like paté. I'm going to serve it on crackers. The president won't know it's cat food, but I will. This pleases me," he said, using a French knife to begin slicing the Spam.

Probably I should have been alarmed and protective of the president, but I wasn't in the right mood for that, and this was starting to seem like an interesting project to me.

"May I ask why," I said, "you're serving Spam and cat food to the president and the prime minister?"

"So they will eat it."

"You could get fired."

"Not unless you tell on me. Are you going to tell on me?" he asked, not even looking at me, but watching the Spam as he sliced it.

"I don't care what the president eats. I didn't vote for him. But Jesus Christ, Abbas—you're serving Spam and cat food to two of the world's most powerful people?"

"Then you are going to tell on me?"

"Possibly not. But why're you doing it?"

"The president pissed me off."

"Isn't he always pissing you off?"

Abbas scowled at me and said, "If he wants to have stupid policies, fine. If he persists in being a jackass, fine. I'm a chef, and it's not my concern what kind of son of a bitch the president is. But yesterday on TV when he ate a hot dog at a Baltimore Orioles game and said he wasn't accustomed to such fine food at the White House, I decided, 'All right, Mr. President. Go to hell. If you insult me on national television, if you demean my skill as a chef, then I too can fix you junk meat.' And this is what I'm doing. I will prepare Spam and cat food for him, which is about the same thing as in hot dogs. I will disguise it in such a wondrous way that the president will eat it at a fine dinner, a dinner fit for monarchs, and dogs and cats."

I had a very faint impulse to stop this, but a stronger impulse to see how well it could work. This was because I knew Abbas would get in trouble, not me.

"How do you disguise Spam?"

"This is easy," Abbas said almost pleasantly, as if he felt safe with me and appreciated my curiosity. "I'll marinate it in lemon juice and herbs, and then bread it, so you can't see what it is, and broil it. To conceal it more, I'll put lemon sauce and slivered almonds on top of it. I'll call it some ridiculous name, like Viennese Veal, and no one will question it. It might even *taste* good. How peculiar."

"What about the cat food?"

"That's very easy. One time, I ate cat food by mistake. I was visiting a friend, and while he was out of the house, I got hungry and found a can of something in the refrigerator that had been opened and had no label. It looked like cheap paté to me, and so I ate it on crackers. It was slightly good, and when my friend got home and started to feed his cat, we discovered that I'd eaten the cat food. So I think the president and the prime minister will like it, too, which of course I don't care about. And so now that you know all this, are you going to tell on me?"

"My job is to protect the president from assassins, not dinner."

I think Abbas and I came to an understanding then,

although what it was, I didn't understand. We were only casual friends, based on the frequent trips I made to the kitchen to get whatever free food he'd give me, but now that we were accidentally brothers in this secret plot, it seemed as if we were closer.

It was odd how, at that moment, at that exact time in my life, I was supposed to be an abstract professional man, concerned only with the immediate needs of my job, directing my mind only to those exact tasks and concerns of the Secret Service, when, honestly, it didn't matter at all to me and I was just being quietly sad, revealing this to no one. Who do you tell this to? It was almost as if the only one I might tell it to was whoever I couldn't find, whoever in my heart was absent. I was trying to imagine her face when Abbas smiled at me and said, "Would you like to help me make the lemon sauce?"

I stared at him and said, "Secret Service agents don't make lemon sauce."

"Why? Are you too masculine?"

"No. I don't have any lemons."

"I have lemons."

"Well, don't tell me any more, Abbas. This is *your* plot. I already know too much, and keep me out of it. If you want to advance your career by being fired, that's your concern, so please don't tell anyone I know about this, or the fuckheads will fire me, too. This is your plot and I know nothing about it."

"You know nothing," Abbas repeated.

I wondered if this was a moral problem. Was it wrong to let the president eat disguised Spam and cat food? The question seemed to wander through my mind with no obvious place to go. It didn't seem like a serious question. The mind, the conscience, knows when something really matters, and in this case, mine was silent. It had no opinions on Spam and cat food. It wasn't so much a spiritual matter as it was an interesting project, and for a while I wasn't sad anymore as I concentrated on this stupid and amusing subterfuge of Abbas's, which I thought presented him with at least a fifty-fifty chance of getting fired, but which I supported both morally and spiritually because there was something vaguely admirable about attempting to ridicule the president without him even knowing it.

What I envisioned—and I had to envision it because Secret Service agents usually weren't needed during dinner —was the president and the prime minister, and maybe the secretary of state, and several other tedious eminences of the highest order, dressed in black tie as they discussed some urgent world matters while holding unimaginably expensive and lovely glasses filled with an enormously costly wine as they ate animal by-products that had come from cans.

It was the most fantastic dinner I was never invited to, but in the morning I was invited to Chief of Staff Gardenaul's office, which was decorated with framed paintings of George Patton, Geronimo, and Julia Child. I sat in a leather chair in front of Gardenaul's desk, pointed to the painting of Julia Child and said, "Which war did *she* fight in?"

Gardenaul didn't smile. "I suppose you know why you're here," he said in a mildly grave tone.

"Yes. This is where I work."

"Were you aware of the Spam incident last night? Gardenaul said in the same grave tone.

"The Spam incident? Was that on TV last night? I didn't watch TV. I was at a bar trying to meet women I'll never know."

Gardenaul glared at me and said, "What if the press finds out about this? What if the *Post* reports that the White House chef served goddamn Spam to the president and the prime minister of England?"

He didn't mention the cat food. I squinted at Gardenaul with what I hoped would look like perplexity and annoyed innocence.

"The president had Spam last night? He never invites me for dinner. I don't know these things."

"Don't feign innocence with me, you little shithead. You were seen in the vicinity of the kitchen last night."

"Little?" I said impatiently. "I outweigh you by about twenty pounds. Whether or not I'm a shithead is a different matter."

Gardenaul slapped his hand violently on the desk and winced, then pretended not to feel the pain.

"You're the one agent I've never liked," he said with quiet anger.

"There's quite a few of them I don't like. I guess you're more amiable than I am."

"Caldron," he said, deliberately mispronouncing my name, "I have no idea which part of reality interests you, but the part you *should* be interested in is that the president is pissed. Seriously pissed."

It made me think of the president standing at a urinal. One time when the president was in a public restroom at a hotel in Denver and a man started to walk in, I stopped him at the door and said, "You need security clearance to urinate."

"Can you explain," Gardenaul said, "why you didn't tell anyone that Abbas was planning to serve Spam to the president?"

I wondered what the best way was to lie. I decided, in

what was probably one of my frequent reckless impulses, to just tell the truth.

"My job is to protect the president and all other assigned people from physical harm. Spam, in my opinion, is incapable of physical violence."

Gardenaul flung his arms into the air and said, "Then you knew! You son of a bitch, you knew Abbas was fixing Spam, and you did nothing to stop him?"

"The president regularly eats food without requiring my opinion of it."

"But Spam? Good God, how can you pretend to tell me you thought it was all right for the president to eat Spam?"

"The president eats fish eggs. If he wants to eat the unfertilized ova of Russian fish, I don't imagine he can pretend to be very sensitive about what he puts in his mouth."

Gardenaul looked contemptuously away, taking a cigarette from his shirt pocket and lighting it as he swiveled impatiently in his leather chair and stared at the pictures of Patton, Geronimo, and Julia Child.

"Caldron," he said.

"It's Coldiron."

"If I don't like your name, I'll call you what I want," Gardenaul said, not even bothering to look at me. "As chief of staff, I have the authority to change your *race* if it suits me."

"Could you change my sex, too? It might improve my chances to be with a woman."

Gardenaul was quiet, probably aggravated that I wasn't obediantly intimidated by him, like nearly everyone else was—the fuckhead.

"Caldron, I don't know how, or by what intolerable set of circumstances, you were allowed into the Secret Service, and although I don't have the authority to have your balls removed and hung from a lampshade in the Library of Congress like I want to, I can at least write a derogatory letter to your boss about this jackass incident. And I will. I'm through with you. You can return to your duties, not that you'll have that many left."

8

As I left Gardenaul's office, walking silently down the hall in my conservative suit and matching 9mm automatic, with nothing before me or behind me but difficulty, in a world where I just wanted to hold somebody, to share my life with a woman who, as far as I knew in my undisturbed ignorance, had no intention of ever meeting me, it seemed as if the only eternal force I'd become intimate with was trouble. I started quietly saying, "Uh-oh. Uh-oh," probably one of the first phrases I learned as a boy, wondering pointlessly and intellectually if, despite the hundreds of languages and dialects that separated humanity from itself, all people were born with the innate ability to say, "Uh-oh."

I thought about Spam. I pictured it in its blue can with the little key you used to open it so you could slosh out the architecturally sound lump of meat. Spam was sturdy enough to both feed and house the poor. I thought I should have said to Gardenaul, "I'm sorry the president didn't like Spam. At least he enjoyed the cat food."

"Good morning, Doyle," one of the White House staffers said as he walked by.

"Uh-oh," I said, since it was the only greeting I could think of.

"Pardon me?"

"Sure. Why not," I said, continuing to walk down the hall.

Every instant of life was an occasion for trouble. Animals millions of years ago evolved or were exterminated based solely on their ability to avoid trouble. And then humans evolved (or at least we assume they evolved, because this is a useful assumption for pissing off all fundamentalists in our worldwide effort to trouble everyone), learned how to walk upright and invented tools, which they used to bang other animals in the head, and humans gradually and fantastically learned how to domesticate wild grasses and animals, and finally invented tribes and clans and civilizations with written languages so they could begin giving proper names to all the countries they stole, or were stolen by. History wasn't a record of advances. It was a record of who stole what. If you looked at all of natural and human history as an inevitable progression of events, you could say that the world was created and life sustained so that I could find myself walking through the White House with a 9mm automatic.

It seemed that I was depressed, or in trouble with one of those emotions you have when you can't have any of the good ones. But then, by the guaranteed randomness of the world, I was distracted by the wondrous buttocks and thighs of Natelle, who walked in front of me in a snug green skirt that simultaneously hid her flesh from view and seemed designed to emphasize every surface I couldn't see and wanted to embrace. It happened again, the way it always did when I suddenly and unexpectedly saw her anywhere. My heart fluttered, its beating seeming to speed up and maybe wobble. And, almost instantly, a warm jolt flashed through me, like something too good to imagine or understand was secretly waking in me, like exuberance and glee and hope were all stirring and crashing into each other in this huge, silent collision in my heart that I never told Natelle about, because she was married, and I wasn't supposed to have secret collisions in my heart for her. But I always did. I looked at her and was jolted. I looked at her and caught my breath. It seemed as if this would never stop happening. I looked at her and felt like I was wakened by every emotion that would ever matter. I wondered if this was love or psychological trauma. I'd accept both.

But I had no hope of ever telling her this, telling the forbidden married woman that I went through intense spasms of elation (Was that the right word, *elation*? Was there ever a word that did more than pleasantly obscure what you felt?), that I was almost disabled by elation, whenever I saw her. So she just didn't know. Unless sometimes in my eyes, or in my obvious eagerness to be with her, she saw everything I never said, and she didn't tell me. Just like I never told her. It was as if our real lives were the ones we never talked about.

I didn't have time for this introspection, particularly since the person I needed to tell it to, Natelle, was the one person I couldn't tell it to. I walked up quickly behind her, feeling the sudden urgency to be next to her that I felt when I saw her anywhere. And, when I reached her and lightly touched her wrist with my fingertips, and she turned and stared into my eyes and smiled, I was home. Of course I couldn't tell her that. This always bewildered me—how Natelle, who was the best thing in my life, wasn't really in my life. This meant that I was always on the verge of Natelle. She had a nice verge. But you couldn't hold a verge, or kiss it.

"Well *Doyle*," she said in a happy voice, and squeezed my fingers with her hand. She grinned, as if a new emotion came into her, and she said, "So what did you have for *dinner* last night?"

"I forget."

"Well if you don't remember what *you* had for dinner, possibly you recall what the *president* had?" she asked, grinning expectantly.

"Cat food," I said.

"Cat food? That's not the rumor I heard," she said in a suddenly quiet voice that went down to a whisper. She leaned her face close to my ear, making me wish I could kiss her neck, and she said, "I heard Abbas fixed Spam with lemon sauce for the president and the prime minister. My God— did he really?"

I wanted to put my lips anywhere between her eyes and neck, strenuously resisted this impulse, and whispered back, "Gardenaul called me into his office a little while ago and said he wants to hang my testicles from a lampshade in the Library of Congress. I don't think it would match the other furnishings."

She looked confused and stunned. "What're you talking about?"

"Furnishings. It's what you put in a room."

Natelle punched me lightly in the stomach and whispered, "I think we better talk in my office, where no one can hear."

"Well, if we can't hear, maybe we should talk in someone else's office," I whispered.

She ground the toe of her shoe into my foot and said, "Come on."

I liked how she could be so familiar with me that she could hit me in the stomach and step on my foot and still know I'd follow her, which I always would.

After Natelle closed the door to her little basement office and stared at me from about three feet away with her lovely green eyes, I realized that again we were alone together and couldn't touch.

"So what were you doing in Gardenaul's office?" she asked in a serious and interested tone.

"Talking about lamps."

"Did you have anything to do with Abbas and the Spam?"

"And the cat food, too. I was a neutral observer. But Gardenaul doesn't think so."

"What do you mean, cat food, Doyle? What else did you do?"

"I didn't do anything. Abbas did."

"Did what, Doyle? What in the hell aren't you talking about?"

"Well, the truth is, I innocently walked into the kitchen last night to see if Abbas or someone would give me a snack, like they always do, and I saw Abbas opening cans of Spam."

"Then he really did it? This is too hard to believe," Natelle said.

"And that's not all he really did. I didn't actually see the cans of cat food, but Abbas told me he was going to serve cat food on crackers. He said it tastes like paté. Not very good paté, I assume."

"My God," Natelle said, opening her eyes wide with disbelief. "What was wrong with Abbas?"

"I don't think anything's wrong with him. I think he just doesn't like the president."

"Don't you think Abbas will get fired?"

"It seems probable. But how did they know it was Spam?

That's what I want to know. Did someone tell them, or did they realize it while they were eating? And if so, did the prime minister lean his head discreetly toward the president and say, 'I think lemon sauce adds an unexpected piquancy to Spam'?"

Natelle breathed in deeply and sighed, staring at me and shaking her head in an affectionate, worried way. "So what did Gardenaul say to you?"

I was looking at her lips, wondering what they'd feel like, and if I'd ever know.

"Doyle? Are you listening?"

"Gardenaul," I said absentmindedly. "He was pissed. He said the president was pissed. I assume everyone else was pissed. I've always wondered what urine has to do with anger."

"Well, are you in trouble?"

I looked briefly at the edge of Natelle's blouse where the very tops of her breasts were pleasantly visible and forbidden.

"I don't think I *deserve* to be in trouble. I'm not responsible for Abbas, and, evidently, Abbas isn't either."

"Well, are you going to be punished, or what?" Natelle said in an impatient but gentle way.

"Probably. Gardenaul said he wants to cut my balls off and hang them from a lampshade in the Library of Congress. I don't think the General Services Administration would allow that."

"What can they do? It's not your fault Abbas fixed Spam, although I'm sure Gardenaul said you should've reported it before dinner was served."

"Yeah. That seems to be the prevailing opinion. But look at the facts. The Secret Service has absolutely nothing to do with the White House chef, unless we think the chef is trying to kill somebody, and Spam with lemon sauce can't be regarded as a weapon. So it doesn't matter what the goddamn chef serves for dinner. But did I know the president and the prime minister would find it insulting or disrespectful or intolerable to be served Spam?"

"And cat food," Natelle said.

"Well, they don't know they ate cat food, so that doesn't count. Let's stick to the Spam only. I'm in no position to second-guess the White House chef, or to suggest menus for state dinners, or . . ."

"Oh, come on, Doyle. You knew they'd be offended by Spam. That's the only reason Abbas fixed it."

"Nuh-uh," I said. "He served it secretly, meaning he didn't want them to be offended. He only wanted them to be defiled. That's different."

Natelle put her hands over her eyes and started laughing quietly.

"You're impossible," she said.

"No. I'm quite possible. In fact, here I am."

She raised her hand and touched my chest, saying, "Yes, you *are* here. But what I want to know is, are you in trouble or not?"

To look at her and not have her was the trouble I was in.

9

After outraging the president, infuriating the chief of staff, having a profound attack of sadness, and continuing to hide my most urgent emotions from the only woman who I wanted to know them, it seemed to me that I wasn't living my life very well.

My head hurt. I felt exhausted and anxious, which could have been symptoms of some new and culturally fashionable disorder called chronic white guy's syndrome, or whining fatigue syndrome. It was in the newspapers and on TV, some recently discovered disorder where white people in their mid-twenties and thirties exhibited symptoms of just generally feeling like shit all the time, although *shit* wasn't the precise medical term. It had the word "syndrome" in it, so all you had to do was randomly add some adjectives or adverbs to it and there you were with a puzzling and ominous new syndrome, such as "being alive syndrome," which was what I thought I suffered from. I could use my medical insurance to go to a doctor and say, "Every day I wake up with the same frightening condition."

"And what's that?"

"Consciousness."

Even the Bible announced in its first book that the first thing you could expect in life was trouble, followed immediately by sorrow, and concluding in death. None of this would have mattered except for consciousness. That's what Adam and Eve got when they ate the apple. So that was my disorder—being aware of my life. And when you fell into the blessed forgetfulness of sleep, it didn't last. You had to wake up. It was odd that while the Bible said sleep was blessed, it didn't say the same thing about being awake.

All these thoughts came to me in great and vivid disorder after I left Natelle's office and sat with repressed agitation at our briefing for the day, where, in my injured mood, everything about my job seemed pointless and wildly extraneous, as if the existence of the entire federal government was just an annoyance. On the notepad on my lap, I started writing a list that I titled "Things That Are Wrong with My Life," as if by listing my major flaws and problems, I might get a pathetically vague insight into how to live well.

1. Not sure how many things are wrong.
2. Is the glass half full, or half empty?
3. What glass?
4. Sometimes I drink too much.
5. Sometimes I drink just the right amount.
6.

My pen ran out of ink. In the chair next to me, Yamato was reaching inside his coat pockets and his shirt pocket and then his pants pockets to find a pen so he could take notes during the briefing.

"Do you have an extra pen?" Yamato said.

"Use this," I said, handing him my pen.

Yamato tried writing something on his pad, then frowned at me and said, "This is out of ink."

"I know. That's why I don't want it."

Doltmeer began handing out dossiers and things about the Queen Mother and some duchesses and other exotic species in town, who we were supposed to protect from potential assassins.

"Do you have a pen that *works*?" Yamato asked.

"That one works. It just doesn't have any ink in it," I said, fumbling through my pockets for another pen for Yamato and me, and then I cupped my hand over my notepad so Yamato couldn't see it and I tried to resume my list of things that were wrong with my life:

6.

The sixth one was too serious. I didn't want to write it. I was going to write what was really true, that, at age forty-one, I'd achieved a number of fairly admirable successes that by themselves meant almost nothing. Sometimes at night I drank beer to make me sleepy, to sneak me into the unconsciousness that otherwise wouldn't come to me. I wondered whether this was depression, or just sadness, to lie hurting in the dark and starting to cry, at first resisting the need to cry, as if someone might see me when there was no one there. That was crazy, not wanting anyone to see you crying because you were so alone, and crying because you wanted someone to see you.

Some nights I'd call out Natelle's name, like an incantation. I'd never been trained in incantations, or religion, or voodoo, or magic, but I seemed to feel innately that when I hurt the most and was almost panicked in my lonesomeness, the best thing to do was say the name of the one person who mattered.

"Natelle."

"Natelle."

I wanted her to come to me, as if just by lying in the dark and saying, "Natelle, Natelle," I could make her hear me from eight or nine miles away, and she'd know with some spiritual intuition that I needed her.

But she didn't. Quietly saying "Natelle, Natelle" didn't travel eight miles. For a spiritual incantation like that, you needed to be right up next to her ear. And then I knew, because there was no reason to dumbly lie to myself all day, that the reason I could get so frighteningly lonesome at night and automatically think of Natelle was that, secretly, in the part of me that was always real and knew without confusion or deception what honestly mattered, I was in love with her. Being in love with someone you weren't supposed to be in love with was like being attacked by a blessing. It was supposed to be joyous, but it made you ache worse than most normal diseases. I couldn't go to a doctor. A doctor would just say stop loving her, and I'd say, "Kiss my ass. I don't want to know how to make love go away. I want to know how to make it work."

Which of course I never told Natelle, even though I desperately wished I could. Somehow, it seemed more moral for me to lie crushed down in this sorrow than to cause Natelle any sorrow by saying *I'm in love with you and I wish you'd love me back.* But no one had to love you back. They didn't even have to know about it.

And so I'd succeeded in having a love affair all by myself.

It didn't work. It gave me headaches and anxiety, as if all of this affection and desire and need that was trapped and swarming around in me kept trying to escape, usually through my head, which I assumed caused the headaches.

Late the night before, when I couldn't sleep and I got up to have a bottle of Mexican beer and see whatever stupid shows there were on TV to keep me company against the night, there was an evangelist on TV saying that if I did everything right, I'd go to Heaven.

"I'd rather go to Natelle," I said.

You had to die to go to Heaven. I worried that reaching Natelle would be harder.

10

The next crucial project entrusted to only the most reliable and ingenious members of the Secret Service was to think of a name for our baseball team. Yamato said we should name the team after an animal that no one had used before in baseball—the Moles.

While it did have a kind of repugnant charm to it, Widdiker said it wasn't unique and that those stupid bastards in the CIA might think of the same name, especially since some of them probably were moles. So he suggested instead that we call our team the Burrowing Rodents. We discussed this at an imitation French restaurant downtown called Maison de Maison, where you could buy affordable French wine from Albania. Also, Widdiker said there'd be a lot of attractive women there for us to look at and never meet, although I thought looking at one woman you'd never meet was sufficient. We drank glasses of red Albanian wine and ate French croissants baked fresh that morning in Ohio, as I wrote down potential team names on the same notepad that had my unfinished list of "Things That Are Wrong With My Life."

"If we're going to name our team after an animal, the Burrowing Rodents is good, since I think in a game between us and the CIA, you'd want a kind of upsetting, disturbing name," Yamato said. "After all, both the Secret Service and the CIA are associated with assassination, war, and revolution."

"Basic American themes," Widdiker said.

"But we need more animal names to choose from, and not any dumb ones, like the Orioles or the Tigers."

"Can we name our team after an insect?" I said.

"Which insect?"

"The assassin bug. That's some bug in South America. They assassinate other bugs, but not for political reasons. They eat them."

"I don't want to be named after an insect," Yamato said.

"I won't name you after an insect. I'll keep calling you Dutch."

"How about the Scorpions?" Widdiker asked.

"That's good. Kind of."

"Well, if you want to name our team after something small and repugnant, we could call ourselves the Horse Ticks," I offered.

"Don't write that down," Widdiker said.

"I'm writing it down," I said. "And also, why do we have to name our team after an animal? Why can't we name our team after a plant?"

"What plant?"

"Blue Mold."

"The Warthogs!" Yamato suggested. "Write that down."

"A warthog isn't a plant."

"Just shut up and write it down."

"Don't tell me to shut up. This is *my* notepad. Eat me."

"I know what. We could call ourselves the Blowfish," Widdiker said. "Write that down."

I shook my head and said, "You can't just keep thinking of simple animal names, such as the Warthogs and the Blowfish, as if the name itself is sufficient. You have to modify and embellish the names, like the *Slavering* Warthogs. It makes it sound more refined. And you can't just say 'the Blowfish.' You have to add a word, make it more impressive and thoughtful. Such as the *Avenging* Blowfish."

"That's excellent," Widdiker said, and patted my back. "Have you ever thought of a career in public relations?"

"Maybe the public has relations, but I don't," I said.

"What other names can we think of?" Yamato said.

"Jackals," Widdiker said.

"All right. And what kind of jackals?"

"The usual jackals," Widdiker said impatiently.

"That's a good name—the Usual Jackals."

"I didn't mean that," Widdiker said, shaking his head. "I mean whatever kind of jackals you usually have. Your standard jackals."

"I'll write that one down, too. Your Standard Jackals. These are some neat team names."

"Fine," Widdiker said, meaning he was tired of trying to explain himself.

"And now we have to think of at least one plant for a team name," I said.

"Why?" Yamato said.

"Because it's too ordinary to just think of animal names."

"I can't think of a single plant that would make a good team name. Name one," Widdiker demanded.

"Botulism."

"That's a plant? That's not a plant."

"No, but it's caused by toxic spores, I think, which come from plants."

"Well, if we're going to name our team after a disease, I'd prefer something more colorful."

"Yellow Fever?"

"I don't like yellow."

"Scarlet Fever?"

"When I was a boy, I always thought it would be neat to get purple fever, since no one else had it. And then I wanted rainbow fever. Even if I was sick, I'd at least be pretty to look at," I said.

"Can't we stick to the subject?"

"Why're you so cranky? Have you got a fever?"

"I think we have plenty of names to choose from," Widdiker said. "Let's just look at the list and decide which one we like best."

"But what do we do after we pick one? Are we going to have the name stitched on our jerseys?" Yamato wondered.

"I don't think we should. We don't want the CIA to know which team we are."

"Well then, why do we need a name?"

"So we can keep it secret."

11

What I imagined was that, on game day, a huge and adoring crowd gathered in the bleachers we didn't have would cheer exuberantly as we came out onto the field in our uniforms while the stadium announcer said, "Ladies and gentlemen, let's give a big welcome to the Avenging Blowfish!"

In reality, there was no such thing as an avenging blowfish, which made it a perfect name for a covert baseball team preparing for a game that might not exist. What I also imagined was the president standing on the pitcher's mound to throw the ceremonial first pitch, but we wouldn't give him the ball.

"Where's the ball?" he'd say.

"We've hidden it, Mr. President."

"And what the hell for?"

"This is spookball, Mr. President. We've decided to make the game more competitive by hiding the ball."

"Well, how in the hell do you expect the game to start?"

"With a search for the ball, Mr. President."

The president probably wouldn't think that was funny. He didn't think Spam was funny. The trouble from all that was just beginning, with the news that Abbas had been fired. And what for? For feeding the president something that millions of Americans ate every day, not including the cat food. As far as I knew, the cat food was still one of the better parts of the meal.

Before I could look for Abbas or talk with anyone in the kitchen, I was summoned by Doltmeer for a special meeting in his office, where, after arriving promptly and adopting a somber expression for this unpleasant occasion, I found Doltmeer feeding flies to a little garden of pitcher plants. I didn't know he had pitcher plants. In his navy blue suit, white shirt, and yellow bowtie, Doltmeer looked strangely proper to be gently stuffing dead flies into the mouths of carnivorous plants. My impulse was to say, "What're you doing with those fucking flies?" although I cautiously said nothing and waited for Doltmeer to acknowledge my presence and announce whatever kind of trouble he had selected for me.

"I'd offer you a seat, but I think your visit here should remain uncomfortable," Doltmeer said.

Uh-oh.

"You're in trouble," he said, then apparently waited for me to respond, which I wasn't going to do. I thought there was no point in responding to the obvious. I decided to seem indifferent.

"Aren't you going to say anything?" Doltmeer asked irritably.

"I assume you are," I said.

Reaching into a small brown bag for a fly, Doltmeer said, "I'm informed that because of your reckless negligence, the president and the prime minister dined on Spam."

"I don't think reckless negligence had anything to do with it," I said. "I think when the White House chef cooks food, he does it deliberately."

"And you'd like to blame the chef, wouldn't you," Doltmeer said in a slightly angry voice.

"Blame the chef for cooking?"

"Goddamn you, Coldiron! You were there when that bastard chef decided to serve Spam to the president, and don't say a goddamn word about how the Secret Service isn't responsible for the president's food! You *knew* it was wrong, you *knew* Abbas was going to do it, you said nothing to *any-one* to prevent it, and it resulted in a serious embarrassment to the president."

The only part of the argument I didn't like was the part where I got in trouble. I didn't think you could say I was morally or ethically responsible for the imagined crime of serving Spam to the president. I wondered if defending myself was possible. I decided to try.

"Spam is made of ham," I said. "It might not be made of the finest cuts of ham, but I think when you're talking about an animal that's been violently killed, there's nothing very genteel about which part you eat, anyway. Whether you eat it raw, like a hyena, or cooked and spiced, like a president, you're still eating the same animal."

Doltmeer put his bag of dead flies down and said, "Good argument. Too bad I don't give a goddamn."

"I knew you wouldn't."

"Yes, but you had to try, and I almost admire that. Except I don't. So don't argue with me. Don't try to be reasonable and correct, because I don't care. We both know the only reason Abbas served Spam to the president was to offend him."

"Not really," I said quietly and with a detatched interest in the subject. "Abbas was meticulous in trying to conceal the Spam. I wasn't there when he did it, but he told me about marinating it and breading it and topping it with fresh lemon sauce. So he didn't want the president to know what it was. As I figured out later, he didn't want to offend the president. He only wanted to defile him. That's purely psychological. Like I said, it wouldn't have made any difference if the president had eaten smoked ham or processed ham from a can. It was simple snobbishness. The offense didn't come from the ham."

"Very true," Doltmeer said in a calmer voice, as if he agreed with me and couldn't be quite so mad at me anymore. "But I think you're missing the point. The president is expected to be a snob. And you knew he wouldn't like the Spam. Therefore, you're screwed. And do you want me to tell you why?"

"No."

"You're screwed because you've gotten a lot of people pissed off at me. I personally don't care if the president eats stray dogs with lemon sauce. But when I get people leaning on *me* because one of my goddamn agents thought it was funny to serve Spam to the president, I'm going to be as vengeful as anyone wants me to be. Do you understand? If Gardenaul wants your balls hanging from a lamp, I'll send you to the store to buy the lamp."

12

I was walking across the White House lawn after getting back from Doltmeer's office, ready to go protect the life of a man who didn't like me and who maybe wanted me fired, and aching to talk with Natelle because I was in love with her and she was my refuge, only I couldn't tell her she was my refuge. So if I went to open my heart to her, I had to make sure it remained closed.

There was an instant of dizziness as I thought about that, and something started rushing through me, like there'd been a rupture inside me, as if everything I hadn't told anybody just silently blew up in me. My skin began to tingle and sweat as, in a vague panic, I felt again, like the first time this happened to me, that every choice I'd ever made was somehow wrong, that I didn't belong here, that whatever I was supposed to be doing in the world had always been hidden from me and was irretrievably lost, and no direction I might go would matter right then.

I stopped walking because there was no reason to go anywhere. The normal sense that I should be going somewhere was absent, as if I really didn't belong anywhere, not even where I stood. Possibly I was going crazy, which at first didn't seem much more troubling than anything else I'd gone through recently. In my college psychology class we briefly studied neurosis and psychosis, and I wondered which of the two I might be experiencing. Given a choice, I wanted neurosis. I could tell as the panic squashed in on me that I didn't have a choice. You can't choose your horrors. They just come. I felt frighteningly remote from everything, as if the air around me, and the massive, dark trees with glittery leaves, and even the blue, vacant sky stretched out in its vast sameness, were all suddenly alien to me, like I'd never seen the world before, and every common detail of existence was appearing to me for the first time.

It seemed likely that I was going crazy. But having never gone crazy before, how could I recognize it? So there was just the tiniest, shortest moment, then, at the height of all this panic and unreality, when I paused to wonder, for the sake of intellectual clarity, if I was going crazy and how I'd know when I achieved it. It was like only part of me was going crazy and the rest of me was an astonished spectator.

I rejected it. Maybe insanity was going to consume me anyway, but not with my permission. As I sweated and tingled and knew that no one in the world was waiting to see me and smile when I appeared, I closed my eyes to all this chaos and said, "No, no, no!" as if I was right at that instant when the chaos would fully come into me, and I had to tell it no. That was all I had left.

No.

And it began to recede, to roll back away from me, as if my refusal had stopped it, and it could only consume me if I let it. With my eyes still closed, the panic slowly left me, like a wind dying down, and the sweating and the tingling stopped, and I was exhausted, just from standing still and trying not to go crazy. It seemed as if I'd won. I was returning to normal.

Normal wasn't an especially good place to return to. I still felt desperately sad. I still wanted to hold Natelle, which wasn't allowed. And whatever had just tried to scatter me into little shards of psychic debris was still in me, maybe renewing its strength for a more brutal attack. Being normal wasn't a victory. It was just more manageable. Possibly all of this was a mystical or religious insight. I prayed not to have any more insights. *Dear Jesus, if you're showing me that every human ambition is extraneous but the giving and receiving of love, please don't give me a nervous breakdown to show me that. I already believe it.*

Of course, I didn't know if I was talking to Jesus or just talking to the sky. Neither one tends to answer you.

My panic had been replaced by a deep and soothing sense of confusion, as if it was a blessing to not really realize what I'd just been through. In the Bible, when people briefly went out of their minds and had a vision, they were called prophets. In the twentieth century, they were called mentally ill. I didn't want to be called either.

I wanted to tell Natelle about all this, but if I told her that one of my insights was the sorrowful absence of her in my life, *she* might panic.

Panic. When all other emotions have abandoned you, panic remains loyal.

I thought of walking into Natelle's office and saying, "Something terrible has happened to me. I'm normal." But of course I wouldn't. I was wondering what to say to her, if I should say I'd just had a brief mental breakdown, or a religious insight, or just way too much sadness. All of it seemed possible, and I wanted to tell her about it. When you tell something that frightening to someone, they either back away from you instantly or they hold you.

When I walked into Natelle's office and tiredly smiled at her as if I were normal, she had no idea how bad normal was. She smiled back and held up a letter she'd been reading.

"Sometimes I love answering the president's mail. It's so strange," she said, and started reading the letter aloud, as if, like her, I was ready to be amused:

Dear Mr. President:
This is to inform you that our new organization, *Women for A Sane Future,* is compiling materials for an exhaustive research library to prove that the single most sinister force active in the world is testosterone. Research from respected and renowned scientists shows that the dominant cause of nearly every act of violence on every continent is the male hormone, testosterone. Accordingly, our research group is preparing detailed proposals to ask the White House and Congress to allocate urgently needed funds to be used by the Centers for Disease Control to study the effects of testosterone and recommend effective plans to eradicate this most odious compound. We hereby welcome your cooperation and opinions on our soon-to-be universal task—neutralizing the male hormone.

Natelle looked up at me and laughed, saying, "The Centers for Disease Control? I wonder what this woman is thinking. Now that we've wiped out polio, men are next? Oh, good God. This would almost be hilarious if it wasn't so ominously serious. I told you a lot of women in America are angry. This one's really pissed off, which I can sometimes understand, after being married for two years. Sometimes I think the only reason people get married is that they're tired of suffering alone. Is it really best to suffer in unison?"

It seemed like she wanted me to answer that, and I said, "I guess if you can't have simultaneous orgasms, you can at least have simultaneous pain. But I wouldn't know. I'm simultaneously alone."

"Are you all right?" she asked, staring at my eyes. "You look pale." She put the letter down and stared at me with some kind of worry or affection. I loved her for that and wouldn't tell her, because it wasn't the right time, and maybe never would be. People didn't want you to love them all the time. They wanted you to love them at exactly the right time. And then they wouldn't tell you when that was.

"Things are awry. That's normal," I said, sitting in the steno chair next to Natelle.

"What's awry?"

"It's when things don't work."

"I knowww that, Doyle. I mean what's awry with you?"

"I'm not sure."

"Well, tell me what you think's wrong. You really look pale. Have you got a fever? I hope it wasn't the letter. I won't let anybody study you at the Centers for Disease Control," she said, putting the back of her hand against my forehead.

I liked it when she did that. Too bad I had to have a nervous breakdown to get her to touch me.

"You do feel a little warm. What's wrong?"

"I think I had a nervous breakdown for about sixty seconds."

"What? What're you talking about? How could you have a nervous breakdown for sixty seconds?"

"You don't need one longer than that."

"Will you please tell me what happened?" she said in a slightly anguished voice, as if I needed new proof that she cared about me, and there it was. Also, she put her hand on top of mine, which meant more to me than I could safely explain to her. It might have been a simple gesture to her, I didn't know. To me, it was a blessed intimacy having her hand on mine. I wondered if we were having the same emotions but we just didn't say so. I wasn't interested in my nervous breakdown anymore. I was interested in Natelle.

"What happened?" she repeated.

"Oh," I said. "I'm not really sure. I think it was like the panic attack you told me you had one time."

"You panicked?"

"I panicked a lot. It overwhelmed me. I was just walking across the grass after being told . . ."

I stopped because there was too much to say.

"After being told what?"

"I can't remember. Maybe now I have amnesia. That'd be great. First you have a nervous breakdown, then amnesia. Maybe I should just go home and sleep. I'd probably get insomnia, though. Then I'd stay up all night with amnesia, unable to remember why I got insomnia."

Natelle squeezed my hand and smiled woefully, as if I was sadly funny.

"I feel better, now," I said.

"But you haven't even told me what happened. You think you had a panic attack?"

I shook my head yes. "I've had a few before, too. But this was different. It was like a panic attack with insights to explain why I panicked."

"You had insights? What insights?"

"I can't remember."

Natelle's head drooped and she started laughing. "You mean you had a nervous breakdown that gave you insights you can't remember?"

"Nervous breakdowns aren't funny."

"Yours is," she said, laughing lightly as she leaned nearer to me to put her arms around me and rest her head against mine. The one insight that mattered the most was now holding me. I wished I could tell her that. It wasn't time, and I began trembling a little bit and I was crying.

"What's wrong?" Natelle said quietly with her head next to mine, and it was like having someone you didn't have at all.

"You go ahead and cry," she whispered. "I've got you."

True, but she didn't know how completely.

13

I think Natelle loved me and she wasn't going to say so. When she held me and said, "I've got you," she didn't say anything else and kept holding me for the longest time, as if it was important to soothe me and important mainly to hold onto me, not just because I wanted it, the sense of her flesh, but because she wanted the sense of mine, too. She kept her cheek pressed against mine and it seemed like she didn't want to let me go, and I wanted to sink into her and become part of her.

Natelle's husband was named Gabriel. One night I prayed that Natelle would divorce Gabriel, since she'd talked about it a little bit with me. I closed my eyes and prayed, "Please let Natelle be divorced," as if God would say, "Okay." The difficulty in praying for a divorce was both the church wedding part and the part in the Bible that says, "Let no man put asunder what God hath joined together," as if Natelle and Gabriel were joined together by God.

Well, then, maybe He made a mistake. He seemed to make them all the time. There were millions of people who shouldn't have been joined together by anybody, particularly by God. If it was ungodly to get divorced, you'd have to say the godly thing was for badly matched people to remain together in pain and despair. A divorce that worked was more holy than a marriage that didn't, and I told that to God, as if I were His consultant. Probably He didn't want consultants.

But if He was really omniscient, why was He joining together so many millions of people who, after years of sorrow and anguish, would find it a joy to be put asunder? If the church wedding didn't work, why couldn't you have a church divorce? At the altar, the priest would say, "All right. Give him back your ring. And you give her the ring back, too."

And as the organist played a cheerful dirge or sonata, the priest would say, "I now pronounce you asunder."

I secretly remembered all this when Natelle decided to cheer me up and look after me by taking me with her to an art fair on the Mall down by the Smithsonian. She said, as if to explain why she wanted to go somewhere with me, that art was good for nervous breakdowns,

"You mean to cause them?" I asked.

She squeezed my hand and said, "People say most art comes from neurosis anyway. Let's look at the art and see if we recognize any of our neuroses."

What we discovered among the rows of watercolors and paintings and sculptures was an exhibit of police sketches. Someone from the police department decided to display about three dozen charcoal sketches of suspects being sought

in unsolved crimes. So in one row you could look at land-
scapes and abstract art, and in the police row you could look
at composite drawings of fugitives. This was so ludicrous it
cheered me up.

We stopped in front of a sketch titled "Arson Suspect."

"It reminds me of Rembrandt," Natelle said as she studied
the drawing.

"Rembrandt was an arsonist?" I said.

A police officer walked up to us from a few feet away and
said, "Do you recognize him?"

"Sure. That's Rembrandt," I said.

"I have no idea who it is," Natelle said, shaking her head at
me.

"You said it reminds you of Rembrandt," I said.

"Is that a first name or a last name?" the cop asked.

"Rembrandt's dead. He's not a likely suspect," I said as
Natelle pulled me away and said, "Stop that. I don't think
the police like you joking with them."

"Well, the police have no business putting on an art show
anyway. If their arson suspects look like Rembrandt, they're
not drawing very well. They've probably got an arrest warrant out for Raphael."

"You seem to be in a better mood. Art must be good for
you," Natelle said, smiling.

"You're good for me. Art's okay. But it wouldn't matter to
me if we were looking at rows of trash stapled onto easels.
I'm just glad I got to go somewhere with you," I said, realizing that what I'd said was possibly too honest, that it
sounded like a description of love, which it was, and now
what did I do?

"I'm glad, too," Natelle said, not looking at me, but lightly,
almost barely, grasping my hand in hers for a second, then
letting it go, as if she was handing me her emotion and I had

to know what that meant. I wasn't sure. I wanted to fall on top of her and stare into her eyes and kiss her until I couldn't breathe.

And I wondered what she was thinking, if she wanted to lie down naked on top of me with one of her breasts in my mouth, if she only wanted to put her cheek against mine, if she wanted to divorce Gabriel so she could marry me, or if she just hoped I was her friend. You never knew what someone else was thinking. Maybe we were walking in the same direction toward different places. You could only hope— only hope that, by a prolonged and astonishing accident, somebody in the world would want you. I wanted this to be Natelle. And then I sighed, because a sigh was the only thing I could think of saying to the woman I wasn't supposed to tell anything to.

This was how you got nervous breakdowns. Apparently successful with my first one, I was qualified for at least one more. Probably a better one.

For lunch we bought hot dogs from a street vendor and ate them on a wooden bench near a tree where some squirrels were sitting on their hind legs eating popcorn.

"I wonder if they prefer plain or buttered," Natelle said.

"I think they like it with dirt on it," I said.

We watched the crowd wander around the art fair, and watched some children flying a kite in the shape of a dragon or a salamander or a Polish sausage. It was just this long, indistinct shape, so if you wanted to say it was a Polish sausage, you could.

"I've stopped taking the pill," Natelle said quietly and abruptly. I didn't know why she said it, because we'd been sitting on the bench being peaceful and happy together, and now when she said she'd stopped taking the pill, this brought to mind an image of vaginas and penises, which wasn't an image we'd shared before. This meant we were close enough that Natelle felt she could tell me anything in her heart, or almost anything, and I was happy to be that close to her. But it also made me think of Gabriel having sex with her, and I was jealous. I wanted to have sex with her.

"You have?" I said.

"There's no reason to. Gabriel and I haven't been sleeping together for weeks," she said.

I was glad. I didn't want her sleeping with her husband. Something I realized again was that Natelle and I had never even kissed, but I wanted to be with her for the rest of my life. Once more I was having urgent thoughts about the only person who needed to know them, and who I couldn't tell.

"What's wrong?" I asked.

She made a quiet moaning sound and sighed loudly. "What isn't wrong?" she said, looking down at her hands in her lap, right next to a part of her I was trying not to think about. "Oh, I shouldn't talk about this. You just got over a nervous breakdown or something and you don't need some-body else's pain."

"If I have to have somebody else's pain, I want yours."

"That's sweet."

"I'm not trying to be sweet. You and I have to share each other's pain. I mean, I *want* to. The one thing you and I share is our lives and that includes the pain. So tell me what's wrong. The worst it'll do is give me another nervous break-down, and I'm getting accomplished at those. Now tell me, please."

She closed her eyes and smiled in a sad way, as if she were glad to be with me to help the sorrow rise up in her so we could both look at it and maybe drive it away, although I knew better than that. You don't usually drive sorrow away.

You just study it and pass some around, and then everyone has it.

"I'm going to tell you some things," she said, "some very difficult things, because I think I need to, or at least I want to. I want you to promise me that you won't run away," she said, and put her hand on mine.

"Run away from you?" I said. "I'm more likely to run toward you."

I did it again. Revealed too much. I might as well have given her a Hallmark card, if they had one about nervous breakdowns and love.

"You might change your mind," she said. "You might think I'm terrible."

"I'll never think you're terrible."

Her eyes closed again and she said, "I went to confession today. This morning, before I picked you up. Gabriel was already gone. To work, I think. I have no idea. I don't want to have any idea. I wasn't really sure why I was going to confession. Not because I'd committed a particular sin, but I've been very uneasy and restless and unhappy for a very long time, and I just needed to tell someone, like I'm telling you now. Or trying to. In the confessional, I told the priest that I'm not having a very good marriage. I told him . . .

"This is too hard. This is too much to remember," she said.

I put my hand on the soft part of her shoulder. "Tell me whatever you need to."

"I told him that Gabriel, as a practicing psychologist, has been having women at the apartment. He calls them his patients, but sometimes his patients have sex with him. I'm sure he does this during the day, when I'm not home. Twice I've found panties in the bedroom that aren't mine. I don't know what happened. I don't know when love starts failing, why it happens secretly in someone and they don't even care to tell you. Gabriel and I haven't been really close for a long time. I think it first happened without me knowing it. I think he loved me in a shallow way, and at some point it stopped being convenient for him. And instead of just giving me up, like he should have, he decided to *keep* me, the way you keep a pet.

"About a month ago, I found the second pair of panties in the bedroom. I was too hurt, too sad and frightened, to ask Gabriel what the hell was going on, to have to ask my own husband why we were losing our marriage and he didn't even want to tell me about it, as if he thought, "Well, the marriage is over, but there's no reason to tell my *wife.*' And what I did was mean and stupid, but I didn't care, I wanted to be mean, I wanted him to feel some of my pain. What I did was take the panties and fold them up neatly and put them on the dinner table under Gabriel's fork, like a napkin. I served him his dinner that way. He didn't say anything. He put the panties on his lap and ate dinner. And we never talked about it.

"I think I started to hate him then. It was like, as if, it didn't matter that I loved him. Like it had suddenly become an old and distant fact that I loved him, and this was now buried in me, and useless, as if it became a new part of me I didn't understand, that I was loving this stranger who sat across the table from me with a woman's panties on his lap and said nothing. Like he thought that was what I deserved. Nothing. One day, the reasons we got married had vanished, and he hadn't even told me. And I thought about killing him. Last weekend he came home drunk and with the fragrance of perfume on him. He went to bed with his clothes on and passed out in bed beside me, where I could smell the perfume, smell that he'd been rubbing up against a woman who wasn't me. He had absolutely no interest in how he was destroying me, and I thought of stabbing him in the throat with a pair of scissors. I thought the world wouldn't be better if he died, but I would. I stood in the doorway of the bedroom, looking at him, the way you stare at a wild animal. I didn't honestly want to kill him, but it was like I was dreaming and having thoughts that weren't really mine, and I had a simple vision of stabbing him in the throat, as if that was one possibility. And I didn't feel any remorse or sadness or compassion for him, as if long ago he stopped being human, and now he was just this animal with bones and flesh who remained in my life every day to hurt me. And he doesn't even want to hurt me. He doesn't plan it or hope for it. To him, it's merely an uninteresting result of how he lives.

"I told this to the priest, thinking that I'd committed a sin by imagining stabbing Gabriel in the throat. He said that maybe it was a sin, but it was certainly an understandable one. He asked me if I'd seen a counselor. I said 'My husband is a counselor.' He had nothing to say then. He said, 'Oh.'

"And now I don't know how to tell you the rest of this, or if I even should. It's probably stupid, like everything else I've been doing for my entire adult life. But I've thought about this for days or weeks. I can't remember. And I told this to the priest. Maybe I shouldn't tell it to you, but for the sake of understanding, for the sake of not having this in me alone, I just want to tell you, and you'll see why. After I knew that Gabriel was seeing other women, when I began to feel thoroughly alone and betrayed so much that sometimes I got sick to my stomach, I needed to be close to someone. I needed desperately to be safe with someone, to have someone hold me, and then I had fantasies of my own infidelity. I've never cheated on Gabriel, or anyone in my life. But even then, to think of cheating on Gabriel—and I told this to the priest— if there wasn't really a marriage left, what was there to cheat *on*? You can't be faithful to someone who's left you. Why should I feel guilty for needing someone when I've been betrayed?

"But I did feel guilty. There was a particular man, someone I've known for a long time, someone I feel safe with . . ."

Suddenly I was dizzy and starting to feel sick with sadness that Natelle was telling me about some man she needed and it wasn't me. Without ever having had her, I seemed to have lost her again.

Natelle kept talking about this man I never wanted to meet or know anything about.

"Sometimes I'd just have simple fantasies that he'd hold me, as if possibly we'd make love, but not then. Not yet," she said.

"Well, don't do it. You'll make me jealous," I said.

This seemed to startle Natelle. She blinked at me.

"You don't even know who it is," she said.

"And don't tell me. I don't want to know his name."

"You already know his name," she said gently, as if I could possibly like the son of a bitch.

"I do? Well, I'll try to forget it, whatever it is. And don't tell me."

"I don't think you should be jealous of him. You get along with him. He's someone you see every day."

"Don't tell me that. I don't want to guess his name. Damn it, Natelle, haven't you ever guessed that maybe I like you enough to be jealous over you? I know I'm not supposed to feel this way, but, damn, I've even been jealous of Gabriel, and I don't feel like politely hiding this right now. When you told me you and Gabriel haven't been sleeping together, I thought, 'Good. I don't *want* you to.' So now you know that. And now you're trying to tell me about some goddamn man you've had a few fantasies about? Please don't. You'll just hurt my feelings."

"I don't think so, Doyle."

"Take my word for it. I have too many feelings."

"Well, I'm going to tell you anyway."

"I won't listen. I'll put my fingers in my ears and hum," I said, and then I put my fingers in my ears and started humming.

Natelle grabbed my left hand and pulled my fingers from my ear.

"Stop humming."

I hummed louder, and then gave up.

"Please don't tell me his name."

She looked at me and said, "It's you."

I was dizzy again, and my stomach tingled.

"It's me?"

"Yes. You're the goddamn man you don't want to hear about."

A stunning rush of elation flashed through me like a drug, like my heart taking a disabling dose of happiness, and all I could do was weakly stare into her eyes, to see if she was joking, to see if there was real affection there, aimed at me only. It looked like there was. She still held onto my hand and said, "This doesn't mean I'm in love with you, although I'm not sure what it does mean. I know this has to be very upsetting to you."

"Upset me. I like it."

"Maybe it was stupid to tell you this."

"Sometimes being stupid is the right thing to do."

"I don't want you to think this means we're going to become lovers," she said, as if I were the one having the sexual fantasy and not her.

"I have no idea what this means," I promised.

"I'm telling you this because I wanted to be honest—as dangerous as that is—and because I needed to talk with you.

And, Doyle, there really were some horribly sad times in the last few weeks, when all of this was crashing down on me, and it just happened, it just happened to be true, that sometimes I sort of automatically or intuitively thought of you, not like we were going to be lovers, although maybe like that. Like I could be safe with you. And mainly," she said, sighing and looking down at our hands together, "mainly I don't know. That's the one thing that hasn't been damaged in the last few weeks. My ignorance. Are you mad that I told you this?"

Although I wanted to kiss her, I just put my hands on her cheeks so we were staring at each other, and I said, "I don't know which emotion I'm having, but it's one I don't want to stop."

Her eyes were bright and glistening, as if she'd started to cry, as if at last she'd let me know she loved me but there was no way we could proceed, no touch that would work. We just looked at each other awhile, staring hard into each other's eyes, touching each other that way. It made my stomach warm, the way I'd felt before when I'd been in love.

"My stomach's warm," I said.

"It's probably the hot dog," she said.

"No."

"Was it something I said?"

"I think I'm mesmerized. I like your eyes."

"I like yours."

"I'll let you have them."

"Then how would you see me?"

"I guess I'd better keep them."

"You'd better."

"In your fantasies, was I a gentleman?"

She smiled and said, "What do you mean?"

"Did I open the door for you?"

"That's not what you mean."

"No," I said. "In your fantasies, what did we do?"

"I didn't even tell the priest that."

"Well, it's none of his business what we do in your fantasies."

"And why do you want to know?" she said teasingly.

"Because I was there."

"You don't remember much about it, do you?"

"I guess, in your fantasies, you didn't give me a memory."

"Have you ever had any fantasies about me?"

"I'm having one right now."

"And what are we doing in your fantasy?"

"We're sitting on a bench, looking at each other."

"That's not a fantasy."

"Thank God."

She smiled at me, still staring deeply into me, and said, "I can't make love with you. I'm a Catholic."

"I'll be a Catholic."

"Do you realize what we're talking about?"

"Yes. I think we're talking about all the wondrous things we're not going to do."

"Why do you think it would be wondrous?"

"I refuse to imagine anything less than that."

"I haven't even told you what my fantasies were. Why do you assume we made love in my fantasies?"

"Because it's the only place we could do it and not get in trouble."

Looking away from me, she exhaled wistfully or forlornly and said, "Well, we did."

"We got in trouble?"

"No. We made love."

With this confession, she became quiet and sad, as if she was guilty of the incomplete crime of having me. I wanted

to hold her, but thought that might scare her, and I was starting to cry. I put my little finger around hers, like we could at
least touch in the smallest way, and she squeezed my finger,
as if our fingers were sentences and we were just learning to
talk that way. I didn't want to leave her, and everything was
simultaneously better and worse, because now we almost
had each other, but we realized that we weren't supposed to.
The one good thing in the world was bad.

After I couldn't stand being quiet anymore, I said, "Thank
you."

"For what?" she said.

"For looking for me," I said. This was supposed to make
her feel better, but it didn't seem to, as if she was depressed
about having told me a secret that, just a few seconds earlier,
had drawn us together. Now I couldn't tell if we were sitting
together or sitting apart. I wanted to say the one thing that
would soothe her and draw her toward me, but had no idea
what that was.

"What's wrong?" I said, desperately wanting to hear her
talk.

"Nothing. Just my whole life."

"Are you upset because you told me about your fantasies?"

"Yes. Don't you think that's the same thing as adultery?"

"Maybe. But if I committed adultery with you and I wasn't
even there, I'm going to feel cheated."

She smiled with her eyes closed, lightly squeezing my
finger.

"That's what I said to the priest," she said. "I said 'Do you
think I committed adultery in my heart?' He only said that
seemed possible. And, for some reason, I was in a cranky
mood, like I wanted the church to help me but I didn't want
the church to criticize me, and I said something like 'Well, if

adultery is a sin committed by two people, and only one of them does it, then that's not adultery at all. It must be an entirely new sin.' And instead of getting mad at me, the priest said there are no new sins. They're all repeats. Of course, this didn't settle anything, and I don't know why the hell I expected a priest to settle anything having to do with sexuality, since priests aren't supposed to have sexuality or know very much about it. And then he changed his mind. After I told him about Gabriel, about his abandonment of me and his various infidelities and his refusal to even acknowledge it, he said he couldn't remember what my confession was. I go to confession and the priest forgets my confession. But I couldn't remember it, either. I said I thought my confession might have been that I committed adultery in my heart. The priest said it's amazing that I still have a heart. I said, 'So I haven't committed anything?' He said, 'If you have, I don't recognize it.'

"Well," she said, staring at me again. "I'd heard of unforgivable sin. I guess now we have unrecognizable sin."

"Really? What happens when you commit an unrecognizable sin?"

"I think they take points off your driver's license. I don't know, Doyle. I just thought it was strange that a priest would invent the category of unrecognizable sin. So we didn't settle that, and then he asked me if I wanted to save my marriage. I thought about this. I said, 'Father. That would be like saving a tumor.' We didn't talk much after that."

"Have you thought seriously of divorcing Gabriel?"

"The Church doesn't recognize divorce."

"Well. They don't recognize divorce and they can't recognize certain sins. Your church is having trouble recognizing things."

"I think I will divorce Gabriel. I'll need a lawyer. I don't know why. Now it's going to cost me hundreds or thousands of dollars to get out of a bad marriage. Will you help me find a lawyer?"

"Of course I will. But remember—I'm biased. I'm the one who doesn't want you sleeping with your own husband. Does that bother you?"

"Sleeping with my husband? Yes."

"Will you tell me something?"

"What?"

"When you had sexual fantasies, what did we do?"

"*Doyle*," she said, as if she was scolding me, then she grinned. "Are you starting to get pornographic?"

"Pornographic? They were your fantasies. I just want to know what we did. Did we like it?"

"And I suppose you've never had sexual fantasies about *me*?"

"Yes. I have."

"Well, what did we do in *your* fantasies?" she demanded politely. "Who was on top?"

This shocked and elated me. We'd never discussed sex before, and now we were discussing it as if we might have it.

"On top of what?" I said.

"Was I on top or were you on top?"

"Sometimes we were sideways."

She seemed embarrassed by her own boldness and said, "Did we have dinner first?"

"Dinner? I didn't have fantasies about food."

"I think we better talk about this later," she said, sighing for about two or three seconds as if we *were* having sex. I wanted to help. My penis was already more optimistic than it should have been.

"All right. We'll talk about it later. I guess we should go

look for lawyers in the Yellow Pages," I said, kind of dizzily happy that we were even closer than before, as if we were on the verge of a romance that we were making sure we weren't talking about. And now that we were closer, I still didn't know what we were closer to. If Natelle knew, she didn't tell me. That was the problem about being alive. Things happened secretly in people. No one ever knew it unless you told somebody. I was going to pray that Natelle be in love with me, but then I remembered that the Church wouldn't recognize that. Maybe Natelle would. I looked at her and prayed, *I wish you'd love me,* and she didn't say anything. Maybe she was praying at me, too, and I didn't say anything. Frequently the world didn't work, and we only acted like it did.

"This isn't a happy way to be an adult," Natelle said as we both stood up to walk away. "I never thought when I was a girl that one day I'd get married and then go looking for lawyers in the Yellow Pages."

"I'm sorry," I said.

"Let's not talk about it anymore. Let's talk about something pleasant, if there's anything pleasant left in the world. How's your baseball team doing?"

"Oh, that. I guess you're referring to the Avenging Blowfish," I said as I held Natelle's hand and wished I never had to let it go.

14

Doltmeer assigned me to protect the ambassador of the People's Democratic Socialist Republic of Indizal, an almost imperceptible island nation off the coast of West Africa. All I knew about Indizal was that its primary export was its citizens. In size it was no bigger than Milwaukee, and it excelled only in its willingness to seek foreign aid. It wasn't even a Third World country, but hoped, by gloomy persistence, to rise to that status. Being assigned to protect the ambassador from Indizal was an honor to be resisted.

"Am I being punished?" I asked Doltmeer.

"We have an obligation to protect all of the foreign ambassadors in this city. It won't do you any good to brood."

"Who am I protecting the ambassador from?"

"Assailants."

"You mean his citizens?"

"I don't expect you to be rude to the ambassador."

"What's his name?"

"I haven't learned his name. It's written down some- where," Doltmeer said, pretending to search for a piece of paper on his desk that he had no interest in finding. "You're expected at the embassy at ten o'clock this morning."

"What do I say? 'I'm here to protect the ambassador. Will you tell me his name?'"

Doltmeer opened a folder on his desk and said, "Aramilo."

"So he does have a name? This'll make it easier to address him. Do they speak English at the embassy?"

"They speak Spanish."

"I don't."

"Ambassador Aramilo speaks English. He has a degree in music from the Philadelphia College of Textiles and Science."

This was too ludicrous to accept, as if Doltmeer didn't care if I knew anything true about my next assignment, since they were dumping me into it anyway.

"Really? He studied music at a college of textiles and sci- ence? Why should I believe that?"

"Don't argue with me. You're in enough trouble already."

"Is the president still mad at me?"

"The president doesn't even know you exist."

"I'll send him a postcard."

"Don't fuck this up, Doyle. The only assignment lower than this is looking for a new job."

So they really were punishing me. I was going to say something clever and sardonic, but I decided the cleverest thing I could do was be quiet.

SOMETHING I thought of as I morosely drove to the Indiza- lian Embassy to meet with Ambassador Hobar Aramilo was that, again, I was involved in extraneous and pointless pursuit: my job. What I did, if you looked at it abstractly, was wear a suit and carry guns to protect the lives of influential people who probably didn't deserve their influence and weren't any more valuable than the millions of people who had no influence at all. Probably I was an egalitarian who believed that all people were equal, but my job was to protect people who were thought of as better than equal. Even the people who wrote the Constitution were aristocrats. It was kind of darkly comical that a famous American saying was that all people were created equal, when it would have been more honest to say, "All people were created equal, but you don't have to stay that way." Equality was something to endure until you overcame it—like being an ambassador from a third-rate country whose gross national product came from foreign aid.

I was pretty cranky when I got to the embassy, but I repressed it all, as I always did, hiding nearly all of my human impulses so I'd seem professional. As I walked through the handsome embassy, I wanted to say to everyone, "Well, I'm here to protect you stupid fuckers from the enemies you probably deserve," but it was important to remain at my current level of trouble and not accumulate more, so I was quiet and polite and as inhuman as professionally necessary.

A fat woman who identified herself as the under-ambassador led me into Aramilo's huge and remarkably pretty office where I saw a skinny little man who at first I thought looked like a member of a religious sect, someone who might try to sell me incense and tamper with my soul. It was the ambassador.

"I am told to expect you," Ambassador Aramilo said in an unidentifiable accent, something like Spanish-Indian.

"Yes, sir."

He was so small, about five feet, weighing about the same as a sixth-grader. I'd never before seen a man of power who looked so weak. He had a grayish-black moustache, like Omar Sharif, and sort of looked like him if Omar had shrunk a lot and was bald. He wore a brilliant blue robe that, even if it was part of the national dress of Indizal, looked like a maternity gown. Aramilo had a pleasant and earnest smile, as if he might really be a nice man. He looked so frail and harmless I thought that if someone wanted to kill him, they could probably do it with a rock.

"My name is Hobar Aramilo, although why am I telling you that, since obviously you know?" Aramilo said as he shook my hand with the grip of a small boy.

"Yes, Mr. Ambassador."

"Oh, I appreciate your formality, but you needn't be that way in private. You're certainly free to call me Hobar."

"Certainly, Mr. Ambassador."

This made Aramilo laugh, so I decided he might not be a son of a bitch.

"Please sit down," Aramilo said in his distinct and unclassifiable accent, pointing to a big green sofa next to a window overlooking a neo-colonial gas station. "May I fix you a drink?"

A beer would've been nice.

"No, thank you. We're not allowed to drink while on assignment."

"I understand. You must remain alert and sober. I don't. I hope you don't mind if I fix a vodka tonic."

"It's not my role to mind anything. It's your embassy."

"Indeed, and a very agreeable one," he said, unscrewing the top of a bottle of costly Russian vodka and pouring about two inches into a glass. He neglected to put any tonic water in it.

"So now," Aramilo said, seated across from me in what looked like an antique chair, "since you're here to intimately guard me from the many possible enemies who lurk somewhere and would like to overthrow my government, may I ask how familiar you are with Indizal?"

"You export rice, manganese, and diamonds, which I assume aren't the ingredients in a casserole."

"Well, you do know something," he said, tipping his head back and laughing. "I don't think manganese is suitable for cooking."

"Tastes vary."

"Undoubtedly. But I assure you we don't eat metal in Indizal. Our favorite spice is curry, which we use to season chicken and fish and rice. Our national anthem is 'Carry Us Home to the Sea,' which I happen to have written myself. Unlike many ambassadors, I assume, I received no formal schooling in statecraft or the political sciences. I was but a penniless student studying piano for a few years in Philadelphia before returning to my home in Indizal. This was before the revolution. Do you know of that?" Aramilo said, smiling as if he'd asked too hard a question.

"The world has too many revolutions. I haven't memorized them all, but I'll assume yours was a good one."

"It was, in the sense that it worked."

"I think that's how we measure revolutions. They're good if you win."

"You are perhaps teasing me," he said in an amused but slightly wary tone.

"No. We're not allowed to tease anyone with diplomatic immunity."

"Oh. You seem to be a very proper Secret Service agent."

"The properest."

"You don't look that conservative," he said, as if examining my eyes or facial features.

"I'm as conservative as my employer needs me to be."

"Why don't I believe you?"

"I'm not authorized to analyze your beliefs."

"Most *in*-tresting. Most intresting," he said, grinning and then swallowing a half-inch of vodka. "But you don't have to remain so professionally aloof from me. While you're assigned to ensure my safety, I think, at least in private, we can converse as one human to another, if that suits you."

"In the Service, whatever suits us is none of our business. But if, as a condition of our professional association, you'd prefer for me to show some evidence of humanness, we're authorized to engage in such aberrations."

"You certainly work for an awfully rigid organization, I think."

"I have no opinions."

"No? Well, you should get some."

"I have no access to opinions."

"This is starting to get maddening. I want you to have a drink with me. Will your superiors allow you to drink if I insist on it?"

"If it will aid the atmosphere of cooperation between sovereign nations."

"Do you like vodka?"

"If I'm requested to like it."

"All right. Then I insist that you have a glass of vodka and like it."

"I guess I have to. Do you have any lime?"

Thirty minutes later, while Aramilo was on his third glass of vodka without tonic, he wanted to play some songs for me on his baby grand piano.

"I should probably be out in the hallway guarding you," I said.

"I'm not out in the hallway. You should guard me in here. Have you heard this song before?" Aramilo said excitedly, and began playing a peculiar melody as he sang:

> When first I saw you in the factory hall
> You reminded me of the love scene in *Das Kapital*.
> And when we embraced in simple seduction
> You put your hands on my means of production.

"I made that up myself," Aramilo said.

"Sounds like it."

"Do you know what it is?"

"I promise I don't."

"I put the economic theories of Karl Marx to music. It's called the 'Lumpenprole Waltz.'"

"Oh. A waltz for the dispossessed. That means you can dance to it, but you aren't invited to the dance?"

"Ex-*act*-ly!"

"That's nice. Do you know any other communist folk songs, like 'Home, Home on the Gulag'?"

Aramilo shook his head. "And you said you weren't allowed to tease anyone with diplomatic immunity."

"I'm sorry. I must've misplaced my protocol. It might be under the couch," I said, glancing down at the floor. "I'm not sure if you should keep playing piano. We should probably discuss your security arrangements for a while, if that's all right." I sipped from my second glass of vodka without tonic, realizing from my giddiness that I was only slightly drunk. "Who's trying to kill you?"

"Someone's trying to kill me?" Aramilo said in a slightly alarmed voice.

"If not, then why am I protecting you?"

"The PDF might want to see me dead."

"Who's the PDF?"

"I don't know."

"You don't know?"

"They haven't told us. In Indizal, they commit acts of violence and terrorism against my government, and they never say who they are. It's just PDF."

"Could it stand for People's Democratic Front?"

"That's fine with me."

"Well, I'm not asking for your approval, as if we're recommending suitable names for a terrorist group. You know, if it's the People's Democratic Front against the People's Democratic Socialist Republic of Indizal, it makes it sound like the people versus the people."

"Yes. It would sound like that."

"In America, we have a saying. I wish I could remember it."

"Is it about people?"

"Yes. That's right. The saying is, 'You can fool all of the people some of the time, and some of the people all of the time, and when you get good at it, you're reelected.' "

"Is that really a saying?"

"It is if you say it. But why would the PDF want to see you dead?"

"My favorite American saying is 'If it's broke, don't fix it.' "

"I've never heard that saying before. You must be from a different part of America. Overseas, for example. Tell me . . . are you politically valuable enough to be shot?"

"And what's that other American saying? I can't think of it. It's like, 'We earn our money the old-fashioned way—we raise our prices.' "

"You're not paying attention to me. How am I supposed to protect you if I have no reason to believe you're worth being shot?"

"In Indizal, we have a saying: 'The blowfish is tastiest that isn't eaten.'"

"Blowfish. What a coincidence. We've started a covert baseball team called the Avenging Blowfish. We've scheduled a game against the CIA, if we can ever find out where it is. Do you play baseball in Indizal?"

"No. The ground isn't flat enough. We have mountains."

"Really? I didn't think Indizal was big enough for a mountain."

"They are little mountains."

"You're a young country. They'll grow. Do you have ski resorts?"

"We have no snow."

"No snow? Well, how the hell do you expect to attract rich American tourists to exploit your economy and make you resentful?"

"Well, we do have our own culture, you know. Have you read any of the works of our famous national writer, Gara de Sayo?"

"If I'm familiar with him, I've managed to not remember."

"It was Gara de Sayo who wrote: 'We are born with all the ignorance we need. We never run out.'"

"That's a nice saying. It reminds me of another American saying: 'The two things that all people have in common are ignorance and something I can't remember.' But Hobar, you know what?"

He leaned his head forward and said, "What?"

"If I'm supposed to protect you from your enemies, you better go get some."

"That's not my responsibility. Your government is paying you to find my enemies," he said, then turned back to the piano and began playing a uniquely drunken chord.

"I know who your enemy is—the *New York Times* music critic."

He ignored me and continued playing a song in which his skill was apparent but badly impaired. He was drunk, and this was my new job—to protect a high-ranking drunken pianist.

15

I was brooding, sitting back like a sullen spectator, regarding my recent misfortunes, and I decided my newest mission was to retaliate against the president. I had been relegated to guarding a high-ranking drunken pianist, and Abbas had been fired because the president was served food meant for a lower class of people: the American public. Spontaneously I envisioned a long headline in the *Washington Post*: "White House chef fired for Spam incident; President scorns food fit only for voters." Someone could nail the bastard that way. Tell the press that the White House chef was fired for serving the president a food that millions of Americans eat every day. Not the cat food, of course. No one would have to know about that. Anyone would have been justified in firing Abbas for serving cat food to the president. But they didn't *know* about that.

They fired him for the Spam, which was the same thing as saying the president felt degraded by being made to eat like a common American. Someone could nail him good for that one. Now I only had to find that someone.

My search for Abbas, who I hadn't seen since the evening he marinated Spam with lemon juice, led me to the Valley of Sleep Funeral Home and Burial Park, near the Goddard Space Flight Center. I wasn't going to ask him why he was there, since it was none of my business how he ruined his life, but he explained that he'd found temporary work in afterlife marketing for his Uncle Jamal, who owned the Valley of Sleep.

"It's just temporary," Abbas said.

"The afterlife?" I said.

"No. I mean my working here is only temporary. With my resume, I'll soon be working at one of the finest restaurants I don't know about yet. They'll call me soon. I hope so. I hate being around dead people all day. Death is too morbid for me. Uncle Jamal says death is a living. I wish he'd be quiet. Did you come here to visit me?"

"I have a way for you to get even with the president."

"How?" he said doubtfully. "I already got even with the president. That's why I was fired."

"True. But you didn't get even very well."

"No. I failed. But for a while it worked. They at least ate the food, and probably enjoyed it for a few minutes before they realized they shouldn't enjoy it."

"I got in trouble, too, Abbas. I wasn't fired or anything, but they demoted me. Well, not really demoted. Gardenaul said that, because I knew you were fixing disguised Spam for the president, I should've reported you, and so they hold me responsible."

Abbas suddenly looked sad, or spooked, like he felt guilty for me. "What did they do to you?"

"They assigned me to protect an eminent drunk."

"What?"

"Have you ever heard of Indizal?"

A distressed and bewildered expression came over Abbas's face. "Isn't that a country somewhere?"

"That's precisely where it is. It's one of those little island nations built on a volcano that doesn't work anymore. I have to protect the ambassador from Indizal. He's a nice guy, I guess, but all I can tell about him now is that he gets drunk and plays Marxist waltzes on the piano."

"And is this bad?" Abbas asked.

"It is if you don't like Marxist waltzes."

"I mean, you're being punished by being there?"

"It's not a good assignment. The ambassador's regarded as a trivial diplomat whose presence in Washington means virtually nothing. It's not good to be assigned to virtually nothing."

"Oh. I'm sorry. And it's my fault, isn't it?"

"Don't start that shit. What you do is your fault. What I do is mine. We'll both get over it, especially if we get even with the president, and I know how."

"Tell me," Abbas said, staring intently at me with his fierce brown eyes, as if his animosity toward the president was still healthy.

"The good thing about my plot is that you do all the work and I do nothing. That's because you've already been fired and can't be fired again. I can. So you're the one who has to do it."

"Do what? Tell me."

"First I want you to sign this agreement," I said, pulling from my coat pocket an agreement I'd written that morning. I showed it to Abbas as I read it aloud: "I, Abbas Amal, rationally and soberly swear that if I agree to the terms of the confidential plan being proposed, I will never publicly or privately reveal that Doyle Coldiron had anything to do with it, on my honor as an occasionally pious Muslim."

Abbas gave the agreement a troubled look and said, "I'm not a Muslim. I'm an Episcopalian."

"You are? But you're Arabic. How the hell can you be an Episcopalian?"

"You just join. Why do you stupid Americans think everyone from the Middle East has to be a Muslim?"

"What do you mean 'stupid American'? You're an American, too."

"Well, I'm not a Muslim. I grew up with Islam, of course, but when my family moved from Jordan to Nebraska and found out Americans didn't like Muslims, we became Episcopalians."

"That's the hardest church to spell."

"I know. But my father didn't want to be a Baptist, which is easier to spell, because Baptists can't drink. My father wanted a church where you could drink."

"But if your parents grew up in Islam, where no one drinks, why'd he decide he wanted to drink?"

"My father was a professor, not a cleric. He liked whiskey."

"In Islam?"

"Whiskey is good anywhere. And so my father embraced a religion that tolerated whiskey."

"Well, I apologize for calling you a Muslim. I'll scratch that out and write down that you're an occasionally pious Episcopalian."

"But what's your plot?"

"Okay. Here's my plot. Go to the *Washington Post* with documents proving you were the White House chef and that you were just fired by Gardenaul. Tell them the simple truth, without any exaggerations, and tell them this is what it means: It means the president felt degraded because he had to eat the same kind of food as the people who elected him."

"What's wrong with that? It's just snobbery," Abbas said in a confused tone.

"Don't say that, Abbas. Let's not try to undermine my plot to humiliate the president."

"Well, what's wrong with snobbery? That's why we even have chefs like me."

"Abbas. You're undermining my goddamn plan. Stop it. The president fired you because he's a snob. Are you defending that?"

"Of course not."

"Well then, let's get the son of a bitch."

"But people don't care if the president's a snob. They expect him to be one, don't they?" Abbas said with growing confusion.

"Maybe so, but there's a paradox about politics. Maybe the public does expect the president to get into office and act like an aristocrat at state dinners, and even if everyone secretly imagines how they'd like to be in power and act like an aristocrat, they also despise the idea that the president thinks he's better than they are. So if you can go to the paper and prove he fired you for treating him like a common American, he'll be embarrassed for weeks."

Abbas's eyes widened with delight. He smiled and said, "This might work."

"Of course it will. It'll be in all the papers. It'll be on the morning news and the evening news. You'll probably be invited to the 'Phil Donahue Show.'"

"This is a good plot. Will you come on the 'Phil Donahue Show' with me?"

"No. No one's supposed to know I had anything to do

with this, Abbas. If you tell anyone, I'll kill you. I have guns, remember?"

"That's right. That's how you protect the president. Why do you protect the president if you don't like him?"

"I don't. I protect a drunken pianist."

16

With a naïveté I found endearing and lovely, only because it was mine, I imagined Natelle would promptly get a divorce and be in love with me, because I couldn't imagine anything more wondrous than that; as if, in an instant never before seen in human history, the likelihoods of daily life would vanish and be replaced by this miracle—what I wanted.

It wasn't going to be.

"There are two problems," Natelle said, staring wearily at me across the table at the Nevermore Bar & Grill, where we were having dinner. "Gabriel might contest the divorce, and the Catholic Church doesn't recognize divorce. Some priests do, but the Church in general doesn't. So for all I know, I might spend months trying to get a divorce, and when I finally do, the church will say I'm still married."

"Screw the church," I said.

"That's not very good advice."

"I withdraw it. But what do you mean Gabriel might contest the divorce? Did he say that?"

"No. He didn't say anything. When I told him Tuesday night that I'd contacted a lawyer to file for divorce, he didn't say anything. He didn't even look at me. He was just sullen and withdrawn. I told him my life had been ruined long enough and I was going to stop it. I was terribly rational and calm and sick to my stomach. I didn't know I could feel so bad, that I could feel worse, but I can. Do you know how, when you're in love, you think the emotion can't get better, but it does? I think pain's the same way. Right when you think it's unbearable, it gets worse. I don't think you can just get rid of someone you were in love with. It's like having a ghost in you. It's a ghost you don't want anymore, but it's still there.

"And I want it to go. I don't love him anymore. There's nothing between us but contempt and sadness and anger, and I want it to just stop, go away, get the hell out of me. But it's all there in me, unresolved and frantic, like some hidden struggle going on in me that I don't even know about. And it scares me. I'm not even sure what emotions I have anymore. I'm only sure that I wish they'd stop, and I know they won't."

She put her hands against her cheeks with the tips of her little fingers holding her eyes shut. "Do you think I need to see a psychiatrist?"

This scared me, that she'd asked me—a man who probably needed psychiatric help—if *she* needed help.

"Maybe we should go together," I said.

"Would you hold my hand?"

"I'd hold both of your hands. I'd hold your wrists and your elbows."

She smiled a little bit and said, "Would you hold my ears?"

"And your feet."

She put her hand on mine on the table, and I wanted to tell her I loved her, so I did.

"I love you," I said, looking hard into her eyes, as if the words alone weren't sufficient and had to be made true by my eyes, and all of the truth began to escape out of me like the wind.

"You love me?" she said in a sad and wondering voice, as if this wasn't what she needed, but she wanted to examine it.

"Yes. Yes, I do."

"Does that mean you want to go to bed with me?"

Knowing that it was the wrong answer, I said, "No." Then I said, "Well, technically, yes."

"Technically?" she said. "You want to go to bed with me technically? I think you must be trying to say something else."

"I think this is a bad time for me to try to make sense."

"Well, let's not . . ."

"I didn't mean to scare you by saying I love you."

"I'm not sure that you did scare me. Like I said, I'm not sure which emotions I'm having anymore. But when you say you love me, does that mean *love* love, or *sex* love?"

"Why do the two have to be different?"

"I think you're not answering my question."

"I'm pretty sure I'm not either."

"Are you hiding something, Doyle?"

"I'm always hiding something."

"Then you do want to go to bed with me?" she said.

"Well, it wouldn't have to be a bed," I said.

"Doyle!" she said in astonishment, her cheeks looking a

little flushed. "Are you telling me you're waiting in line to be my lover?"

"You mean there's a line? Everything gets harder."

"But you can't . . . this is . . . what're you saying to me?"

"Not very much so far. All I mean is, I just want you to know I love you, and of course I'm sexually attracted to you. I always have been. I just never told you before because you were married. And I'm sorry I blurted it out. Well, no, I'm not. I love you, and I won't take it back. But it doesn't mean I'm waiting in line to be your lover. What line?"

"I didn't mean a real line. I just meant . . . so this isn't purely Platonic, your feelings for me?" she said, and sipped some wine.

"Let's keep Plato out of this."

"Doyle. This is a bad time to try to fall in love with me."

"All my life has been a bad time to try anything. If I wait for that one good day, I might be dead. Still, I'll leave you alone."

"Stop it," she said, and touched my hand. "Don't leave me alone. Don't leave me."

"I'd never leave you, even though I've never had you."

"But I can't go to bed with you."

"Bed, bed, bed. It's just a piece of furniture, but the paramount piece of furniture in human history. Did I use that word right?"

"Bed?" she asked.

"Never mind. I'm not trying to take advantage of you."

"I won't let you," she said, smiling at me in a troubled way.

"And you can't stop me from doing what I won't attempt. All I mean is I love you. You can take that for every possible meaning, because that's probably how I mean it. And you can't hurt me. I already am. Well, actually, you could hurt me. It's remarkably easy. But I think all I mean, if I can just think of . . ."

She put her hand over my mouth, just lightly, as if to hush me, as if to let me taste her fingers. She said, "I left Gabriel today. I moved into an apartment by myself. It's the start of a new life I don't know anything about. And I'm scared. I'd like you to come over and keep me company for a while, on my first night in the abyss."

It looked like she might cry. I wished I could stop it. I kissed her fingers and said, "The abyss? Is that like a studio apartment?"

And she laughed, even though I was sure that when she said abyss, she meant herself.

IN THE living room, which only had a couch and some curtains and a little portable TV resting on an end table or something, Natelle put her coffee cup of wine on the floor in front of the couch, then put one of the pillows on my lap and lay down with her head in my lap and one of her hands on my stomach. She did this without saying anything, not asking if it would be all right, not wondering why it seemed best now to be together this way, which we'd never done before, and which to me was euphoric or blessed, as I tingled with sexual love and regular love and love I didn't know about, and the simple, astonishing wonder of being touched by her.

Even with her eyes closed, Natelle looked exhausted, and I decided that what we were doing wasn't the least bit erotic, but we were sharing the sanctuary of each other. I started thinking, *I love you, I love you, I love you,* like she'd hear me thinking. People always wanted magic. Reality didn't seem quite sufficient. Reality didn't work well enough. But then, magic didn't work at all. Still, I wanted some, thinking, *I love you. Please know this.*

Maybe she was in love with me, too, but there was no way for her to say it, because, all the time we'd known each other, she'd been married, and happily married at first, and then badly, horribly married. And everything Natelle and I had done together was restricted by taboo. So even if we were released from it now, the force of always never having each other was still there, like gravity or something. Of course, maybe she wasn't in love with me and never would be. Then I was a stupid goddamn idiot. I had experience at that. I knew how to be one.

I put my hand lightly on her cheek, and she didn't speak. She breathed regularly, as if she felt safe with my hand on her cheek. I started to pray, *Our Father, who art in Heaven,* but that wasn't the right prayer. 'Give us this day our daily bread' wasn't at all what I had in mind. It was 'Give me this day Natelle.' I didn't know a standard prayer for when a woman was lying in your lap, and since it would've been a prayer that involved sexual climax, there wasn't one in the Bible for that. As hard as I was trying to be spiritual, I realized I was trying to pray for something exquisite I wasn't supposed to have: a married woman.

I thought, *Jesus, she hired a lawyer.* It didn't seem as if Jesus would be amused, and I quit thinking about Him, as if I could pray to somebody else—a more reasonable savior. It didn't seem fair that you'd have to pray for the one thing you needed, to love someone who loved you, that it didn't have to be granted to you and you could live your entire life in unresolved sadness. As if God thought that was just fine. I didn't think it was just fine. Of course, it didn't matter what I thought. Most of the time, reality did what it wanted, and joy and sadness were the occasional accidents randomly given to us. Still, I had hope—whatever that was.

I looked down at Natelle's face and was enraptured with

every part of it, looking at her closed eyes and her lashes and her nose and her lips and her cheeks, as if she was the most sacred gift I maybe wasn't supposed to have. I looked away and looked back at her, and I was enraptured again. I felt a swarm of affection that I needed to give to her, though there was no proof yet that she even wanted it. She was asleep, and didn't look like she was ready to be swarmed, so I didn't.

In front of the couch, the TV movie was over and the evening news was starting, with a woman saying, "Our top story of the night: White House officials refused to comment on a report today that former White House chef Abbas Amal was fired last week after having served disguised Spam to the president and a group of foreign diplomats during a state dinner at the White House. In a story being printed in the *Washington Post* tomorrow, Abbas Amal—seen here in a file photo serving barbecue to Pope John Paul the Second— claims that he secretly served the popular American luncheon meat to the president as an act of minor vengeance after the president ate a hot dog at a Baltimore Orioles game and reportedly told journalists at the game that he didn't eat that well at the White House. Chief of Staff Clark Gardenaul declined comment. Amal, reached at his home in Washington today, admitted his part in the Spam incident, but claimed it was justified."

They showed Abbas in front of his garage. "Possibly it was a mistake to serve Spam in disguise to the president, but it was a mistake I liked," he said. "I felt, in my opinion, that the president was insulting me on television and in the newspaper to say an ordinary hot dog was better than my meals. And so I decided, hey, if the president likes processed meat, I'll give him processed meat. I marinated it in herbs and lemon juice, and breaded it and prepared a light lemon sauce for it. Undoubtedly, it was the best Spam the president ever ate, and I was fired for it."

"Mr. Amal," a female reporter said, "why did you choose to publicize your apparent misfortune at the White House?"

"Apparent?" Abbas said. "I lost my job. I think that's worse than apparent."

"Were you trying to embarrass the president?"

"Let me offer another view. If you recall that, as I'm told, Spam is one of the most common foods of the American public, then this is what it means: I was fired for treating the president like an American."

I wondered if I should wake up Natelle and tell her this wonderful news that would get me fired if Abbas talked too much. But she needed to sleep, to not have to think about her escape from Gabriel and her ruined life. She was asleep with three of her fingers tucked under my shirt, and I felt her ribs and part of her breast pressing onto my leg as she breathed. Even if she was only touching me in her sleep, unconsciously, I at least wanted that. I put my hand on the pillow in front of her nose to feel the warm flow of her breathing. That was all I had: a sleeping woman and her breath. It seemed like a lot.

17

Seated on an antique chair near one of the windows in Aramilo's office, ostensibly guarding Aramilo from an imminent threat that so far had failed to be either imminent or a threat, I faced the general direction of Natelle's office in the White House and silently prayed, *Please let Natelle and me love each other for the rest of our lives,* aiming this prayer toward Natelle without knowing her longitude or latitude, imagining the prayer rushing by her like an inexplicable and pleasant breeze that she'd feel around her—realizing intuitively that it was my prayer—and that she'd love me for it.

Probably not, though. She might not even be in the White House then, and my prayer would be one more hope uselessly fired off into nothing. I wasn't sure that praying even worked. Maybe God just listened to idiots like me, and, as the prayer whooshed into God's omniscient ears, God said: "Doesn't interest me. Try again." It didn't seem like God ever granted me anything I prayed for. It wasn't like I was praying for a new car or a washing machine. I was praying for love. Prayers didn't get any more sacred than that, or any more pointless, either. It never worked. Sometimes I thought prayer was just talking to yourself and hoping someone else was listening. Maybe, instead of praying to God, I should pray to Natelle. At least she'd listen.

As I stared distractedly out the window, Aramilo began playing some jackass song on the piano, saying, "Do you recognize this?"

"I'm trying not to," I said.

Aramilo smiled boyishly and began playing piano with one hand as he sipped vodka from a big glass. It seemed like that was his job as the ambassador, to stay drunk and play piano. I wished he'd be quiet.

"Would you be quiet?" I asked.

"I'm the ambassador. I don't have to be quiet."

I wondered how the whole world had so developed that the effects of all humanity resulted in this particular building in this particular town with me aiming my heart several miles away at a woman I only wanted to love, with little proof that this could possibly work. And instead of attending to that, which was the one thing in the world that mattered, my life was so arranged that I carried a machine gun to shoot at people who probably weren't going to attack the ambassador from Indizal, who joyfully played songs I didn't recognize or want to.

Playing a new song I didn't know, Aramilo said, "Have you heard this one before?"

"No."

I looked toward where I thought Natelle might be and I

prayed, *If she gets divorced, I'd like to marry her. Will anything work?*

"Do you want me to show you how to play piano?"

That wasn't what I prayed for. Maybe God decided that instead of love, I needed piano lessons.

"Sure," I said. "And I'll show you how to fire a machine gun."

"Would you?" Aramilo said in a delighted voice. "I've always wanted to shoot a machine gun."

"Okay. You teach me how to play a Mozart sonata, and I'll show you how to shoot the doors off a Greyhound bus."

"But I don't know a Mozart sonata."

"You're screwed, then."

"Oh please. I don't want to be screwed. I could teach you how to play 'Begin the Beguine,' by Cole Porter," Aramilo said hopefully.

"What's 'beguine' mean?"

" 'Beguine'?"

I looked at Aramilo and said, "Well, if you're going to begin the goddamn beguine, shouldn't you know what a beguine is?"

"It's just a song," Aramilo said defensively. "I don't know what it means. And anyway, it's an Am-ER-ican song. You're an American. Don't you know what a beguine is?"

"Maybe it's a car. You're going on a trip and someone says 'Okay. Someone go begin the beguine.' "

"Ha," Aramilo said smugly. "You have no idea what a beguine is."

"Well, if my ignorance duplicates yours, you can hardly feel superior."

Someone knocked at the door and walked in. It was Maria, the chargé d'affaires, carrying some papers. "These are the trade agreement proposals, Mr. Aramilo," she said. "I've told the senate subcommittee staff that the proposals will be ready by this afternoon, if you'll just examine them for me, please." Maria placed the papers on top of the piano and waited for a reply.

"What's 'beguine' mean?" Aramilo asked her.

"Pardon me?" she said.

"'Beguine,'" Aramilo said as he flipped some pages of sheet music.

Maria looked mystified and impatient. "The senators would like to begin studying the proposals tomorrow," she said.

"Of course," Aramilo said. "But we need to find out what 'beguine' means first. Just leave the papers on the piano. Do we have a dictionary?"

"I'll confer with you this afternoon," Maria said as she turned on her heel and walked out of the room, gently slamming the door as if giving us a lesson in being elegantly rude.

"I guess she doesn't know what 'beguine' means," I said. "I don't think anyone does. I've lived in America all my life, and I never saw anyone begin a beguine."

Aramilo walked over to the massive bookshelf he never used and said, "Here's a dictionary."

"What about the trade agreement?" I said. "I didn't know Indizal had anything to trade. Do you guys have baseball cards?"

"How do you spell it?" Aramilo said, holding the dictionary open.

"'Beguine'? I think it's b-e-g-u-i-n-e."

"Yes, yes."

"Don't tell me what it means. I want to guess. 'Beguine' means . . . I think it's a casserole. I'm hungry. Did anyone begin the beguine yet?"

"It's not a casserole, you fool. Look. It's a *dance*," Aramilo said.

"A dance?"

"Yes. It's a 'vigorous popular dance of the islands of Saint Lucia and Martinique that somewhat resembles the rhumba.' Now will you teach me how to shoot the doors off a Greyhound bus?"

"No. You're an ambassador. Ambassadors are supposed to play tennis, not shoot machine guns."

"During the revolution . . ."

"Oh no. Not any more about the goddamn revolution. Please! Practically everybody's had a goddamn revolution by now. What's so fun about shooting at people, anyway? I shot at people in Vietnam and they shot at me. I don't remember anyone saying 'Boy, that's fun. Shoot at me some more.'"

"You were in Vietnam?" Aramilo said, staring at me with a surprised, serious look. He put the dictionary down and walked back over to his vodka on the piano. "You don't look old enough to have been there."

"I was nineteen. That's not very old."

Aramilo almost looked sober, now, and fascinated, staring at me with his big, dilated pupils. He seemed to sip his vodka respectfully. "Were you a patriot?" he asked.

"I was 1-A."

"What's that?"

"It's an unwilling patriot," I said, standing up to go to Aramilo's refrigerator and get a bottle of Dutch beer. "I was drafted."

"Drafted?"

"Conscripted. You better go get your dictionary again," I said, walking back to my chair with a bottle of Grolsch.

"I thought you weren't supposed to drink while guarding me."

"I'm not guarding you. I'm on break."

"When were you in Vietnam?"

"In 1971. We have a government agency called the Selective Service. They decide who is eligible for military service. Back then, the people who were the most eligible were designated as 1-A."

"The *best*?" Aramilo wondered.

"No. You must be confusing 1-A with A-1, which is a steak sauce. That's different. Although I wish they had declared me A-1. I'd rather have been steak sauce."

"You still didn't tell me what 'draft' means."

"The draft means you're fucked. If you got drafted, meaning the Selective Service had selected you to be in the Army, your friends would throw a big going-away party for you, with party hats and balloons and a big banner saying 'We Love You. You're Fucked.' "

"I don't believe that part," Aramilo said, trying to smile and still look serious.

"Well, you shouldn't. I did have a party, but it would've been rude to put up a sign saying I was fucked, especially when everyone knew I was. What I remember about the party," I said, staring at Aramilo to see if he was interested, and it looked as if he was completely serious, as well as drunk, "was that I wanted to get real drunk, and then be alone with my girlfriend and maybe make love with her before I went off to die. But I didn't have a girlfriend. That was all screwed up. Usually when soldiers get ready to go off to war, they're supposed to hold their wives or lovers and tell them to wait for them. But I didn't have anyone to wait for me. So I told this girl who I knew from high school, Rachel, to wait for me. 'But I'm not your girlfriend,' she said. I said, 'Well, you don't have to do anything. Just *wait* for me.' She said she would."

Aramilo somberly sipped his vodka, perhaps sadly imagining me asking Rachel to wait for me. "Were you shot?" he said.

"Not at the going-away party. There weren't any guns there."

"Were you shot in Vietnam?"

"No, and I still find that surprising, when you consider how many hundreds or thousands of bullets and mortars and rockets and things were fired toward me, and not a one of them hit me. And you think, 'Jeez these fuckers are bad shots,' which of course isn't the truth. I probably fired off a few hundred bullets at random, having no idea what I'd hit or if I hit anything at all. I'm sure I hit some trees. Sometimes we'd joke about that and say, 'Those trees won't be attacking us again.'"

"I assume this means you were in combat," Aramilo said in a respectful voice.

"That's what it's called when people shoot at you. Yes. And I think, you know, I used to think, maybe a few times, after there'd been a firefight or something, and we'd been shooting randomly into the trees again, that I'd get the Congressional Medal of Gardening for killing more trees than necessary."

"Were you ever injured?"

"Yes. Yes, I was. But I don't like to tell that story because it requires facts."

"Well, I won't know if what you're telling me is factual or not. Will you tell me?"

"Sure, I guess. We were in a firefight somewhere in Vietnam. The reason I specify 'somewhere' is because we had no idea where it was. Do you know what a firefight is?"

"No. I don't know that word."

"A firefight is when two groups of armed strangers surprise each other and spontaneously start shooting at each other, not because they've done anything bad, but just because they're there. And I think that's what war is. When you find somebody conveniently nearby, you shoot them. So that's what we were doing. But we weren't so much shooting each other as we were shooting *at* each other. We were on opposite ends of a rice paddy, just shooting and shooting and shooting, like in a movie where everybody fires their guns just to increase the noise, but there were enough trees and things to hide behind that, at least on our side, no one got hit. And then eventually we stopped shooting, both sides, not for any tactical reasons, but I think because we all realized that no one was winning and no one was losing. We were in a Mexican standoff in Vietnam. I love geography. Don't you? Anyway, what we were doing then was sullenly hiding from each other, and, presumably, trying to think of the most rational way to kill everyone on the other side. And then I saw a huge green spider about the size of a coffee cup on my leg. I hate spiders. I fear and detest and despise spiders, especially one so big and one that's on me. I was going to brush off the spider with my hand, but I thought it would bite my hand. I could've stood up to shake my leg and knock the spider off, but someone would see me and shoot me. It looked like the spider was staring at me. It kept walking up my leg, so I raised up my rifle and viciously slammed the rifle butt onto the spider. This squashed the spider and broke my knee. This also meant I could go home. Not right away, of course. We still had a firefight to resume, which we did. But eventually both sides snuck away, as if we didn't mind being in a war as long as we weren't being shot at. And that was the end of the war for me. I found out that you don't have to defend the world against Communism if you break your knee. Of course, then all the other guys wanted to break their knees with their rifles. One of the officers threatened to take their rifles away. It was a fun time. About a week later, I was back home in Kansas, limping around like a war hero, with people asking if I'd been shot by the Viet Cong. And, you know, it just doesn't sound heroic to say you defended world liberty by breaking your knee in an attempt to squash a spider. I mean, you're not going to be invited by the American Legion or the PTA to give a speech at a dinner about how you made the world a little safer by squashing a spider. So I just told people I didn't want to talk about it. And that's how I helped save the world from Socialists like you. You are a Socialist, aren't you?"

"What happened to Rachel?" Aramilo asked. "The woman who was waiting for you."

"Oh. Rachel. I don't know. I think she decided to wait for me somewhere where I couldn't find her."

18

One of the most secret things I'd ever done was go to a psychiatrist to see if my 60-second nervous breakdown meant I was crazy. Maybe it just meant I was efficient. Instead of having a nervous breakdown that lasted days or weeks, like most people, I got mine done in a minute. Although what did "crazy" mean anyway? Did it mean someone was incapable of having sustained, rational thought? If so, practically everyone in the world could be regarded as crazy, as if people went into and out of sanity several times a day, which maybe they did.

I was going to talk with Natelle about this, about going to see a psychiatrist, but I didn't want to hurt her with new worries, right when she was hurting about as much as she could stand because of her attempted divorce, a process which was like a formal acknowledgment of a ruined life.

Also, I knew that one reason, if not the main reason, I'd had my 60-second nervous breakdown and my earlier attacks of sadness seemed to be that I desperately needed to love someone, and it was Natelle. I didn't want to tell her I loved her so much I needed psychiatric care.

So I didn't tell her. And because I didn't want to tell anyone else, either, there was no way to ask anyone who a good psychiatrist might be. So I was forced to search for one at random in the Yellow Pages. There were dozens of them, as if insanity was a pretty big industry. Since I didn't know any reason to prefer one psychiatrist I didn't know over another one, my impulse was to pick someone whose name I liked. I picked Dr. Marilee Boulan, because her name sounded nice. Marilee. It sounded like she'd have flowers in her hair and offer me some pie she'd baked. And then she'd tell me that even if I was crazy, I was still a very nice man. "Mr. Cold-iron," she would say, "you might be as unstable as a new-born calf, but I think you're sweet."

She didn't have flowers in her hair when I met her in her office. She was about my age, with short black hair, and wore silver earrings in the shape of squids. I was glad they weren't real squids. At first I was afraid to tell her very much, as if I didn't want her to think there was anything wrong with me. I thought that, even in front of a psychiatrist, you ought to seem sane, as if whatever was bothering you actually wasn't very serious, so that all of a sudden you wouldn't need to see a psychiatrist.

And then she spoke. I knew that was going to happen.

"What would you like to talk about?" she asked politely.

"Baseball," I said.

"Are you having a problem with baseball?" she said with gentle skepticism.

"No. I have no problems with baseball, which is probably why I'd like to talk about it."

"It's perfectly normal to feel nervous in a psychiatrist's office."

"Do you?"

She smiled and said, "I sense that you're trying to gain a degree of control, which is a good sign. It means you're aggressive rather than passive."

"In my job, you have to be aggressive."

"And what is your job?"

"I can't tell you."

"Oh. Do you work for the government?"

"Which government?"

"The United States government."

"Yes. That one."

"Well, I certainly don't have to know anything about your profession, unless it's related to why you came to see me. Your secrets are yours."

"That's why I came to see you. Some of my secrets shouldn't be mine."

"Oh? And what does that mean?"

"It means I need to share them with somebody, but there isn't anybody. I don't think I have a very interesting psychiatric problem for you. I don't hallucinate. And why should I? Reality's strange enough. At least hallucinations go away. Reality won't. But I don't mean I want reality to go away. I just wish it would work better."

"Which part of reality doesn't work well for you?"

"The part where I wake up every day and I know the only person I can share my life with is me. I mean, I like myself. I think I'm a pretty nice man. Usually. But I've come to hope that I deserve more than just me."

"Are you suffering from loneliness?"

"I'm not benefitting from it. I told you it wasn't a very interesting problem."

"All suffering is important. You don't have to pass some qualifying round to talk with me. Loneliness can be one of the most debilitating, agonizing conditions a person can face. You don't have to apologize for not having the right kind of pain, as if there's a superior sort of pain; there isn't. But earlier on the phone, you said you thought you might have had a nervous breakdown?"

"Yes. For about a minute."

"A minute?"

"That was long enough for me. Do you think it's possible to have a nervous breakdown in 60 seconds?"

"Well, I've never heard of one that short, but I'm sure it's possible. There aren't time limits on nervous breakdowns."

"If I'm the first person to have a nervous breakdown in 60 seconds, could I get a ribbon or an award?"

"I don't think anyone gives awards for suffering."

"I'd at least like a ribbon. A red one."

"Before we honor you . . ."

"Or a green one."

". . . for your rapid suffering, it would be helpful if you told me what happened to you during what you describe as your nervous breakdown."

And so I told her about the overpowering sense of unreality, my sense of alienation from everything immediately around me, and the general feeling—almost like a sudden and horrifying realization—that everything I'd been doing in my life was shallow, pointless, and wrong, and that I urgently, desperately needed someone in my life, and there was no one, how it was like I was having almost a mystical insight in which all of the dulling layers of ordinary existence and ambition and sensibility—my public self—briefly vanished, and the only truth I saw was that I needed to love someone, and there was no one, as if the universe finally told me an awful truth: *All you have is you.*

Dr. Boulan silently listened to all that and stared at me with somber concentration. She said that what I described, including the overall sense of uncontrollable panic, at least resembled a nervous breakdown, but whether or not it could be called a nervous breakdown didn't matter, because I obviously had something. And it didn't matter which name you called it. It mattered that I survived it and was trying to live my life well.

She didn't say what color ribbon I'd get. She assured me that I seemed perfectly sane, although I said "perfectly" was obviously an exaggeration. She said, "Yes, but the only people you'll ever meet who might enjoy undisturbed sanity are babies, because they haven't had to face anything yet." She recommended that she and I talk at least a few more times if I was serious about examining why my emotions could become so concentrated and explosive in me, and if I wanted to deal with my loneliness. She said people liked to trivialize and dismiss loneliness, as if it were nothing more serious than feeling sorry for yourself, which often it wasn't. But she said that being alone, or being too alone, was unquestionably one of the most unnatural and damaging conditions in human experience. Meanwhile, as I was busy being unnatural and damaged, she said I ought to think about doing some kind of community or volunteer work, at least for the time being. Since I didn't seem to have a woman in my life, I could meet other people and help them, which maybe wasn't the sexual love I was hoping for, but it could be a way to find and give love.

THE ONLY kind of volunteer work I really wanted to do was volunteer to have Natelle lie on top of me, which undoubtedly would have to wait, and which I hoped wouldn't be a community project anyway. But probably it was a good idea to go out into the community and work with someone who might genuinely need my help, since it could distract me from my morose self-interest and maybe make me a little more human. Dr. Boulan had suggested I try the Literacy Council, and I went there for four training sessions to learn how to teach adults to read and write well enough to at least fill out applications for the wretched jobs they applied for. These people were the working class, or the underclass, or the great huddled masses of immigrants who hadn't even been assigned a class from which they'd like to escape. The literacy classes were held in a church basement. The student I was assigned to was Mria, whose name I thought was supposed to be spelled M-a-r-i-a, but she spelled it "Mria," as if for all of her life the first "a" had been missing from her name and no one had told her. I thought that possibly her mother or her father, both of whom I assumed were illiterate, sat down years ago with great affection to show their little girl how to misspell her name. So I decided that now wasn't a good time to injure what little pride she had left by telling her a letter was missing from her name.

Before our first lesson, before I could show Mria the alphabet and help her practice writing the letters, Mria told me exactly what she wanted out of the class.

"I need to learn how to write a suicide note," she said.

Disbelief and anxiety rushed through me, as if no one could have really said such a thing. I said, "What?"

Mria stared at me with a patient and almost peaceful expression on her young face and said, "I need to learn how to write a suicide note. Can you show me that?"

I looked across the room for one of the supervisors, but they weren't there. I didn't know what to do. She didn't look desperate or crazed. She just looked like a pretty Hispanic woman in her early twenties who was politely waiting for me to speak. I said, "I'm supposed to teach you how to write so you can have a better life. I'm not sure suicide is a better life."

"No, no no no no noooo," Mria said quickly, shaking her head and smiling in an embarrassed way. "I don't want to kill myself. I only want to write a suicide note. Just a note."

"Killing yourself and suicide are pretty much the same thing, and I don't think I'm supposed to get involved in that. Maybe you should see a psychiatrist. They're in the Yellow Pages. But then, you can't read the Yellow Pages. I could show you."

"You don't understand," Mria said in an exasperated tone. "I'm not going to kill myself. That would be crazy. I only want you to help me write a suicide note to Diego, so he'll love me."

"Who's Diego?"

"He's my lover."

"If he's your lover, doesn't he already love you? And why would a suicide note make him love you?"

"Diego's seeing another woman, and if I threaten to kill myself, he'll know how much I love him and maybe he'll come back to me," Mria said in a sad and honest tone, and I was astonished that someone I didn't even know was telling me her most painful truths. And then I thought of something.

"Can Diego read?"

Mria looked puzzled and uncertain. "I don't know," she said. "I've never seen him read anything."

"Well then, how could he read your suicide note?"

Mria put her hands over her eyes and moaned, and I felt sorry for her.

"Maybe Diego could come here and take classes," she said in a hopeful voice.

"So he could read your suicide note? I think he'd want a different reason than that. Anyway, I don't think suicide is the basis for a good love affair."

"I want to learn how to write anyway," Mria said defiantly.

"Okay. Good. We'll start with the alphabet."

"And will you write me a suicide note to take home with me tonight?"

She was so innocently morbid and grotesque that I started sniggering. I was supposed to be helping someone toward self-esteem and self-reliance, and this woman just wanted a goddamn suicide note for her illiterate boyfriend. The world wasn't meant to make sense. I said, "Mria, if I wrote you a suicide note, how would you know what it said? You can't read."

"Well, it's not for me. It's for Diego," she said.

"He can't read, either."

"But you could tell me what it says and I'll memorize it and tell Diego what it says."

"Well if you're going to *tell* him, there's no reason for a note."

"Then you won't help me? I only need a simple note that says 'Diego, you pig, you bastard, I love you. And because I've given you my heart and you don't want it, tonight I will take my own life.' But I won't kill myself. I just want Diego to miss me."

That was the only thing Mria and I had in common. We wanted someone to miss us. And there wasn't anyone to do that. So I felt kind of close to her then, because we shared the same sadness. And even though I regarded her as pathetic and ludicrous, I decided I'd at least write her stupid note for her, the way you give a child a worthless gift that the child nonetheless finds invaluable.

On lined notebook paper, with Mria solemnly watching me, I began writing: "Dear Diego, you pig, you bastard, I love you."

19

The president, the dominant force and instrument through which the nation sought to realize its noblest ambitions, was shown on the television news eating a grilled Spam sandwich at a district attorney's barbecue in Provo, Utah. He ate Vienna sausages at a firefighter's picnic in Little Rock, ate Beanie-Weanie casserole at a church supper in Peru, Indiana; and ate fried pig intestines at a military show at Fort Bragg, North Carolina. If it came from a dead animal and was held in low culinary esteem, the president made sure he was seen eating it.

The obvious explanation was that the president wanted to be seen as a regular guy, a peer of the common Americans who, by habit or economic coercion, routinely ate second-rate food that even they didn't like very much. The public had reacted with so much derision and contempt over the firing of Abbas that the president conspicuously sought to counter it and ingratiate himself once again.

But there was another and more fascinating truth to this. I had manipulated the president. Oh, he manipulated me first, by reacting with petty scorn over the elegantly disguised Spam he and the prime minister ate. I had been transformed by him into the bodyguard for a drunken pianist with diplomatic immunity. But while the president manipulated me quite directly and crudely, my manipulation of him was more insidious, and therefore more pleasing. And this was my power: the president was putting unpalatable things in his mouth.

Abbas had the glorious part. All he did was lose his job because of his own willful recklessness. Because of my plot to humiliate the president, Abbas had already been a guest on two national news shows and three national talk shows, for which he was paid thousands of dollars to light into the president. Losing his job had actually been quite profitable, and I was jealous. All I got was free beer for guarding Aramilo from the unknown political assailants who, in my opinion, wanted to kill him for playing Cole Porter songs, since that was almost all he did.

Abbas had been elevated into a kind of chivalric national hero for demonstrating that the president "really wasn't going to tolerate being treated like an American," which was the phrase he memorized for every talk show and newspaper interview. You really had to appreciate the logic. I did, since it was mine.

The president responded by gallantly eating every vile food he could find on his various trips across America. People became less interested in what the president's position was on unemployment and global chaos than in what his position was on corn dogs. The presidential diet became a national obsession, and hundreds, if not thousands, of people mailed bizarre recipes to the White House, inviting or daring the president to try them. Natelle made photocopies of some of the stranger recipes, such as the one for artificial tofu made from beef, which was supposed to be for vegetarians who liked meat.

One of the recipes was called "Threatened Species Gumbo." It was sent in by a man from Port Sulphur, Louisiana, who said that the main ingredient was "some animal that the Wildlife Commission doesn't want you to eat." There was no way to know which recipes were genuine and which were purely ludicrous inventions meant to taunt the president, but the recipes included Gila Monster Omelette, Pan-Fried Salamander, Sweet and Sour Skunk, Blackened Sea Cow, and Venison de la Rue, which Natelle and I decided meant a deer found dead on the side of the road. Natelle said we could compile some of the recipes into an American cookbook. If we did, I wanted to call it "Cooking Without A Conscience."

My own role in all of this remained secret, but I was alluded to in a *Washington Post* story about the Spam incident in which an anonymous White House official said that "a Secret Service agent was reassigned as a result of the president's unhappy meal." I think this made me famous in the same way that the Unknown Soldier was, except I wasn't given a tomb.

Every day I read the paper and watched the television news to see if Abbas would screw up and mention me, which he didn't, and to see what else the president would put in his mouth that day in some obscure neighborhood where offended and mistrustful Americans waited to see if the president would insult them by not eating their food. Finally it happened, at a goat roast near Tulsa, that a woman offered the president a plate of breaded and fried pig testicles. I thought the president should have smiled graciously and said, "Actually I prefer my testicles without breading," but he didn't think of that. And, for a while, as I watched the brief report on television, I felt sorry for the president. There's something wrong with a country whose citizens think sex education shouldn't be taught in public schools because it's indecent, but who think it's fine to eat pig genitals.

Gardenaul was standing next to the president and said, "I'm sorry, ma'am, but the president can't eat anything that hasn't been tested by the Secret Service," as if Widdiker and Yamato were going to eat balls. You could see them standing next to the president and shaking their heads. It looked like Yamato was going to pull out his machine gun and kill the woman. And who could criticize him?

"She was holding a plate of testicles in a threatening manner. Naturally I shot her."

I missed being on the road.

MRIA DROPPED out of the literacy program right after I wrote the suicide note for her, and I nervously studied the newspaper and watched the television news to see if she'd either killed herself or been murdered by Diego. I worried that maybe she really had intended to kill herself, or that she or someone else read the suicide note aloud to Diego, who, after hearing himself described as a beloved pig and bastard, went into a rage and killed her. If any of that happened, it never showed up in the paper or on TV, which was good, although what it meant was that Mria was still illiterate and I hadn't made even the tiniest fragment of the world better.

My next student was a 46-year-old schizophrenic alcoholic street person named Dark, who said he wanted to write children's books about a dead pigeon he owned. To be conversational, I said, "You have a dead pigeon?"

"Me too," Dark said, and I could smell acrid wine on his breath. "I'd like to write children's books about a dead pigeon that has a fear of heights, so it won't fly."

"There's already a book about that," I said, hoping this would dissuade Dark from talking about it anymore, and suddenly I decided the best thing I could do was make sure he never learned how to write. So, already, my first student had dropped out of class, and my second student was threatening to write grotesque children's stories that I wasn't going to help him write. I wondered if Christ ever felt this way when he went out into the world to help people, if he just wished they'd go away and suffer somewhere else. I asked my supervisor if I could at least have one student who was sober and who didn't want to write about the lives of dead animals, and my supervisor, a woman named Grace, smiled at me and said, "You've already driven away two students."

"So you're pleased with my speed? Thank you," I said.

She got me a new student who was sober and who seemed at least moderately sane, a 31-year-old maid named Keesta who said she wanted to learn how to read so she could read stories to her six children, two of whom were already teenagers and didn't want anyone reading stories to them. But finally I had someone I could work with, someone whose simple and backward life I could help a little bit by showing her the alphabet, which to me was just ordinary, trifling—second nature—but to her was the same complex wonder that a four-year-old encounters. Keesta, who at least knew how to spell her own name and the names of her children, stared with confusion and uncertainty at the printed alphabet I showed her.

"Where all these *letters* come from?" she said, as if she'd never seen all the letters in a row before.

"The store," I said. "Not really. I think they're Arabic, or maybe Greek, mixed in with some other Indo-European crud that we don't have to talk about. It's not that many letters. You can learn them pretty easy. I'll show you."

She kept staring at the letters and said, "*Air*-bik? Isn't that foreign? I need to learn *Eeen*-glish."

"Well, this is English. We got some of our letters from ancient cultures thousands of years ago, but then we changed it into our own language. You don't have to learn all that. You just have to learn these letters."

"How come," she asked, pointing her finger at the letters, "some of these is big, and some of these is little?"

"The big ones are for adults. You have to be at least eighteen to use those. I'm kidding you, Keesta. The big ones are called capital letters, and the little ones are just called little ones."

"Like babies?"

"Like babies. But you don't have to feed them, and they don't cry."

It was hard for me to speak on the same level as Keesta, since I had no idea what that level was, but even if I'd confused her, she at least smiled at me.

"You a strange one," she said in a mildly amused way. "You sure you know English?"

"Frontwards and behindwards. I studied political science and English in college. By the time I'm through teaching you everything, you'll be able to write speeches for the president, since he has no idea how to write his own."

And then I began the maddeningly slow process of showing an adult how to memorize the alphabet, draw the letters, and tediously arrange them from meaningless chaos into the simplest of words. This was supposed to make me feel good, and it did, a little, but not very much.

"Now I want you to practice drawing all the letters. What for? Well, you have to memorize them. What for? You can't have words without letters. So you have to draw each letter over and over until you memorize them, and then I'll teach you some words."

"Which letter do I draw first?" she said.

"I recommend the A."

"Which one is that?"

"The first one."

I think we were moving as rapidly as possible, which was pretty slow, and even though I wanted to feel nothing but kindness for this woman, she was already getting on my nerves, which I disguised completely, of course, but she stared with almost somber perplexity at the alphabet chart and then spent nearly five seconds just drawing an A.

"What does that spell?" she asked.

"It spells A," I said. "That's the shortest word in the English language. Pretty soon, we'll work our way up to B."

Making the world better sure was slow. You couldn't even tell it was happening.

20

One night at home when I was sad and anxious because I hadn't seen Natelle in a week and I didn't know what she was doing and I needed her—and, for the anesthetic and psychic effect, I had mixed my emotions with about four or five beers—there was a news report on TV about the Stealth bomber, with a videotape showing one of the bombers gliding high up over some puffy clouds, which reminded me of flying a kite. It occurred to me that I should build a Stealth kite. And I did.

I wondered if Natelle would like it, if the aching of my heart would stop if I got to look in her eyes again, if whatever sadness she felt in these days of her ruined life could be eased a little if she looked in *my* eyes. This was always my project, to see if she'd be in love with me. So I called her to ask if she wanted to go with me to the Mall near Capitol Hill and fly my Stealth kite with me.

"Stealth kite?" she said, sounding skeptical and amused.

"We shouldn't talk about it over the phone. This isn't a secure line," I said.

"What're you talking about? What's a Stealth kite?"

"It's a kite you can't see. At least I don't think you can. I haven't tested it yet. I just thought of it today when I saw a Stealth bomber on TV, and I decided to make a Stealth kite. It costs less than a Stealth bomber. It's made out of a clear plastic frame and Saran Wrap. You should see it. I mean, you shouldn't see it. I think if you get it high enough in the sky, no one'll have any idea there's a kite up there."

We decided to launch the Stealth kite in the Mall, between the National Gallery of Art and the National Air and Space Museum.

"Some day this kite will be in the Smithsonian," I said. "Or maybe on the Smithsonian, if it crashes."

Natelle went into a fit of giggling, wagging her head like a girl and sort of stooping over as she giggled, letting the Stealth kite droop down toward the grass.

"You have to hold it up," I said, holding the spool of transparent nylon fishing line that was attached to the kite.

"I'm trying, I'm trying."

"It's drooping. I didn't design it to be launched from a droop position."

"All right, all right," she said, taking a big breath and standing up straight with the kite held above her head in the wind. The transparent plastic Stealth tail, made from an old couch cover, slapped at Natelle's legs and stomach, and I was envious of the kite, which got to touch her.

"Are we ready?" she said.

"Not until I say 'Red Alert.' "

"Why would you say 'Red Alert'?"

"It's what I thought of."

"It sounds too militaristic."

"All right. What color alert do you want?"

"I don't think we should have an alert. Kites aren't dangerous."

"One thing I could say is 'Go.' "

"All right. That's fine," she said, stepping back a few feet to get the line taut as the kite wiggled and fluttered in her hand, and I announced the crucial command.

"Go!"

I started running and letting the line spin out as the wind caught the kite and lifted it into the sky above Natelle's head.

"It's working!" she shouted, staring straight up at the kite as it slowly gained altitude, and I realized I could stop running and the wind would pull the kite up. I stood still and let more line spin off the spool, and already the kite was maybe thirty feet up and rising in a pretty strong wind. More importantly, it was hard to see the kite. Only a tiny amount of sunlight reflected off of its transparency. Natelle ran up to me laughing, staring at my eyes with exuberance, then staring back up at the kite, saying, "Look! You can hardly see it!"

"I know! Isn't it neat?" I said, gleeful that the Stealth kite was working, but looking with wonderment and affection at Natelle, who'd been hurting so much, and now she was happy to be with me and my dumbass little toy.

I wanted to marry her. That was all I could think right then. I wanted to marry her. It just came to me from looking at her face, from a swarm of emotion I didn't understand and couldn't name and didn't care to, that I wanted to marry her. It wasn't rational. I had no interest in being rational. I just wanted Natelle, and prayed, *Please let us love each other,* as if none of my other prayers had worked but maybe this one would. Why did you pray for something so seemingly good, and never have any idea if it worked?

"Look at it, Doyle! It's getting harder and harder to *see* it!" she said.

I wanted to tell her what I'd just prayed, but it might have hurt her worse than she already was. And so the only person I could talk to was the one I had to hide from.

"It is getting harder to see," I said, wondering if I was talking about love or the kite. Still, it was a wonderful, silly time, watching the transparent kite drift farther up into the pale summer sky, with Natelle and me standing together and squinting harder and harder until it didn't matter anymore.

"I can't see it," Natelle announced. "I mean, I know it's up there. You can feel it," she said, pushing her hand down on the fishing line that curved way up into the sky and seemed connected to nothing. "This is really weird, flying an invisible kite."

"It's sort of stupid. I like it. Do you want to fly it?"

"Yes! Yes!" she said, carefully taking the spool from my hands and laughing when she felt the invisible kite tug against her. "This is incredible. It's like magic or something. I can feel it pulling on me, but where is it?"

I could feel it pulling on me, too. Not the kite. Natelle. It was strange to be filled with such powerful emotions for someone who, even though she stood right next to me, had no idea this was happening. It seemed like I was radiating affection and sexual desire with the intensity of refined uranium. Natelle should have been radioactive by then.

"This is wonderful," she said. "I don't know why, but it's wonderful. Thank you for letting me be with you today."

"Letting you? Goddamn it, Natelle, I always like to be with you. When will the obvious seem obvious to you?"

"All right," she said, leaning over and kissing my cheek, and I didn't know what it meant, but I tingled.

For a long time we took turns flying the kite and wondering where it was. It seemed to be about three hundred feet up, but who could say?

"I can assure you, the Russians don't have a kite like this," I said.

"Are you going to share this technology with the Pentagon?" Natelle asked.

"Aw, fuck those guys. Let them build their own goddamn kites."

One time I decided to maneuver the kite and said, "I'm going to tug on the line and make it do acrobatic tricks." Then I tugged rhythmically on the line.

"It just did a figure eight," I said as we looked at the vacant blue sky where maybe the kite was.

"Make it do a figure nine," Natelle said, laughing when I tugged on the line from side to side, saying, "Wait a minute. That was a seven."

"Make it write my name," she said.

"Okay."

I began weaving my arm, raising it and lowering it, as if gesturing far into the sky, where I commanded the invisible kite.

"There. I wrote your name," I said, staring into her eyes, which it almost hurt to do.

She began laughing, and stood behind me with one arm suddenly around my stomach and her other arm resting on my arm that was flying the kite, and her chin was on my shoulder as she pressed her body lightly against me, perhaps all in innocence and unknowing of her effect on me. It felt like she was floating into me. I started to cry a little bit, at the unexpected rapture of being held by her, as if she finally had me without realizing she did. She couldn't see me crying because she was behind me, but she put her fingers on my cheek where it was wet, and I thought I'd get in trouble, that she'd know I was crying only because she held me, as if I were the lover she didn't know she had, and it wasn't a secret anymore. I thought she'd push away from me and grab onto the line as if all we were doing was flying a kite, and I pretended to be looking up at the kite that neither one of us could see, giving her time to let go of me and act like none of this was happening, the way adults do when the truth is too true. But she didn't let me go. She rubbed her fingers along my cheek where it was wet and held onto me a little tighter. And we stood like that without saying anything, pressed together. I let the kite go. I didn't even know if Natelle realized that. It didn't matter anymore. I think we were flying each other.

21

Ecstasy doesn't last very long. Two hours after Natelle held me to her, just silently holding me for several minutes in the grass as we breathed together and shared the joy of touching each other for no other reason than that we wanted to, she went to some restaurant to have dinner with her husband, her goddamn husband, who I had seen only a few times at dinners and parties and who I wished would be beamed up by the particle transformer on the U.S.S. Enterprise on "Star Trek" and transported several million light years away where he'd do me the favor of vanishing. I at least wanted to kick his ass, which was mean and inexcusable, but I wanted to kick his ass, because he represented the ruin of Natelle's life and the single breathing obstacle between Natelle and me. She said she was having dinner with him to talk about the divorce and the remains of their marriage, and now I sat by myself in a bar, drinking Mexican beer and waiting for Yamato to show up and help depress me the way single men did when they hung out with each other morosely in the mateless, dateless night, idly getting drunk and staring wistfully at women they'd never meet. They talked about goddamn baseball games and other pointless distractions whose pleasures were real enough and yet far inferior to the inexpressibly wondrous warmth of being held by someone like Natelle.

She'd held me like I shouldn't go away, and now that was gone. I wrote on a white paper bar napkin, "Ecstasy doesn't last very long." It made me feel like Aristotle or Voltaire or Colette, writing some universal truth you wish you hadn't thought of. Looking at my truth on the napkin made me think of the Bible, which said that in Heaven what you'd do is worship God for eternity. Maybe that was a practical arrangement for Heaven, but I had no interest in going there. I'd rather see Natelle. Maybe if Natelle and I died and we went to Heaven and everyone was standing around worshipping God, I'd take Natelle's hand and go for a walk.

Mark Twain pointed out in some book that every description of Heaven in the Bible hinted that there'd be no sex there. Why would you want to be resurrected for a life of eternal celibacy? On my napkin I wrote, "Maybe there's no sex in Heaven, but for some of us, there isn't any here either."

There *was* masturbation, one thing that nearly everyone did, then pretended that someone else did it. Masturbation was like having a date with yourself. And in the morning, you wouldn't be embarrassed at who you woke up with. Just sad. I remembered vividly a time in high school when my health class teacher, this middle-aged woman, told us somberly that being by yourself and masturbating was wrong. I looked at the boy in the seat next to mine and whispered, "Does that mean you're supposed to do it with someone else?"

Actually, a woman whose name I couldn't remember anymore, maybe it was Eisell—my girlfriend for maybe five months when I was about 24—did that to me. For me. With me. She was afraid to have sex because of all the emotional complications, as if she was waiting for the perfect moment of undisputed love, although every other kind of sex was fine with her, as long as the penis didn't actually go inside her. That was the rule, like Robert's Rules of Sex. It was like parliamentary sex: *I move that we have sex. Motion seconded, with the stipulation that your penis not actually go inside of me.*

It was hard to make love that way.

And why did people make love anyway? The word "orgasm" wasn't even in the Bible. Maybe the Greeks put it in there and the Christians took it out. Except for The Song of Solomon, the only references to sex in the Old Testament were always about some old man "spilling his seed." It made them sound like clumsy farmers.

"Yoo-hoo. You spilled your seed."

"Why, thank you. I hadn't noticed."

It produced the imagery of sex as agriculture. The man was the farmer and the woman was the field. On my napkin, I wrote:

> Old MacDonald had a farm
> Ee, yi, ee, yi, oh
> And on his farm he spilled some seed
> Uh, uh, uh, uh, oh.

Thinking of farms made me think of bread, which made me think of making love with Natelle while she was in her kitchen making bread. She'd be kneading a big gooey mound of dough on the kitchen table, resting her left knee on the table, and I'd walk up behind her and begin massaging her through her orange sweatpants, and as she squeezed and folded the dough and hummed a childhood song, she'd put her other knee onto the table, with her legs apart, in front of me, and I'd slowly pull her sweatpants down and begin kissing and gently licking her as she hummed "The Farmer in the Dell." And she'd say, "After you eat *me*, you can have bread."

I wondered if this meant I was too sexual. Although, if I hadn't made love in five years, how could I be too sexual?

And now I wanted bread. I had to stop thinking that. I ordered another beer and when I picked it up I felt my holster rubbing against my ribs. I wished it was Natelle's hand rubbing against me, and I had to stop thinking that. It looked like I was going to have to completely stop thinking, and go into a religious, mystical daze where no thoughts entered or left my mind, which you could achieve by meditation or by drinking about nine or ten beers.

Alcohol was a strange thing. I looked around me at all the well-dressed, handsomely dressed, showily dressed middle-class people who would've found it horrifying, or at least indiscreet, if someone came up to them now with a bag of cocaine or LSD or opium or Ecstasy and said, "Would you like to get high?"

"Get away from this goddamn table, you son of a bitch!" they'd say, and then take a big swallow of their white wine or bourbon or vodka. Americans were people who thought using most drugs was pathetic and destructive, and they'd tell you so over cocktails. We were at war with the Colombian drug lords, not because they were selling drugs, but because they were selling the wrong drugs. If the drug lords opened breweries in the United States, they'd be praised as level-headed capitalists. Probably in this crowd tonight I could find several men and women drinking wine who'd say they didn't drink to get drunk. Lying was an honorable American tradition.

Suddenly I missed Natelle again. It must have been fifteen or twenty seconds since I'd last thought about her. Was that how you knew you were in love with someone—you were always thinking about them? And you always missed them? And the rest of the world seemed stupid? The rest of the world always seemed stupid. It seemed like a place to just wander through and be alone while you looked for someone to love. And when you finally found someone, there was no reason for that someone to want to be found. It was always possible to finally find the wrong person. I'd spent all of my adult life finally doing that. As if I should say, "At last! I've again found someone I wasn't supposed to find!"

Oh, good. I'd depressed myself again.

Melinda, the bartender, walked up to me and said, "Are you all right, Doyle?"

I smiled at her and said, "Sure. I'm a healthy adult male in the prime of my life sitting here by myself in a bar surrounded by people with wives and husbands and dates who'll go home with them, but not me. I'm fine."

Melinda leaned on the bar in front of me and said, "I'm sorry. What happened to that woman I saw you with here last week?"

"Oh, she's out having dinner with some jackass. Her husband."

Melinda looked shocked.

"Don't worry. I'm not having an affair. I'm not having anything."

"Well, it's none of my business anyway," Melinda said sympathetically.

"It's none of my business, either."

"You look depressed."

"It's just my emotions. They'll go away."

"Well, you shouldn't sit here and just drink."

"At a bar? Who would think of that?"

"Let me get you something from the kitchen. On the house. What would you like?"

"Bread."

"Is that all?"

"I like bread. It reminds me of something."

What worried me now that I was eating French bread was that every time I ate French bread I'd get an erection. And what for? It wasn't anything I could use.

Yamato showed up with his smiling face and further depressed me. Yamato was good-natured and even-tempered and almost chronically cheerful. When he sat next to me I looked at him and said, "What're you smiling about? You depress me."

"I'm just in a good mood," he said, still smiling at me, and he ordered a *rotch on the skocks*, which was what he said one night when he was drunk and trying to say scotch on the rocks, and everyone else started ordering *blasses of geer* and *tin and gonic*. Someone was going to order *cum and roke*, but it sounded too vile.

Yamato sipped his drink and said, "This really spits the hot."

He was too amusing for me to remain fully depressed, so I looked at him and said, "Shut up."

"And I'm so happy to see you, too," he said. "What are you depressed about?"

I couldn't show him my napkin that said "Ecstasy doesn't last very long," because I didn't want him to think Natelle and I were having an affair. And I sure as hell wasn't going to tell him about my fantasy that I kissed Natelle's vagina as she sang "The Farmer in the Dell." Maybe I should have picked a different song. I couldn't even tell Natelle about that. At least not soon. Possibly the only person I could tell it to was Dr. Boulan. Was my life so secret I could only share it with strangers?

"Well anyway," Yamato said, "it's good to talk with you, even though you're not saying anything."

"I'll say something in fifteen or twenty minutes."

"Are you depressed about your job?"

"I love my job. It's an honor to protect drunken diplomats who play Cole Porter songs all day."

"Cole Porter?"

"He wrote 'Begin the Beguine.' "

"Begin the *what*?"

"No one knows what a beguine is. That's why you can't begin it."

"What're you talking about? Have you lost your mind?" Yamato asked indifferently.

"No. I remember where it is."

"Which doesn't necessarily help."

"Not often."

That was how we talked. We strayed from everything that mattered and kept it in that region. I think this was because we both wanted to be with women and we both weren't. So I drank my beer, and Yamato drank his rotch on the skocks, so that at least we could numb our brains so severely we'd have no idea what was missing.

Sometimes I wondered if I was an alcoholic. To me, this was the same as wondering if I was part Norwegian. Did it really matter? Maybe I was only part alcoholic. So I could say I had some Norwegian in my blood, and alcohol, too. I looked at Yamato and said, "How do you become an alcoholic?"

Yamato frowned, as if thinking, and said, "I don't know. I think you have to fill out an application."

"Do you ever worry about becoming an alcoholic?" I said, and took a big drink of beer.

"I haven't even applied," Yamato said serenely.

That was the thing about alcohol—it was like liquid emotion. You drank it, and soon you had different emotions. Glee. Serenity. Euphoria. Those sounded like women's names.

"If I ever have a daughter, I'm going to name her 'Glee,' " I said.

"Really? What made you think of that?" Yamato said.

I looked at my beer bottle and said, "Or maybe I'll name her 'Moosehead.' "

"That's a good name for an infant," Yamato said. "I think I'll name my daughter 'Glenlivet.' "

I remembered thinking, before, that alcohol was a substitute for love. That was probably why I drank. I never had the euphoria of being touched by someone who loved me. And so alcohol was my lover, and I swallowed her, and went home to fall into my liquid, dreamless sleep. And in the mornings, my lover tried to bite through my head to get out of me.

Whether or not I was part alcoholic or part Norwegian, I had one more beer to sustain the ones I'd already had.

At ten o'clock I went home and was a little bit drunk, pleasantly and not badly, and I knew what was missing and I looked out the window toward Natelle's apartment across town. There were buildings in the way. I was going to call her, but I was afraid she didn't need me, that because she'd already seen me a few hours earlier it would be annoying to her that I needed her again already. If she was in love with me, she wouldn't be annoyed. I picked up the phone and listened to the dial tone, then quickly hung up, in case she was trying to call me at that very instant and she'd get a busy signal. The phone didn't ring. She might not even be home. Possibly she was home listening to the dial tone and hanging up. She could be watching TV. Maybe she met a man, someone I didn't know. I wasn't especially needed. If anyone in the world needed me, they hadn't said so. They. *They* was Natelle. She might be asleep, sadly asleep after she called me and I wasn't home and she was afraid to call back because it might annoy me. But if she was asleep, what if she got mad because I woke her up and I wasn't her lover and why was I acting like I was?

I didn't know. There was something wrong with me. I missed her. I was anxious. I wanted to see her face, to touch her fingers, to have her breathe on me. I wasn't going to cry. Yes I was. No, I wasn't. It seemed like I was. I called her.

The phone rang. Rang again. Rang three times. What if she was mad? She might not be home. Rang again.

"Hello?" she said.

"It's me." I didn't know what to tell her. *There's something wrong with me. I love you.*

"Doyle. How are you?" She sounded tired.

"I'm fine. I just wanted to call and see how you are. Did I wake you up?"

"No. And thank you for calling. I'm a little anxious tonight."

"Me too. What's wrong?"

"I thought you said you were fine."

"Did I? I was wrong. I'm anxious, too."

"What's wrong?" she wondered.

I couldn't just suddenly say something as reckless as the truth, that I missed her, and thought of her voluntarily and involuntarily, and wanted to hold her face in my hands and fall asleep with her breath on my neck.

"I don't know. Yes, I do. I miss you."

"You do? I think I miss you, too."

"You think? When will you be sure?"

"I'm sure."

"That was fast."

"I'm glad you called. I'm lonely. It's not very late. I have some wine. Would it bother you if I asked you to come over and visit me for a while?"

"Why would I come visit you just because I miss you?"

"Do you remember how to get here?"

"Do I re-mem-ber? Do I re-*MEM*-ber?"

"You're repeating yourself."

"I'll be there in fifteen minutes."

HER COUCH, where we'd been talking and drinking white wine, was just twenty feet from her bedroom, where I assumed we weren't going, because of perfectly good reasons that we wouldn't talk about, so I wouldn't know what they were. She had her life and I had mine. And in the spontaneous rush to blend our lives together for one more night, seldom with any real certainty about what had been shared and which parts of us were still strangers to each other, she fell asleep in my lap, with her head resting against my erection in my pants—my stupid, foolish erection, which was obviously waiting for an event in someone else's life. I wondered if she could feel it, if she liked that sensation, if she felt something like it herself that we'd talk about some other day. The Farmer in the Dell. I was the farmer. She was the dell. With her head on my erection, I was feeling highly agricultural. I thought of waking her up and saying, "Natelle. We need to farm."

But she slept.

Except for the persistence of my erection, which I knew

would give up eventually and go away, I felt peaceful. Kind of exultant and peaceful, as if finally my life was working, when really it wasn't. She'd wake up and go away. I didn't have her. For her to have fallen asleep in my lap didn't necessarily mean she was in love with me or even close to it. It might only have meant she was sleepy, and felt safe enough with me to sleep in my lap, free from such predatory forces as me and my futile erection. And so, once more, I was a stupid man, gratefully holding this woman like a gift I hadn't been offered yet. This was as close to having her as my lover as I'd ever been, just holding her in the night as she slept and didn't even remember she was with me. Very gently I put my hand on her chest above her breasts, to feel her warmth and her softness and the rising and falling of her chest as she breathed. She moved a little bit and didn't open her eyes. I was afraid she'd sense my hand on her chest so close to her breasts, and she'd be mad at me, as if I was trying to satisfy some concealed lust while she slept, and she'd think I was reprehensible. She didn't say anything. With her eyes still closed, she put her hand on top of mine and slid my hand onto her breast. She didn't move anymore, and seemed to be asleep, or returned to sleep. I wondered if she'd mistakenly put my hand on her breast. No, I decided, a woman knew where her breasts were and when they were being touched. That was what she wanted. Ecstasy didn't last very long, but it sometimes came back.

22

Early in the morning when I'd woken and Natelle was asleep in my lap with her nose against my stomach, my hand was still on her breast. And we'd done nothing, as if we were having a secret love so exquisitely hidden that even we didn't know about it. I'd felt her breast under my hand and her breathing against my stomach, and I had tingled and was dizzy, almost like I was falling through her and into her in some spiritual descent where I'd realized I was part of this sleeping woman who didn't know any of this was happening. I had thought of waking her up and whispering, *I'm part of you, now.* But she was still married, and that would have been like having two ghosts in her—one leaving, and one just arriving. The similarity between insanity and love wasn't as disturbing as it probably should've been.

I remembered this now, in Aramilo's office, where I was overcome with the warm disorder of missing Natelle and wondering if she missed me, or if she regretted our newest and unexplained closeness, or if in her office she wistfully imagined lying down on me and couldn't stop thinking of me, or already had. Life wasn't presented in any understandable fashion. It just happened, and you either knew what it meant, or painstakingly misunderstood it all.

I felt my forehead to see if I was hot. I wondered if Natelle was feeling her forehead. I wanted to feel it for her.

Aramilo sat at his desk, quietly sipping a cup of hot tea and vodka as he read some kind of government report and simultaneously watched a PBS documentary on television about the cowboys of Indonesia. That's what it sounded like when I asked him what he was watching. Either his speech was slurred, or my hearing was. Someone knocked twice at the door and opened it. It was Maria, the chargé d'affaires, looking more somber and preposterous than usual.

Aramilo said, "What?" an Americanism he'd picked up. Instead of saying a complete sentence, such as, "Maria, what do you need to tell me?" Aramilo just looked at her and said, "*What?*"

"May I speak with you in private?" Maria said insistently, and I left the room to stand out in the hall. About two minutes later, Maria opened the door and walked somberly past me, saying nothing. I walked back in to the office to see Aramilo at his desk staring into the distance.

"Bad news?" I asked.

"We're at war," he said.

"Who is?"

"The PDF attacked Rio D'Iguana."

Rio D'Iguana was the capital of Indizal. This was the first time in my life I'd ever been in the presence of someone who announced the start of a war, and I didn't know what to say, as if I should buy Aramilo a Hallmark card that said "Sorry about your war. Hope you feel better." I already had my war. I wasn't interested in another one.

"The PDF," Aramilo said with curiosity. "We don't even know who they are, and they're attacking us. They attacked part of the city this morning with rockets and mortars and automatic rifles. Maria says our own troops repelled them, but we can expect more fighting. And now I'm a target."

"You?" I said. "Who'd want to kill you?"

"Why?" Aramilo said. "Don't you think I'm worth killing?"

"I wouldn't want to be."

"Do you think I'm not important enough to be killed?" Aramilo said resentfully.

All he did was play piano. People weren't usually killed for that. But I didn't want to hurt his feelings, so I said, "I'm sure your death would be widely acclaimed."

Ignoring me, Aramilo stood up to look at the world map on the wall behind his desk, and I walked over beside him to look at the map, which was embarrassing. Indizal was such a new country that it wasn't printed on the map. Someone had used a pen to draw a little blue dot in the Atlantic off the coast of West Africa to show the existence of Indizal. It probably wasn't much bigger than Walt Disney World and didn't have any rides. Aramilo looked anxious and confused, and I wanted to make him feel better.

"I'll call my government to let them know about the fighting," I said, trying to comfort him. "They'll issue orders for some kind of surveillance and intelligence-gathering in Indizal. We have networks to find out if there are any plans for violence here in Washington. I wouldn't worry. The PDF couldn't be very big. I doubt they could afford to send somebody over here."

Actually, the Secret Service and the CIA probably had no reason to care about a tiny war in Indizal. They probably wouldn't order any surveillance. They'd probably ask me to be "more alert," and that would be the extent of our security.

"Do you think anyone will try to kill me?" Aramilo asked.

"If they do, I'll kill them first. That's what I'm trained for."

"Are you sure?"

"Am I sure what I'm trained for? Yes."

"No. How do you know you'll kill them first?"

"It's the sequence I prefer."

"Did you ever kill anyone in Vietnam?"

"I don't know."

"You don't know? You were in a war and you don't know if you killed anyone?"

"I shot at people. I assume I hit them sometimes. And when they were dead, I didn't want to know who killed them. I didn't want to look at a body and say 'That's *my* corpse. I did that.' That's crazy, Hobar. I have a lot of flaws, but I don't think I'm crazy."

No, I wasn't crazy. Unless you counted my nervous breakdown. Unless you counted the fact that I was deeply in love with a woman who might never want me. But that wasn't crazy. That was just my normal life.

"Well, I assume you're highly qualified to shoot people," Aramilo said apologetically.

"Thank you for your faith."

23

A dog was glancing at me unpleasantly. It was a big Rottweiler on a leash held by a foreign-looking man whose nationality I couldn't identify. He and the unpleasant Rottweiler gazed at me in front of the embassy while I waited for Aramilo to come out and get in the limousine to go talk with the deputy secretary of state or someone about the war in Indizal and possible PDF terrorism in Washington. As innately suspicious of all humans and animals as I'd been trained to be, I regarded the dog and the man as a threat to Aramilo, and therefore to me. The dog and the man stood still on the sidewalk, not taking a walk but staying there, waiting. The dog, which I estimated to be about 110 pounds—just 60 pounds lighter than me— seemed to stare at me with ill will, as if he knew I was in the Service, as if he knew Aramilo was coming. The man, who wore sunglasses and a white windbreaker, under which any number of guns could be concealed, stared off toward the other side of the street, as if uninterested in me, although there was no reason for him to just stand there. I wasn't going to let him. This was the crazy part of my job, where I had to be suspicious of everyone, without reason, because it was impossible to look at a stranger and know if he or she was harmless, which nearly everyone was, or if the stranger was preparing to kill me and whoever I was protecting.

"You have to move," I said loudly to the man, as if I knew this as a fact and I was educating him. I walked down the embassy steps toward the man and the dog. The dog looked at me more unpleasantly and growled. I had my arms crossed over my chest with my hand inside my jacket, holding onto my machine gun. The man stared at me with a slightly troubled or curious expression.

"Pardon me?" he said in an accent unlike Aramilo's but which I couldn't name. He didn't move, and the dog was still growling.

"You have to move. You're standing in a secure area. It's not allowed."

"It's not? And who the hell are you?" he said in a more combative tone.

"A foreign embassy is private property protected by the federal government, for which I work. I recommend that you move."

"Well, I don't give a goddamn who you are. I'm an American citizen. You can't tell me where to stand on the sidewalk."

"Yes, I can. I can have you arrested. I can have your *dog* arrested. The best thing for you to do is walk away. Now."

"You can have me arrested for standing here?" he said in a tone that seemed to make the dog growl more.

"Sir. Don't fuck with me. It isn't safe," I said, pulling back my jacket far enough to show him part of my machine gun.

He flinched, and stepped back a few inches.

"This is a lovely city. You and your dog should go walking through it. Pretty far from here."

"I don't like being threatened," the man said.

"Then leave."

"This is outrageous. This is un-American."

"Foreign embassies are all un-American. Don't argue with me. Just leave."

"I'll be back with a lawyer, by God."

"Even a dumb lawyer would tell you not to come back here," I said, watching the man and his dog walk away, and I felt a little bad about it all, having to intimidate presumably harmless people. But that was my job. As the man and the dog walked down the sidewalk, I wondered if I was just being too cautious and suspicious because of the war. It didn't seem like anyone from the PDF would have any serious interest in killing Aramilo, unless they didn't like Cole Porter.

The front door of the embassy opened and here came Aramilo, this tiny, almost comical-looking man in a black and red robe billowing out like he was a foreign diplomat going trick-or-treating. He looked nearly serene. I knew it wasn't serenity. There was vodka in his tea. Sometimes I wondered if I should tell on him; tell the State Department or someone that Aramilo was almost constantly drunk. But if you expelled all the drunks from Washington, the government might collapse. I wanted some vodka myself, or a beer, to calm me down from the tension of thinking I might have to shoot someone, which was stupid. No one was going to shoot Aramilo.

There was a shot, somewhere close behind me. Fear and

anxiety rushed through me as I ran up to Aramilo and knocked him down flat onto the concrete steps, where it looked like his nose smashed into the concrete and he screamed and there was another shot as I tingled with intense panic and dizziness during which I saw Natelle's face and her eyes clearly, and I wanted to hold her as I pulled out the machine gun and spun around toward the sound of the shots, thinking I didn't want to die, that I at least wanted to tell Natelle I loved her, and I saw, down and across the street as I aimed my machine gun in that direction and prepared to kill someone, a white man firing a pistol into an old Volkswagen. The man seemed to wobble as he stood near the Volkswagen, which didn't seem to have anyone in it, and he fired again, into the door. Three of the embassy guards were dragging Aramilo toward the front door of the embassy. Aramilo's nose was bleeding pretty badly, and he stared at me with horror and bewilderment. The man across the street fired again, then simply held his gun pointed at the car, like he was trying to shoot once more but he was out of bullets. He kicked the car with his shoe and yelled something, then lost his balance and fell backward into the street, dropping the gun, which landed under the car. I had no idea what he was doing. I assumed he was drunk. My panic wouldn't go away, the horrifying sense that I could be dead and couldn't be held by Natelle again because some lunatic drunk was shooting a parked car. Two of the guards came back outside with machine guns and aimed them at the man sitting and yelling in the street.

"I think he's out of bullets. His gun is under the car. Did you call the police?" I said.

"Yes. They're coming."

"He was wobbling. He fell down. I think the fuckhead's drunk," I said.

"Fuckhead?" one of the guards asked. They were from Indizal and weren't familiar with American obscenities. Possibly they thought a fuckhead was the name of a political organization. This wasn't a good time for linguistics.

"What should we do?" one of the guards asked.

"Stay here while I go kick the fuck out of him," I said, handing him my machine gun and walking across the street toward the man with my automatic pointed at him as he sat in the street yelling, "I fixed your car, Connie! Come down and drive it! Hey, Connie!"

The man looked confused and sullen when he saw me, as if his world was bad and I wasn't welcome in it.

"What the fuck do you want?" he said.

I pointed my gun at his face. "Does this make you nervous?" I said.

"You a cop? You can't shoot me," he said contemptuously.

"Did you ever see 'Dirty Harry'?"

He scowled at me and said, "You mean that Clint Eastwood movie where he points a .44 magnum at some man's face? You ain't got a .44 magnum."

"No. This is only a nine millimeter. It won't blow your head clean off. It'll just blow it about three-fourths off. But I don't mind fractions. Do you?"

There were sirens nearby, getting louder, and the man said, "You can't shoot me in front of everyone. I know my rights. I'm entitled to a lawyer."

"Fine. I'll shoot you in front of your lawyer."

"Are you crazy?" the man said apprehensively.

"Don't use that word. My psychiatrist doesn't like it."

THE SECRET Service gave me a letter of commendation for breaking Aramilo's nose. The letter praised me for acting professionally and quickly in keeping Aramilo out of the line of fire in a potentially lethal situation, although mainly what I did was cause trauma to Aramilo's nose. He looked awful. His skin was blue and purple around his swollen nose and along the lower ridges of his eyes, which you couldn't see completely because his nose was taped up over a nose brace. The press found out and did a brief story in the paper, mentioning the war in Indizal and saying that the "gunman" apparently had no connections with the PDF.

"Why would the PDF send someone over here to shoot a Volkswagen?" Aramilo asked the next day as he was reading the *Post* and sipping his daily cup of Ethiopian coffee and bourbon. He wasn't mad at me. I apologized to him a few times anyway.

"Will you stop that?" he said in his new, nasal voice. "Better you should break my nose than someone should shoot me. But did you have to throw me down so hard?"

"I'm sorry. But we don't practice throwing people down gently," I said.

The biggest threat against Aramilo so far was his drinking. Every morning at eight-thirty, he had a cup of freshly brewed Ethiopian coffee, to which he added about an ounce of Wild Turkey. But no sugar. He said sugar was bad for you. With his breakfast, which usually included fresh fruit, croissants, and some exotic omelet, he had a glass of fresh orange juice with genuine Russian vodka. He refrained from drinking again until lunch, when he always had one or two vodkas with tonic, unless he was at a working lunch where no vodka was available. Then he'd have bourbon or wine. At three o'clock every afternoon he had his traditional Earl Grey tea with vodka, presumably to clear his head of any residual sobriety. At four in the afternoon, when his work was either done or had been forced on someone else on his staff, he began drinking as much vodka and tonic as he wanted while he played piano. Everyone on the staff knew he was an alcoholic, but he was an eminent alcoholic, and therefore beyond reproach. One afternoon when Aramilo fell asleep on the couch from being vodka-saturated again, and I was just looking at that pale little man who, amazingly, hadn't destroyed himself yet, I thought that the best way for the PDF to attack him was to send him vodka. I wondered if, as a Secret Service agent sworn to use every bit of intelligence and degree of vigilance and effort to protect Aramilo from harm, I should shoot every bottle in his liquor cabinet. If I did, I'd be fired for guarding his life, although I was praised for breaking his nose.

The war in Indizal looked, so far, like a series of minor and inefficient attacks that were ineptly repelled by government troops who probably wondered why anyone would want to steal a nation so small that the Peace Corps wouldn't go there. It was the kind of war in which the victor would be embarrassed for having won something undesired by anyone else. Although I told Aramilo that the CIA was getting daily reports on the PDF, I found out that even the CIA didn't know what "PDF" stood for. No one did. We had a contest in the Service to invent the best meaning for PDF. People wrote down their entries and pinned them on the bulletin board at work. Some of the entries were "Please Don't Fart," "Palestine Dance Fraternity," "Pink Dog Fur," and "People's Democratic Fungus."

Aramilo was a skittish, high-strung turmoil of nerves, which was how he had been before the war started anyway. Each day he asked me what the latest CIA intelligence report was, and I just calmly lied to him and made stuff up, such as, "There's been no unusual activity."

"Could you be more specific?" Aramilo would ask.

"The PDF seems engaged in routine acts of appalling inefficiency. Yesterday, they blew up one of their own supply routes."

This wasn't true, but it relieved Aramilo, who poured himself some more vodka and tonic and resumed his important political project of learning to play "Rhapsody in Blue," by George Gershwin. I think he would have done this—I think he would have maintained his astonishing indifference to reality, his boyish self-absorption—even if he was in Indizal during the war. Someone could have come into his office in the capital and shouted, "Mr. Ambassador! We're surrounded by tanks!" And Aramilo would have said, "I need to finish practicing 'Porgy and Bess.' "

Working at the embassy seemed kind of harmless and amusing, but only if you thought that wasting your life was harmless and amusing. I was forty-one years old. Forty-one. When I asked myself what I had in life, the answer was me. *Me* wasn't very much. I had a few friends who I didn't see very often and who I wasn't very close to, either because they were unmarried men I didn't want to hang out with because the loneliness of men without women was virulent and contagious, or because they were married, or coupled, and they progressed emotionally as couples, sharing the love and sex that I assumed sustained them and which I knew nothing about. It was like they'd reached a higher level of humanness and intimacy from which I'd always be alienated.

Me wasn't very much. Dr. Boulan tried to tell me in one of our sessions that it was quite possible to live a happy and satisfying life without sexual love. She meant well, and was right in the abstract, and was only trying to help me. When she said that, though, I found it to be a bewildering, maddening, stultifying, intolerably solicitous, condescending remark that seemed to knock the wind out of my soul and make me sigh for a few seconds as various responses crashed and tumbled in my head. I looked at her with disbelief and astonishment and said, "You mean I don't *need* my penis? Maybe I should donate it to a less fortunate person in the Third World."

She blushed. Her entire face turned the color of a pale strawberry. It looked as if she was going to laugh, but she decided against it. She obviously didn't know what to say, and I obviously didn't either.

"I mean," I said, "I mean, I mean, I mean God-*DAMN.*"

"I wasn't suggesting . . ."

"Well then, what were you suggesting? That I should be a nun? Might as well change my sex if I'm not going to have any."

"I didn't mean that and you know it. I only meant that for at least part of your life, possibly a few months, possibly even several years . . ."

"I've already done that, and I don't call involuntary celibacy a good policy. I call it a misfortune."

"Not all love has to result in an orgasm."

"Who told you that? Some priest? Mother Theresa? You shouldn't take sexual advice from people who don't have sex. And I never said all love has to result in an orgasm. I just wish that SOMEtimes it would."

"Calm down, Doyle."

"I don't have to calm down. I'm your patient. I'm *supposed* to be upset, goddamn it. And I am. I am! I mean, Jesus, when I tell you about my honest, thoroughly earnest and genuine need to love some woman who loves me—and we know such a thing is fundamentally, unavoidably, wondrously sexual—I don't want to be told sex is optional. I don't want to be told it's some extraneous feature that doesn't really matter, like you could say to me, 'Doyle, you could live a perfectly wonderful life with just one leg.' The point is, I'd be missing something. I *am* missing something. And it's not my goddamn leg. So why *was* I born with a penis?"

"I think you've made your point."

"Are you mad at me?"

"Actually, I think you're very entertaining."

"I'm sorry if I embarrassed or offended you. I won't talk anymore. I'll repress all of my emotions and explode in this chair. You better call a janitor."

"When you say that '*Me* isn't very much,' does that mean you're unhappy with yourself?"

"I'm not talking anymore. I told you that."

"Yes, you are. You enjoy talking. I can tell."

"I'm not listening, either."

"So, Doyle, when you say *you* aren't very much, what exactly does that mean?"

"It means I'm alone."

"Could you tell me more? Explain that?"

"I don't *have* anybody. I just have me. I want to give myself to somebody, and there isn't anybody. The world is filled with millions of people who aren't mine. Isn't that stupid? I don't want millions of people. I only want one. And there is nobody. Sometimes I just wish I could be a boy again, just be this six- or seven-year-old boy again, because, back then, I had no idea I was alone. I was too ignorant and innocent to know what being alone meant. I do now—it means I need to love somebody, with no guarantee, and not even any genuine hope, that it'll work.

"I wish someone would hold me. I'd give up everything in the world, every ambition and extraneous desire, just to know someone would hold me. Sometimes I see women on the street, women in cars, women in stores, women who there's no reason for me to ever know or see again, and I stare at their faces and look at their eyes, as if one of them will realize they want me. And of course they never do. There are times, just odd, unexpected moments in the day, when I wish that, for maybe ten or twenty seconds, a woman would hold me. And that's all. I just wish she'd hold me and make me feel that, even though I don't really belong in anyone's life, someone could at least pretend I do. It wouldn't even have to be a woman I know. Just someone who'd put her arms around me and push my head against her shoulder and then hold me for a while. Theoretically, you're supposed to be able to live your whole life like that. I'd just be grateful for ten seconds. To have the fantasy, for ten seconds, that I mattered to somebody."

It hurt, and I couldn't talk anymore. Dr. Boulan didn't say anything. I had my hand over my eyes so she wouldn't have to see me crying. I heard her stand up and walk over in front of me, like she was going to tell me to grow up and get used to sadness, and just get out of her office and make room for someone with *real* sorrow. I heard her moving in front of me and then beside me. I wouldn't look at her because I was ashamed to have told a stranger how much I hurt. She was kneeling next to me and she put her arms around me. She was soft, and she smelled like flowers. I couldn't tell what kind. She kept one arm around my back and shoulders, and used her other hand to push my head against her shoulder. She held onto me, and I could feel her breathing. I tried to breathe in the same rhythm with her.

"Some day," she said very quietly and slowly, "you won't have to wait for a stranger to do this."

"What day?" I said.

"I don't know what day. Life usually happens without warning."

What she did was hold me, with her softness and her strength, and we breathed together. She was the kindest stranger in my life. Maybe God was answering one of my prayers. But I'd scattered so many of them around, I couldn't remember which one.

24

It would have been easy to assume that the Spam incident was a minor event with no lasting effect on the president, but every day in the mail, and by private express, Americans sent so many cans of Spam to the White House that the Spam had to be stored in a government warehouse. A science writer for the *Washington Post* estimated, without any particular reason for doing so, that if a meteor as dense as all the cans of Spam being accumulated by the White House hit Washington, the city would be vaporized. A professor of astronomy at Georgetown University said in a letter in the *Post* that if such a meteor were made of Spam "it would never strike the city, but would burn up in the atmosphere and perhaps leave an unpleasant odor over North America."

The people who made Spam remained strangely aloof

from all of this and said practically nothing to the press, as if they believed in the separation of Spam and state. But they evidently read the *Post* and were slightly offended by the remarks from the Georgetown professor. A woman who identified herself as a public affairs officer for the luncheon-meat manufacturer said in a letter in the *Post* that "Spam, an American institution for more than half a century, is quite suitable for grilling or barbecuing, and, in the event that it were to be propelled through outer space and burn up in Earth's atmosphere at thousands of miles per hour—which we find unlikely—it would produce a highly satisfying aroma."

I told Natelle I was going to a pet shop to buy her a Spamster. She thought it was kind of funny, but only kind of, because her days were filled with Spam. Cans of Spam. Crates of Spam. Spam-o-grams. I thought a Spam-o-gram was where you X-rayed Spam to see if it had a tumor. Natelle said it was a telegram about Spam sent to the president. She said she worried that all this would result in a serious backlash from the pig people, meaning animal rights activists who cared about the welfare of all the pigs killed to produce Spam, and she was right to worry.

"The pig people are here," she told me on the phone one afternoon when I was protecting Aramilo from the people who wanted to assassinate him for playing Cole Porter. I met Natelle at the White House that afternoon, and we stood on the lawn watching the pig people marching back and forth across the street carrying posters saying "Luncheon Meat is Canned Death," and "You wouldn't eat your dog for lunch, would you?" and "Pigs should be in a field, not a can."

"This is all your fault," Natelle said as we looked at the demonstrators.

"You mean the right to assemble? Thank you," I said. "Are you mad at me?"

"I wish I didn't get five hundred cans of Spam in my office every day."

"You get that many?"

"We ship it out every day to some warehouse. No one even counts it, there's so much. That's thousands of dollars of postage, and thousands of dollars of Spam. We've got people starving in this nation and starving across the world, and as a joke, or a protest, people send tons of Spam to the White House. It's not right."

"What's the president doing?"

"He's boar-hunting in Arkansas."

"Really? Was that one of his campaign promises? 'If you elect me, I'll shoot wild pigs in Arkansas. I don't remember that promise."

"Sometimes I hate working in the White House," Natelle said in a wistful voice.

"What for?"

She stared distractedly toward the protestors and said, "You see everything in the world exaggerated, and nothing clearly. In the White House, it's like the whole point of being alive is overshadowed by the public spectacle of the White House. I mean, I get dozens and hundreds and thousands of letters and cans of Spam, as if all that matters in the world is people reacting to the president reacting to something else, so that they're all reacting to the same pointless thing. And now we have a couple dozen demonstrators here, getting national press attention, as if what really matters in the world is making sure that pigs lead happy lives. And the president? He goes around the nation eating whatever nondescript lumps of regional goo that someone shoves in front of his face so he won't seem to have offended the public just because some goddamn national poll shown on TV says he's losing some of his popularity over a trivial incident that shouldn't matter to any rational person. And now we have maybe twenty-five tons of Spam being wasted in a warehouse because *why*? Because Abbas got mad at the president for saying he liked hot dogs.

"This isn't reality, Doyle. This is so stupid I can't even think of a word for it."

"America?" I wondered.

She looked at me and shook her head yes. "But don't think I'm mad at you. I'm not. In a way, it was a good idea, maybe even a brilliant one, to get even with the president the way you did. Except you didn't really get even. In a few weeks, people will forget this. Something newer and stupider will be on their minds. The president will still be president. Abbas will still be fired. And the people who're mad at you still won't like you."

"I know. I've been thinking about that. It's kind of like having a brilliant success that just doesn't matter. And now," I said, pointing across the street, "the pig people are here."

"I'm just depressed."

"About what? Your divorce?"

"Yes."

"We haven't talked about that in a few days. I think about you a lot. How're you doing?"

"I'm not sure. I've never been divorced before. I seem to be doing it right. I'm depressed all the time, and jittery, like my life is gone but it's not being replaced with anything."

"I'm with you," I said, and briefly touched her wrist, as if that might calm or soothe her, but her facial expression didn't change, so either she wasn't paying attention to me or my announcement of being with her was hardly what was needed. I was beginning to feel disposable.

"Gabriel says he won't contest the divorce," Natelle said. "That means it'll work. I don't know why something so painful should work." She looked off at the horizon, not at me, and said, "I've been thinking of going away. Of going on a retreat. Sometimes I think I need to vanish. To vanish even from myself. I'm not well, Doyle. I feel alienated and betrayed and anxious all the time. The person I loved the most has ruined me. And I haven't even stopped loving him. I thought I did. But it doesn't just stop. It goes on, like bleeding. It feels like someone died, and I don't know who it is, unless it's me. I tell myself, the way you're always so stupidly taught to do, that I should just go on. But on with what? Sadness? Horror? That's all there is to go on with. I think, Doyle, what I've been thinking, is that it's like being in an explosion, and you're all bloody and stinging and dizzy and horrified, and you look around, and you don't know where to go. It's like you're trying to remember what you were doing before the explosion, but you can't remember. It's like you used to have a life, but you don't remember where it went. And then you want to be comforted and held by the one person you love more than anyone, and then you remember . . . that's who blew you up."

Her eyes were closed, like she was trying not to cry, and I held her hand.

"I'll help you," I said, realizing from the limpness of her hand that I wasn't helping her at all, realizing also that the fact that I deeply loved her was, for the time being, the greatest possible gift she didn't want.

IN THE embassy one morning as I drank my Ethiopian coffee and read a copy of the *Weekly World News* with a headline saying "Boy gives birth to baby sister," and Aramilo sat at the piano with a cup of coffee and bourbon as he practiced "Begin the Beguine," Maria walked into the room without knocking, approached Aramilo with a charmingly excited smile and said, "The civil war is over. There is a cease-fire. Many of the PDF have surrendered, or are in disorganized retreat, which I was just this moment told over the phone. There are celebrations everywhere in Rio D'Iguana. People took to the streets and fired their guns in the air, killing sixteen people, unfortunately. The country is ours again."

I thought of a headline: "Sixteen people killed by peace."

Maria left the room, as if she had urgent work unrelated to "Begin the Beguine," and Aramilo sighed gratefully, saying to me, "I guess now no one wants to kill me."

"I guess not."

"And now your watchful security can be relaxed."

"What security? I'm just reading the paper."

"Have a drink with me," Aramilo said in a relaxed voice as he stood up to go to his omnipresent liquor bottles, which I imagined that he regarded not as a liquor cabinet but as an altar.

"I don't drink in the morning," I said.

"Are you saying I have a drinking problem?"

"It doesn't seem to be a problem at all. You can do it under even the most difficult circumstances."

Aramilo laughed as he poured himself a small glass of vodka, and then he sipped from it and held the glass above his head.

"To Indizal!" he said. "To all tiny little island nations!"

I raised my cup of coffee above my head and said, "To the islet of Langerhans!"

"Really?" Aramilo said. "Which island is that?"

"It's not really an island. It just sounds like one. One time while I was watching 'Jeopardy' on TV, one of the answers was the islet of Langerhans. It sounds like some island off the coast of Ireland or Wales, but it's not. The islet of Langerhans is a group of cells in the pancreas, I think."

"To the pancreas!" Aramilo toasted. "Now that we have peace, you know what it makes me think of?"

"Vodka?"

"Noooo, no, no. You know in your Bible, you Christians, there's a saying I've nearly memorized, but not quite."

"Sounds like a lot of Christians, who can't quote a single line from the Bible but say they believe everything in it."

"The saying is something about plowshares and swords."

"That's the chapter about hardware stores."

"I think," Aramilo said, squinting, as if lost in thought, "I think it says we shall turn our swords into plowshares."

"Yeah. And then you know what? Someone will start a war with plowshares."

Aramilo shook his head and said, "Don't be so depressing."

"Well, I guess you should celebrate, now. You could fire my gun out the window and kill people ten blocks from here."

The sudden peace in Indizal reminded me of the general pointlessness of my career. Whatever slight chance there had been of someone wanting to assassinate Aramilo was now gone, meaning that I resumed the punishment of guarding someone who was in no danger. I resumed protecting a privileged man who deserved no privileges and had many; and all because I'd offended an entire hierarchy of privileged people whose privileged lives I was sworn to protect.

Bastards.

I decided to call Doltmeer and ask for a new assignment, which almost certainly he wouldn't give me, unless it was more demeaning and pointless than what I wanted to escape. But I was at least going to ask. When I got Doltmeer on the phone, I said, "The war in Indizal's over. We just heard on the phone. Maria said they . . ."

"What's Indizal?" Doltmeer said.

"That's the country whose ambassador I've been guarding from the assassins who don't like Cole Porter."

"Oh. Yes. *In*-dizal. It always makes me think of Pine-Sol."

"Well, yes. I see the comparison. Pine-Sol is a cleaning solvent, and Indizal is a country. But anyway . . ."

"I was making a joke," Doltmeer said lightly.

"Well *I* know that, goddamn it. And so was I."

"*I* know that. Jesus Christ," Doltmeer said peevishly. "Don't any of my agents have a sense of humor?"

"Humor? I'm protecting an alcoholic pianist from his countless enemies who don't exist on an island nation that rhymes with Pine-Sol. I think I understand humor. But let me digress to the original reason I called you. The war in Indizal's over. Maria said they defeated the PDF and there's a cease-fire, and now that everyone in the capital of Indizal's so happy, they fired their guns in the air, accidentally killing sixteen people."

"No shit?" Doltmeer said curiously.

"That's what Maria said."

"Who's Maria? Someone you're dating?"

"She's the chargé d'affaires at the embassy."

"Oh. That's right. The embassy."

"I work there. Remember?"

"Yes. I sentenced you."

"I was thinking that now that the war's over and the PDF's no . . ."

"Did anyone ever find out what PDF stands for?"

"I don't think we were trying to find out, were we?"

"Not really. I was just curious," Doltmeer said indifferently.

"So anyway, I think what I'm getting at is that I'd like to be reassigned. There's no point in punishing me by having me guard someone who was never in any danger. You might as well assign me to something with at least minor importance that I also won't like. That way, I'll at least be doing something with negligible value, and you'll still be punishing me. Can't we be that practical?"

"I'll give it some thought. But, officially, you aren't being punished."

"Of course not."

"The Service doesn't do petty or vindictive things just because our superiors ask us to."

"Then why *do* you do petty and vindictive things?"

"Don't get on my bad side, Doyle."

"It's too late to avoid that side."

"Yes, but don't bury yourself any deeper. What new assignment were you thinking of?"

"I hadn't thought of one, really. Maybe I could be assigned to protect the ambassador from the islet of Langerhans."

"What's that?"

"It sounds like an island off the coast of Wales, doesn't it?"

"Is it a U.N. member?"

"No. It's a group of cells in the pancreas. At least that's what they said on 'Jeopardy.' Could I be assigned to guard someone's pancreas? It couldn't be any more ludicrous than what I'm doing now."

"That's true. I do hate wasting valuable agents. Not that I'm saying you're valuable. Do you know what you've got to learn? Don't *ever* piss off people in power. They don't have to be nice. They don't even have to be human. You think we're living in a democracy?"

"There are those rumors."

"That's all they are. Rumors. People in power badly want the vote of the common people, but they have no intention of being treated like them."

"Well, *deja vu*. That sounds remarkably like what Abbas said on TV and in the newspapers, over and over."

"And you don't think it pisses off the president even more?"

"I didn't vote for him."

"Well, you better act like you did, or you won't even get to guard someone's pancreas. I'll assign you to someone's anus."

"I don't think I'd like being that specialized."

"Then be careful. Can you do that?"

"I keep learning."

"Good. I'll call you if I can find a demeaning and tedious assignment more pleasing to you."

"Somehow, it doesn't seem appropriate to say thank you."

"It isn't."

25

"The beauty of a line drive van-
ishes when it hits you in the forehead," Widdiker said contemplatively as we all lay in the grass and flowers out in the
outfield where tiny, nearly invisible flying bugs, as well as
honey bees and wasps, buzzed around us and sometimes
landed on our beer cans. We were supposed to have been
practicing, and had been, except we took a time-out after
Deek was hit in the forehead by a line drive that almost
knocked him out and caused him to start reciting the peri-
odic table of the elements.

"Hydrogen, helium, lithium, beryllium, boron, carbon,"
Deek said drowsily when Horner and DeMarco tried to pick
him up from the ground where the line drive crumpled him.
Deek was too heavy, and we left him lying in the shade with
his baseball glove under his head as a pillow.

"Are you all right, Deek?" Widdiker asked.

"Nitrogen," Deek said. "Oxygen, fluorine, neon, sodium, magnesium. I don't know why, but I can remember *everything*," he said with calm amazement, and then he said, "Aluminum, silicon, phosphorus, sulfur, chlorine, argon, potassium, calcium, scandium." And he smiled.

It was all very restful, with everyone lying side by side in the rim of shade from all the big trees at the edge of the outfield, and sometimes you could hear a cow lowing and some birds twittering and Deek saying, "Titanium, vanadium, chromium, manganese, iron, cobalt . . ."

"Don't you think we should take him to a hospital?" Oxler said. Oxler was the one whose line drive whammed into Deek's forehead.

"I'm fine. I just need to rest," Deek said. And then he said, "Nickel, copper, zinc, gallium."

"What if he has a concussion?" DeMarco said.

"Germanium," Deek said.

"He says he's fine," Yamato said.

"Arsenic," Deek said.

"What if he goes into a coma?" Horner wondered.

"I guess we'll need a new outfielder," Widdiker said.

"Selenium," Deek said, smiling up at the wispy white clouds straying across the sky. "I'm a little dizzy, and my head hurts. But other than that, I'm fine. Bromine. Krypton. Rubidium."

"Krypton?" Yamato said. "Isn't that where Superman was born?"

"I don't know. We didn't study that in school," DeMarco said. "We studied where Columbus was born."

"Strontium," Deek said.

"No. I think Columbus was born in Italy, Deek," DeMarco said.

"This reminds me of when I was a boy," I said, staring at the clouds.

"You mean when you were a boy," Widdiker said, "someone got hit in the head with a baseball and named all the elements?"

"No," I said. "I mean just lying in the grass and staring at the sky. In Kansas, where I grew up, there weren't very many trees, so you could lie on your back and look straight up and see absolutely nothing but the sky. Like that's all there was —sky. If you did that long enough, you'd start to get dizzy, and maybe throw up."

"You must miss your childhood," Yamato said.

"No. I don't think you ever really leave your childhood. There's a child in everyone. Especially if you're pregnant."

"Is that what you're trying to tell us—you're pregnant?" Pascal asked.

"Yttrium," Deek said.

"Is he speaking Yiddish now?" Yamato asked. "Maybe we should take him to a doctor."

"Why? Just because he's speaking Yiddish?" Horner asked.

"Zirconium," Deek said. "Niobium, molybdenum, technetium, ruthenium, rhodium, palladium."

"I know what it is," Pascal said. "He's speaking in tongues. It's the end of the world, and Jesus is coming back."

"Well, if he comes here, let's give him Deek's glove and let him play in the outfield," I said.

"Jesus doesn't play baseball," Widdiker said.

"That's right. There aren't any sports in the Bible," I said.

"I thought killing Philistines was a sport," Pascal said.

"Well, if you look at it that way, the entire Old Testament is a sports document," I said.

"Silver," Deek said. "Cadmium, indium, tin, antimony."

"Is this what happens when you grow up?" Yamato asked. "You lie down in a field, mumbling incoherently?"

"Thoreau said most people lead lives of quiet desperation," Widdiker said, as if maybe that was why we were there.

"That's because loud desperation is rude," Pascal said.

"Shhhh," DeMarco said, and all you could hear was the wind, and some honey bees, and a bird calling, and the sorrowful absence of someone you needed who you might not ever have.

And you could hear Deek saying, "Tellurium."

NATELLE INVITED me over to her apartment for burned chicken and an annulment. She had the chicken neatly stacked and burned on the edge of her grill on her balcony when I got there, and there was an empty bottle of pink wine next to the freshly opened one that she used to pour us both a glass. I sat next to her in a folding chair, and she smiled at me in a distressed, dreamy way.

"Thank you for coming over," she said. "I'm drunk."

"I think I can tell," I said. "Did you burn that chicken for me?"

"I'm not sure who I burned it for," she said, pointing her bare toes at the grill. "Maybe we could regard it as a burnt offering to the Lord."

"Is He coming over too?"

"You shouldn't joke about the Lord."

"You just did."

"Well, Doyle, *I'm* drunk."

"I know. Are you okay?"

"Not that I'm aware of," she said, folding her legs beneath her to sit cross-legged. "I talked to a priest today. A gay priest. Father Ruuden. I asked him about getting a divorce.

He said, 'Well, you can't, my dear. The Church won't allow that.' And I thought of saying 'And how long has the Church allowed gay priests to dispense Church doctrine?' But I didn't say that. Although the truth is, a gay priest told me I can't get divorced, because it's a sin, even though being gay is a sin, too. So, are you hungry?"

"Not right now. I need to finish hearing your story."

"I have some chicken. It's burned."

"And what else happened?" I said, touching my hand on her shoulder to reassure her, and also just because of my need to touch her.

"I have some potato salad and fresh strawberries," she said cheerfully. "Do you like strawberries? I do."

"Yes, but you said something about an annulment."

She nodded her head yes. "I've decided to annul myself."

"Yourself?"

"Well, no. I mean my marriage. You see, as Father Ruuden explained, divorce is a sin, because you'd be putting asunder what God hath joined together. But what the Church does, as a loophole, is annul you. They pretend you never really were married. Does that make sense? To say, 'Well, you're married, and the only way to dissolve marriage is to pretend you *aren't* married'? That's what Father Ruuden said. I've been thinking about it all day. Although, . . ." Natelle stood up to look at the chicken on the grill. She said, "It's all burned on one side. I think it's raw on the other. In the Bible they always have burnt offerings. I'm not sure that includes barbecue."

"I don't think so," I said, watching Natelle sway just slightly as she stood. I wanted to hold her and feel her breathing against me.

"Soooo," Natelle said, and sat down again. "The Church has the authority to pretend my marriage isn't a marriage. If

I just up and got a divorce, they'd say it's a sin because I'm married. But if I ask for an annulment, then they'll pretend I'm not married. I guess that's an important theological doctrine."

"What is?"

"Pretending," she said, and smiled at me wearily. "It's awful. I think I'm having a schism. Do you know what a schism is?"

"Yes. It's when you have a different reality than what the Church wants you to have."

She nodded her head and said, "You know what I've decided?"

"What?"

"I've decided to have my own annulment," she said, and very delicately took a sip of wine, as if she needed just the tiniest amount to keep her as drunk as she was.

"You mean do it yourself?" I asked.

"Yes. Technically, some priest or cardinal or bishop or somebody, who knows nothing about me, is supposed to examine my request for an annulment. So a group of strangers gets to decide if I'm really married or not." She looked over at me and said, "I was there. *I'm* the one who lived through all this. Don't I get to decide if I'm married or not?"

"It's fine with me," I said.

"All right," she said, sitting up straight and breathing in some air and exhaling. "How do you do an annulment?"

"I've never done one."

"Do you think I should change my clothes?"

"I think you can do an annulment in shorts."

"All right," she said, taking in a deep breath and exhaling again. "And then what?"

"This is a new ceremony. I think you get to make it up."

She began biting her thumbnail and said, "We had music

during my wedding. Should we have music at an annulment?"

"Well," I said, rubbing my hand on her back, "they also had someone to give you away at the wedding. Do you think we need someone to give you back?"

Natelle's head tilted wearily toward me as she started laughing quietly. "That's right," she said. "You give the bride away. Now it's time to give her back. But who are we giving me back to?"

"We're giving you back to you," I said, wishing I'd never come up with that idea, because now she closed her eyes and sat very still and did nothing except be quiet and let tears trickle from her eyes. I kneeled beside her and put my arms around her and felt her lightly trembling as she cried without sound. I wanted the hurt to come into me, to invade me, like I could transfer it all to me, because I was used to sadness and swam in it. But it stayed in her, and all she could do was cry and tremble in my arms, like something was thrashing inside of her. As tightly as I held her, I wasn't protecting her from anything.

"I'm giving me back to *me*?" she asked almost inaudibly. "Isn't there a better prize than that?"

I wanted to say *Me*, but I was always the kind of prize women eventually discarded, and there was no proof that Natelle wanted me for anything more than the desperate kindness of holding her then. And so I cried with her, and helped her do that.

"All right," she said suddenly, as if waking from her sadness, or just fighting it, and she raised her head up and said, "I'm a big girl. I'm a brave girl. Let's finish my annulment. Get the damn thing over with."

"Okay," I said, since I had to say something, although I had no idea what she was going to do.

"Let's see," she said. "I've never been to an annulment, so this is going to be pretty primitive."

"That'll fit in with the burned chicken," I said.

"Okay," she said. "Okay, so . . . give me your right hand," she said, smiling a little bit.

I gave her my right hand and she held it up and pressed the palm of her left hand against mine. She did the same with my left hand so that we sat side by side with our knees touching and the palms of our hands pressed together.

I said, "Are you sure this is an annulment? It seems like patty cake."

"No. This is an annulment," she said. "You have to do it, you have to touch the hands of someone you love and trust, and press them tightly together," she said, and she pushed and pushed against my hands, and I pushed back on hers. What we were doing was touching each other almost as hard as we could, like she had to fight physically against her sadness by trying to push herself into me.

"Is this how they do it in Rome?" I said.

"This is how we do it at *my* house," she said, grinning intently at me as she used an instant burst of strength to push me backward so hard that I and my chair fell over. Natelle fell with me, cradling her arms around my head so it didn't hurt very much when we both landed on the wooden deck and the chair fell away from me. She lay on top of me, an accident, a harmless accident, and also the first time either of us had ever been on top of the other. The full weight of her was stretched out across me, and I thought maybe it *wasn't* an accident, as she pressed her lips against my neck and, very lightly, only one time, pushed her groin against mine and made no effort to get up.

"Is this part of the annulment?" I said.

"I think that part's over," she said, bringing her lips up

onto mine, and we were kissing. Her breasts were pressed against my chest and she pushed against me again between my legs, no mistake, no accident. Without warning or preparation, we had each other. I worried. I reluctantly thought of my better judgment, and said to her when she lifted her head up to look at my eyes, "Is this what you want to do?" which was a depressingly responsible thing to say.

"Well, I'm not doing this by accident," she said.

"But you've been drinking."

"But part of me's still sober," she said.

"Which part?"

"This part," she said, and kissed me again on the lips.

"Are you trying to take advantage of me?" I said.

"I think it's working," she said, then pushed herself off of me and didn't say anything, as if now she realized she didn't want to do this. She stood up and looked down at me on my back and said, "I want you to go in my room and wait for me."

I was stunned by the idea that she wanted to have sex with me. I looked up at her and said, "What're you going to do? Knock me over again?"

"I might," she said, pulling me up by my hands. We walked into the kitchen together and she said, "Go wait for me. I'll be there in a minute."

It amazed me how familiar we'd become with each other when so much of us was still unfamiliar, like love was a squall and you didn't know it was coming and suddenly it was all over you. I wasn't going to turn her down. I went into her bedroom and sat on her bed and quickly started undressing, tossing my shoes and socks and shirt and pants on the floor.

"Are you ready?" Natelle called out from the kitchen.

And we'd never even had a date. I never understood

anything. All of this was impossible, and unmistakably real.

I said, "I'm not sure what I'm ready for, but yes."

Natelle came through the doorway with only her panties on, pale green panties with tiny red flowers on them. Her breasts swayed as she walked up to the bed and crawled on her hands and knees over me and beside me. It felt like electricity from her skin shot through me, and I was feverish and bewildered and gentle.

"What do you want to do with me?" I asked.

She leaned into me and pushed me down on my back and rolled onto me, kneeling over me as if she'd pinned me, and simply stared into my eyes, both of us staring and never blinking, as if it wasn't possible to see enough and we wanted to see harder; as if what we were really doing was entering each other through our eyes. She leaned her face down and put both of her lips lightly on my top lip and then my bottom lip, kissing me almost reverently, which was how I felt about her weight on me, every touch and nearness of her, gently astounded that she wanted me, feeling the vague sensation that she could pass right through my flesh into me, or at least I wanted her to.

"I want to melt into you," I said, not even sure what it meant.

"I think you might," she said, turning sideways and around on me, still on her hands and knees, moving her head down to kiss me high on the inside of my thigh, slowly kissing me, her own soft thighs and her wet, flowery panties raised just inches above my face as she put her hand between her legs and used two fingers to pull aside the narrow, soaked swatch of her panties while I breathed in her strong fragrance, staring with wonder at the glistening, wet folds of her vagina, which she slowly moved so close that I couldn't see, but then found with my tongue inside her, where I found something she must have gotten from the kitchen: a small, sliced piece of a strawberry. Natelle moaned when I discovered the strawberry and worked to get it with my tongue. She giggled briefly and said, "Do you like strawberries?"

"More than I realized," I said. "Served this way, I'd even eat broccoli."

She almost shrieked with laughter and pounded the mattress with her hand.

"Well, I'm not going to put broccoli there. It's not as erotic as a strawberry."

"And a lot harder to conceal."

"Does it taste good?" she wondered in a playful voice.

"You, or the strawberry?"

"Both."

"I like the strawberry fine. The flavor I prefer is you."

"Good. There's more of me," she said, pushing her fragrant, moist flesh back onto my mouth and gently sliding her tongue along my penis, up to the tip, covering it with her lips. This was more complicated than bliss, this complexity of love and hungry tongues, where you couldn't distinguish the giving from the taking, both seeming the same. And in this way we consumed each other, and made of each other more.

26

Doltmeer was holding a bag of dead flies when I walked into his office for our two o'clock meeting. I knew it was a bag of dead flies because he reached into the bag and pulled out something too small to see and gently stuffed it into the mouth of one of his pitcher plants near the window. I glanced around the room to see if Edgar Allan Poe was with us. We were alone. For a moment, when I should have been concentrating only on seeming properly serious for Doltmeer, I couldn't help remembering having had sex with Natelle for the first time, which should have been a completely wondrous thing except that Natelle had been drunk. There was no way of knowing if she really wanted me, as it had seemed, or if she'd be sober now and regretting her intimacy with me. While to me it was the best thing possible, to her it might have been an aberration, and she'd have to drive me from her life. I wanted to go to the White House, then, and talk to her about it, to find out if I was deeper in her life or about to be pushed guiltily to the farthest edge of it.

But I couldn't just leave Doltmeer's office right when I got there, and I was reluctant to say anything that would make Doltmeer immediately get to the point of why he'd asked me there, since he would either describe to me some new trouble I was in because of the Spam deal, or he'd announce to me some repugnant new assignment. I decided to make small talk.

"As a special treat, do you ever give the plants horseflies?" I said.

Doltmeer glanced thoughtfully at me as he stuffed another fly into a plant and said, "No, but it's an interesting idea. It's hard enough, as you might imagine, just to find a steady supply of ordinary flies."

"I know. I was at the mall last weekend and didn't see a single store that sold flies."

"I get mine from a biology professor at Georgetown," Doltmeer said. He put the bag of flies on his desk.

"How much is a pound of dead flies?"

"Free," Doltmeer said, while looking at some papers on his desk.

It was pointless to keep making small talk about dead flies, so I said, "Is everyone still mad at me?"

"I was never mad," Doltmeer said in a quiet and oddly friendly voice, as if for a while, not long, he'd try to speak to me as a friend, a human. "Personally, I didn't vote for the president and I think he's a son of a bitch. So I don't care what he eats. And I kind of enjoyed it when you and Abbas humiliated him. But professionally, I can't tolerate that. And neither can you. In the Service, we're like courtesans with guns. Do you know what a courtesan is?"

"No, but it's an interesting word."

"A courtesan is a prostitute for the upper class."

"We're whores?"

"Somewhat. We aren't required to have sex, but we are bought off, even more than a prostitute, who can have sex, wipe herself clean, and go home. We can't go home. We practically live with the people we're assigned to, and in some cases, we actually do. So we're expected not only to escort them everywhere and protect them from harm, we're also expected to protect their dignity, even if we don't think they deserve dignity, and sometimes they don't. So that's why I say we're like courtesans with guns."

"Does this mean you're going to ask me to live with someone?" I asked with mild anguish.

"Good Lord, no. I don't think you're civilized enough for that. On my staff, you're one of the fringers. You operate successfully on the *fringe* of order, decency, and sanity. And don't think it's an insult. It's not. The world needs fringers, just like history's always needed explorers, inventors, thinkers and madmen."

Madmen? I wasn't going to tell him about my 60-second nervous breakdown. It might make me seem too authentic.

"So I'm a fringer," I said in a wondering tone.

"We gave you an award for breaking an ambassador's nose, didn't we? That's certainly a characteristic of a fringer."

"Well, that was an accident. I didn't practice breaking his nose."

"And you didn't need to. It was done expertly without practice."

"Thank you. Do I get a raise?"

"Not soon, no. But you do get a new assignment, which, coincidentally, is part of the continuing fallout of that dumb-

ass Spam incident that you'll live to regret, if you're capable
of an emotion as refined as regret. The White House has
received threatening mail from a heretofore unknown animal
rights group calling itself Animad. As far as we can tell, Animad just comes from the *a-n-i* in animal, plus *mad*. Not particularly poetic or clever, but they, whoever they are,
apparently have an office near RFK Stadium, according to
their letter, which was received by the White House today.
Here's a copy," Doltmeer said, opening a folder and handing
me a photocopy of the letter.

Dear Mr. President:
   It was with great shame and indignation that we saw
you on TV and read about you in the papers, traveling
across the nation and eating mound after mound of
innocent, profaned and desecrated animal flesh in an
atrocious attempt to show the public that you, too, are
just an ordinary, fun-loving pig murderer.

I looked up at Doltmeer and said, "I don't think the president actually kills pigs. I think he just eats them."

"Just read the letter," Doltmeer said. The rest of the letter
said:

You have an opportunity, as the most powerful and
visible leader in the nation, to set a moral example of
enlightened vegetarianism for this nation and the world
instead of debasing and debauching us all by eating
every vile and repugnant form of massacred meat cooked
up by the ignorant masses, to whom you pander for
votes. On top of that, the latest media estimates are that
the federal government—the White House—is now
placidly storing in a government warehouse approximately 38 tons of Spam, that canned atrocity, mailed to

the White House so far in a continuing tragedy and indictment of Western Civilization.

"Western Civilization," I said. "Does that mean Roy Rogers and John Wayne?"

Doltmeer grinned slightly, one of the few times I ever seemed capable of amusing him. The final part of the letter said:

> Action is called for and will be forthcoming. The endless and unconscionable slaughter of animals ultimately must stop. You, as President, have it in your power to help end the immorality of wanton predation, the cruel insanity of transforming sentient creatures into lunchbox sandwiches. We urge you to consider this, and advise you that to dismiss us can result in dramatic consequences from the devoted members of Animad.
>
> Seethingly,
> L. D. Krite, President
> Animad

I put the letter on Doltmeer's desk.

"Seethingly?" I wondered.

"He does seem pissed," Doltmeer said.

"Well, what do you want me to do? Waste him?"

"Oh, good God. Have you been watching gangster movies again?" Doltmeer said.

"Let me waste him. I like being wasteful."

"What I want you to do is go talk to him. Find out if he's dangerous. I want you and Yamato to investigate Mr. or Ms. Krite, learn everything you can, see if Animad is an organization to be reckoned with and if the consequences he mentions are an actionable threat to the president or anyone else. And remember . . ."

"What?"

"You started this."

YAMATO AND I found the Animad Institute on the second floor of a decaying old building above the business offices of Psychic Madame de Bollix. Yamato had lost his car keys that morning and he wanted to ask Madame de Bollix where they were. I told him I didn't think the occult forces of the universe had a serious interest in his car keys, and even if they did, the occult forces weren't to be trusted, although, after we interviewed L. D. Krite, Yamato and I could briefly visit Madame de Bollix if he wanted to waste his money that way.

A young woman, maybe in her twenties, with stunning red hair worn in the washerwoman style and almost overwhelmingly pretty green eyes, let us into the Animad office and seemed only a little upset when we showed her our Service IDs and explained why we were there. I could tell by the way Yamato stared at her and looked away and stared again that he probably wanted to date this woman, who in fact was L. D. Krite. It was odd, and reminded me of how much I loved Natelle, that in the midst of our deliberate and coldly precise reality, it suddenly didn't matter anymore to Yamato that he was a government agent searching for any vague or incipient threats to the president, and now he was just Yamato, looking at a woman he might want. Which part of reality was more real? The part you wanted most.

While I was starting to ask L. D. Krite about the letter to the president, Yamato looked at her and said, "Not very many women wear their hair that way. It looks nice on you."

"Thank you," L. D. Krite said uneasily.

"We're just curious," I said, holding a copy of her letter, "about a few of the remarks in here, such as 'Action is called for and will be forthcoming.'"

"I like animals. I have a collie," Yamato said, smiling boyishly and with stark hope at L. D. Krite.

"Really? Male or female?" L. D. Krite said, smiling more warmly.

"Female. Her name is Honker, because when I first got her as a puppy and I was driving her home, she stood up in my lap and kept accidentally honking the horn."

Yamato and L. D. Krite laughed about that.

"While I'm sure the president doesn't agree with the 'cruel insanity of transforming sentient creatures into lunch-box sandwiches,' " I said, abruptly reading from the letter again, "what we're curious to know is what you meant by suggesting there might be 'dramatic consequences' if . . ."

"I have a cat named Bonk," L. D. Krite said happily to Yamato, ignoring me. "When she was a kitten, she constantly bonked her little head on furniture and things in the house, so I named her Bonk." She and Yamato laughed again. I wondered if they were going to fall in love and, as a covenant of their love, kill the president together.

"Do you have a pet?" L. D. Krite asked me.

I was going to say I had a Spamster. It annoyed me a little that she could write a vaguely threatening letter to the president and then act as if she were a darling woman with a lovely cat named Bonk. And there was that son of a bitch Yamato, almost joyously smiling at her and probably having pointless fantasies about love and copulation with a woman we might ultimately arrest. Jesus Christ.

"No. No, I don't have a pet. I hate to digress to the reason we actually came here, but we really do need to discuss this letter a little bit."

"Why? Do you think I'm going to kill the president?" L. D. Krite said brazenly.

"She wouldn't do that," Yamato said.

Oh God. Now Yamato was defending her. This wasn't working.

"I'm not here to accuse you of anything," I said politely.

"Yes, you are," she said. "You're a carnivore, like all the rest," she said in an accusing way. "Are you here to arrest me? Harass me? Intimidate me? Because I'm getting all this on tape," she said, nodding her head toward a small tape recorder in front of her on her desk.

"We're being taped? Well, I might as well say something worth taping," I said, and began quoting a fragment of a poem I'd learned in college:

> She walks in beauty, like the night
> Of cloudless climes and starry skies;
> And all that's best of dark and bright
> Meet in her aspect and her eyes:
> Thus mellow' to that tender light
> Which heaven to gaudy day denies.

L. D. Krite seemed confused and didn't know what to say.

"That was Lord Byron," I said. "Maybe Lord Byron will sound good on tape. Anyway, we have no intention of harassing you. Could you please tell us what you mean in your letter when you say 'action is forthcoming and there will be dramatic consequences if . . .'"?

"Animad has hundreds of members in Washington alone," L. D. Krite said. "It would be relatively easy to stage a large protest at the White House."

"And that's certainly your right," Yamato said defensively.

"May we see your membership list?" I asked.

"Do you have a warrant?" L. D. Krite said.

"Noooo, no, no, no," Yamato said in a cheerful and calming tone, not like an agent doing a good job, but like a cooing prospective lover. He was pissing me off.

"I know you're just the obedient henchmen of the White House," L.D. Krite said.

"Henchmen?" I said. "What's a hench?"

She looked at me suspiciously, with distaste, and said, "You must think I'm awfully stupid if you think I'll just passively tell you any plans we might have."

"Well, you don't have to tell us. But we could easily have a dozen or more agents following you night and day, tapping your phones, investigating everyone you know, and learning how often you brush your teeth every day. It'd just be easier if you talk to us now."

Yamato frowned worriedly, as if I were upsetting his girlfriend.

"Are you *threat*-ening me?" L. D. Krite asked in a slightly hostile tone. "I'm an American citizen. You have no right to harass me for political reasons."

"Fine," I said. "If you have no interest in talking, we'll leave."

As I walked toward the door, Yamato said, "I'm really sorry if we unintentionally sounded threatening. We were just making a routine inquiry."

Dickhead. Why don't you kiss her goodbye?

Downstairs in front of the psychic's office, Yamato smiled at me and said, "She seems like a nice woman."

"You fucking idiot," I said. "You *know* we're going to have to investigate her."

"She's so pretty," Yamato said wistfully.

"And you eat meat. She eats plants, like a sea cow."

"You could almost see her nipples through her blouse."

"Well, I'll be sure to include that in our report."

"It's easy for you to be indifferent. You have a girlfriend, sort of," Yamato said, referring to the occasional times he knew I'd been with Natelle. Actually this hurt, because it wasn't certain that I had Natelle in any sense, and just as she was leaving Gabriel, she could just as easily leave me.

"That's right. I have a sort-of-girlfriend, which is the same thing as having nothing. But you? I don't think you should date women who threaten the president. You should only date women who threaten the vice-president."

"Well. I guess I have to resort to cold professionalism and find out where she lives and stare in her bedroom window with a telephoto lens."

"A matter of national security?" I asked.

Yamato ignored that. "Should we go see Madame de Bollix and find out where my car keys are?"

"Maybe we should ask her if L. D. Krite's going to attack the president."

"That's a good idea," Yamato said, walking toward the psychic's door.

"We can't do that, you asshole."

"Sure we can. We just won't tell anybody," Yamato said, opening the door and walking through several layers of stringed glass beads hanging over the doorway to what I regarded as an ostentatiously dark and eerie office that smelled like incense and fried pork. On an impulse, I followed him. The clinking and jingling and clanging metal things on the strings we walked through alerted Madame de Bollix of our presence; I whispered to Yamato: "If she was really a psychic, she wouldn't need noise to know we were here. She'd predict our arrival."

Madame de Bollix came through another series of hanging glass beads at the back of the room and walked up to the circular wooden table with folding chairs around it. She wore a maroon skirt that went down to her ankles and a black, puffy blouse. In the semi-light of the room—lighted by a single stained-glass lamp hanging a few feet over the table—I saw that she wore a pale orange bandana on her head, like a pirate. She looked to be in her forties and wore lipstick as dark as dried blood. Her bosom, slightly sagging, seemed weighed down by a dozen or more silver and gold necklaces with various peculiar and unrecognizable "things" hanging in a tangled clump, almost as if someone had been trying to capture her by throwing necklaces at her, like lariats, but she had gotten away. She pointed to the table with her left hand, revealing maybe half a dozen rings, and five or six bracelets, on her left wrist alone.

"Sit," she said.

Yamato and I sat. Madame de Bollix sat across from us with her hands in her lap and gave us a somber, aristocratic smile, as if pleased with something wholly unrelated to us.

Yamato didn't say anything. I didn't say anything. Then it was Madame de Bollix's turn not to say anything. I wondered if there was a secret rule for proceeding that none of us knew.

Madame de Bollix lifted her arms onto the table, and she was wearing so many metal bracelets of different thicknesses and shapes that she clanked, just by clasping her fingers together. It looked like she was walking by a jewelry box when it exploded. She stared at Yamato and me with a vague kind of curiosity.

"Are you here for a reason, or did you just wish to sit?" she said.

"I thought you might be able to help us," Yamato said respectfully. "But I've never been to a psychic before. How do I know you're a real psychic?"

"Well, you don't," Madame de Bollix said in what sounded like some kind of European accent that could've been either real or fake. "You look at the sign on the window and what does it say?"

"It says 'Psychic,'" Yamato said.

"Then you must assume that I'm a psychic or that I have the wrong sign up. Which do you assume?"

"I assume you're a psychic."

"Very well. And how may I help you? Are you interested in the future? Do you wish to speak with the dead?"

"No. I have two problems. I need to find my car keys, and I need to know if anyone plans to harm the president of the United States," Yamato said.

"Twenty-two-fifty," Madame de Bollix said.

"What's that—a code?"

"My price. Simple consultations are twenty-two-fifty. You pay me now."

Yamato pulled his wallet from his pants and handed Madame de Bollix a twenty and three ones. She put the money in a blue leather pouch suspended from her waist by a strap. Then she closed her eyes and was quiet. This was all she did, as if closing her eyes and being quiet was occult.

"Aren't you going to light a candle or something?" Yamato asked.

"I'm the psychic. Not you. Be quiet," she said.

I whispered to Yamato: "She owes you fifty cents."

Yamato whispered: "Shut up."

"Stop whispering. I need silence. I need no distractions," she said, although outside you could hear rap music coming from a boom box. Possibly rap music didn't interfere with the occult, but whispering did.

Madame de Bollix remained silent, with her eyes closed, without any movement or obvious results, for at least a minute.

"I think she's in a transcendent state," Yamato whispered.

"Taking a nap," I whispered.

"Your keys are innnnn," Madame de Bollix said suddenly, "the sink. The kitchen sink," she said, raising her hands to her temples, her battery of bracelets clinking and clunking down to her forearms.

"What about the president?" Yamato asked.

"He wouldn't be in the sink," I said.

Madame de Bollix's head swayed slightly from side to side, as if sloshing visions around in her head, and she said, "This is difficult. I see forms unclearly."

"That's because her eyes are closed," I whispered.

"I see . . ."

"Darkness, until she opens her eyes," I whispered. Yamato scowled at me.

". . . the White House. And inside the White House, I see . . ."

"White people."

"Shut *up!*" Yamato whispered.

". . . great disorder."

"Well, that's true, regardless of who's president."

"Will you shut the fuck up?"

"The disorder is caused by . . ."

"Anyone who's elected."

". . . animals. I see animals," Madame de Bollix said, tilting her head back, as if sloshing the visions to the back of her skull.

"*Wild* animals?" Yamato asked. "What kind? Pigs? Goats? Dogs?"

"Lobbyists?" I said.

Madame de Bollix sighed loudly and leaned her head forward, slowly opening her eyes and staring at Yamato and me with a kind of grim confusion. "I don't understand the vision," she said.

"Why? What'd you see?" Yamato said nervously.

"All of the animals," she said, "are in cans."

ANYONE COULD have dressed up like an old woman from the nineteenth century, put on six pounds of jewelry and lipstick the color of dried blood, and, by following the news, predicted trouble in the White House with canned animals. To discredit the old fraud, Yamato and I drove to his apartment and looked in the kitchen sink.

"My keys!" Yamato said, lifting the keys from the sink and holding them in front of me. "Do you realize what this means?"

"I don't want to realize what it means," I said.

"She really is a psychic!"

"Maybe she is, but I'd rather not care."

"But what if she's . . ."

"Don't say it. I don't care, I don't care, I don't *c-a-r-e* if she's a psychic. We're not going to use a goddamn psychic in the Secret Service."

"But what if she's right about the president?"

"All right. Fine. You go up to Doltmeer and say 'We've got to listen to a psychic's prediction of trouble in the White House because she found my car keys in the sink for me.'"

"Well, you can't just ignore her," Yamato insisted.

"Yes, I can. I'm ignoring her right now."

"But why *can't* we use the paranormal in investigations?"

"Because it's not normal."

"You're not funny."

"Yes, I am."

"But if she really is a psychic, like we both believe she is, then she could easily be right about something bad happening in the White House."

"Something bad always happens in the White House.

That's why we have presidents: to screw up all our lives at once, so we don't have to do it individually."

"But damn it, Doyle, she found my car keys!"

"Well, that's just wonderful. Let's go to the White House now and say, 'Everyone evacuate the White House! Dutch found his car keys!' "

"You're forgetting one thing."

"What?"

"The president has an astrologer."

"So?"

"That means he already *believes* in the paranormal."

"Of course he does. That's why he believes that raising taxes on the poor will give them more money, because they'll be inspired to look for new jobs that aren't there to pay the new taxes on the income they don't have. That's paranormal."

"But if the president already accepts astrology, I don't see why he wouldn't accept the advice of a psychic."

"She didn't give any advice."

"Well, no, but she said she saw canned animals."

"And anyone who reads the papers or watches TV would know that."

"But we don't think she's a fraud. She found my keys."

"Dutch, I don't care if the president makes all his crucial decisions based on a fucking Ouija board. We're *not* going to let him know the Secret Service thinks a psychic has correctly predicted a cataclysm of canned mammals."

"All right. Fine," Yamato said irritably.

"And what were you doing flirting with L. D. Krite?" I finally said.

"My personal life is none of your business," Yamato said curtly. "She's pretty. I'm attracted to her."

"Don't do that. Don't flirt with the suspects."

Yamato looked at me with a slightly mournful expression and said, "Sometimes suspects are the only women I meet."

"I know. I know," I said sympathetically. "But what if you started dating her and you had to arrest her?"

"I won't date her," he said in a wistful tone. "I'm an omnivore and she's an herbivore. I'm the wrong kind of vore."

"Yeah," I said as we walked away to continue our investigation. "Also, she probably doesn't believe in oral sex, since she wouldn't want meat in her mouth."

"I know," Yamato said with quiet sadness. "I'd have to tell her to make believe my penis was a plant. They say make-believe is important in lovemaking."

27

The vague and incomplete intuition I was having, one that I'd had repeatedly throughout my life, was that people almost never did what they needed to do. Right now, as Yamato and I were driving to the office to get a Justice Department order to tap L. D. Krite's phones, Yamato was suffering from a spontaneous and doomed affection for L. D. Krite—essentially a stranger, although nearly everyone in the world first saw their lovers the same way, as strangers. But was Yamato doing what he needed to do to find someone to love? No. He was stupidly doing his job, just like I was stupidly doing mine, when actually what I wanted to do was be with Natelle, who, if I was lucky, actually wanted to be with *me*, unless she secretly felt so awful about getting drunk and making love with me that she was thinking of a polite way to expel me from her life. I didn't want to believe that. Rather, I made myself imagine she really did want to be with me, but instead she was at work, stupidly doing *her* job. Maybe this all came from that Biblical passage in Genesis where God said to Adam and Eve that they shall live by the sweat of their brows, as if before the Fall, people simply had love, but after the Fall, they got jobs.

"Did you know," I said to Yamato, who sat quietly and dejectedly beside me in the car, dwelling painfully in his aloneness, "that I just figured out the book of Genesis?"

"That's nice," Yamato said.

"Yeah, so far none of the scholars have figured it out. I did. Just now. In my spare time."

"That's nice."

"Do you want me to explain it to you?"

"No."

"Okay, I will. Adam and Eve lived in bliss in the Garden of Eden, and then they ate from the tree of knowledge of good and evil, and do you know how God punished them? He made them get jobs."

"Oh," Yamato said.

"That's right. They had to live by the sweat of their brows, and what else could that mean but they got jobs? So instead of letting them loll around paradise all day, luxuriating in bliss and stuff, maybe feeling nothing but the love of God—which, frankly, I've always found a little too abstract for me—or the love of each other, God kicks them out of Eden and says, 'Go get a job.' And isn't that what we're doing right now?"

Yamato didn't answer.

"Right," I said. "People are born, carefully nurtured and loved, and then sent to school and transformed into fallen and wretched beings called workers. Like right now: what would you rather be doing?"

"Hearing you be quiet."

"Aside from that, I think what you'd rather be doing is kissing some woman on the lips. Or maybe her breasts. That's up to you. But really it's not up to you at all, and you know why? Because you're living by the sweat of your brow. I think that's what hell is. Hell isn't fire and limestone."

"*Brim*-stone," Yamato said.

"I know. Just trying to see if you're listening."

"I wish I wasn't."

"So right now, instead of being in love with the one person who's in love with you, or something, do you realize what's happening?"

"Yes. You're blathering."

"No, I'm not. The worst thing, the most painful, agonizing thing God could do to separate humans from each other, was make them get jobs. And he did it. He nailed us, Dutch. And that's why we're driving around doing stupid shit right now. We're being punished by God."

Yamato turned his head very slowly toward me, with a morose look, and said, "Oh. Well. Now I feel better. Why don't we just take our guns out and shoot each other in the head?"

"Because we'd get in a wreck, Dutch."

That afternoon, after we'd arranged to tap L. D. Krite's phones and thus put additional surveillance on a woman that Yamato could conceivably date or arrest, I called Natelle at the White House, but she didn't have time to talk with me or see me, because she had to work late. When she hung up the phone, it was like a rope had been tied around my heart and tightened. I couldn't help thinking that, on the morning she sobered up and remembered having sex with me, she had purged me from her life and hadn't yet told me. I went to the refrigerator and got a bottle of beer and swallowed some,

and swallowed some more. I knew why people became alco-
holics. I looked at my walls and I looked at my furniture and
I looked at the window and the pale blue sky, and it was so
quiet I could hear the absence of everything I ever wanted.

"I WAS thinking," Yamato said in the deteriorated and dismal
apartment we'd rented across the street from L. D. Krite's
office to spy on her. He sat staring out the window at cars
and pedestrians going by, which was essentially all we did:
watch pointless events of no consequence and eavesdrop on
harmless, obscure phone calls. "You know the Clapper?"
Yamato asked.

"You mean that thing on TV commercials?" I said.

"Yeah. The Clapper, where you plug this thing into the
wall and you can turn on and off your lights or the TV or
anything just by clapping your hands."

"What about it?"

"I was wondering what would happen if everyone in the
world hooked up their nuclear missiles to the Clapper," Yamato said.

"Why would they do that?" I said.

"So they wouldn't have to walk across the room."

"I see."

"Ultimately, the point of science and technology is to make
life unnecessary."

"Uh-huh," I said, because Yamato needed me to say something.

"Almost every invention we have has replaced some form
of human behavior. Ideally, you'd invent something that
does every-thing humans do. Then you'd buy one, turn it on,
and you wouldn't have to exist anymore."

"I like to exist," I said. "I can't remember why."

"Yeah," Yamato said listlessly, looking out the window at

nothing of any significance. We were assailed by boredom, the enforced wastefulness of our lives, like modern Bible characters lamenting the vanity of existence, except we didn't have God to talk with. God quit talking with people a few thousand years ago. You'd think that, every now and then, from somewhere up in the heavens, God would just say, "Hey," and then everyone would wonder who said it. The *New York Times* would print a story saying: "Theologians speculated that God said 'Hey' yesterday afternoon, but no one knows why."

Yamato looked at me thoughtfully and, as if sharing his own deep musings caused by severe boredom, he said to me, "If dogs wore bras, they'd have to wear three of them."

"I know," I said, as if I'd thought of that long ago, but I hadn't.

"I wonder," Yamato said, "why it is that human females only have two breasts, but other species have six."

"That's an old question," I said, "first posed by Martin Luther during the Reformation."

"I know," Yamato said.

"You're thinking about L. D. Krite, aren't you?"

"She doesn't have six breasts."

"No. But you're thinking about the two she does have."

"You're wrong. I'm just thinking about one of them."

"You're not supposed to date suspects, Dutch."

"Shut up."

Through my headphones I heard L. D. Krite making a call. I pointed one finger at my ear for Yamato to see, and I said, "She's making a call. Do you want me to tell her you're thinking about one of her breasts?"

Yamato gave me the finger.

A man answered the phone and L. D. Krite said, "Skip. We're doing it."

"For sure?" the man who might have been Skip asked.

"For sure. I decided this morning. There's no reason to wait anymore, no reason to keep being cautious."

"All right. I agree. I'm ready. When do we do it?"

"Tomorrow, at eleven."

"Eleven."

And they both hung up. Yamato heard the conversation over the speaker on the tape recorder, and he and I looked at each other wonderingly, almost imploringly, as if staring at each other in our common ignorance might explain what we just heard.

"Goddamn it! I hate this!" I said. "Why couldn't they just plainly say here's what we're doing and here's all the details? I hate surveillance! I *hate* it when people are secretive and covert, like we are. Bastards."

28

L. D. Krite and some man we hadn't seen before, presumably "Skip"—with whom she was going to "do it"—left the Animad office at approximately nine-thirty in the morning and got into a black Japanese sports car that Yamato and I tried to identify to the others in our surveillance group over our walkie-talkies, but we didn't know what kind of car it was.

"I think it's a Honda GLC," I said, having no idea.

"I don't think so," Yamato said into the walkie-talkie. "It looks like a Nissan Centro."

"That's not a car," I said.

"Well, maybe it's an Isuzu Bolero," Yamato said, naming a car we'd never heard of before.

"Well, what goddamn kind of car is it?" agent Peffler asked over the walkie-talkie.

"Black," I said.

"We think it's a Mitsubishi Al Dente," Yamato said.

"Or the Infiniti ad Infinitum," I said.

"You guys don't know what the fuck it is, do you?" agent Peffler said jeeringly.

"We're secret agents. Not car dealers," I said, as Yamato and I got into Yamato's silver sedan that I didn't know the name of, and we began following the black Japanese car down the road.

"Do you guys even know what *street* you're on?" Peffler asked.

"I don't think that's any of your business," I said. I looked at Yamato and said, "You're Japanese. What kind of car is it?"

"I'm Japanese-American," Yamato corrected me cheerfully. "The Japanese make thirty or forty kinds of cars. I have no idea what it is. Does anyone?"

"I think it's a Toyota No Comprendo," I said over the walkie-talkie.

"Just follow the car and be quiet," Peffler said.

"Upon further surveillance, I think it's a Nissan Mons Veneris," I said.

"What's that?" Yamato asked.

"It's that soft, comfortable spot between a woman's legs."

"They named a *car* after that?" Yamato said dreamily as we drove on, trying to stay far enough back from the black car that we didn't seem to be conspicuously following it. We weren't wearing the suits that L. D. Krite had first seen us in; we both wore blue jeans and T-shirts with light windbreakers to hide our shoulder holsters. Yamato had on a Kansas City Royals cap and I wore an Oakland A's cap, so we'd seem like ordinary Americans in the summer, except when you saw men wearing windbreakers on a hot summer day with no wind, you could assume they were hiding something, such as .357 magnums. There was no summery way to wear guns.

L. D. Krite drove slightly above the speed limit, like almost everybody in the world, going away from downtown, away from all the government buildings, and finally out into the stupid mixture of suburbs and woods and shopping centers of what might've been called the wilderness of Maryland, turning at last down a side road that we knew led to a huge private warehouse where the White House was storing most of its extraordinary tonnage of Spam.

"This is it," Yamato said as we turned onto the side road.

"It?" I asked.

"It's going down," Yamato said. "Say that on the walkie-talkie."

I picked up the walkie-talkie and said, "It's going down."

"What's going down?" Peffler said.

"Nothing," I said. "We're just using police jargon from the movies."

Yamato tapped my shoulder and said, "Tell him this: 'The eagle has landed.' "

So I did. "The eagle has landed," I said.

"What?" Peffler said.

"That's what one of the astronauts said in 1969 when they landed on the moon," Yamato explained to me.

"Where are you guys?" Peffler said.

"Maryland," I said.

"Could you be more specific?"

"Southern Maryland. We just turned onto Crouton Road."

"Crofton Road," Yamato said.

"The warehouse?" Peffler asked.

"That's right," I said. "Do you want us to bring you back some Spam?"

"Let us know if anything happens," Peffler said.

As we drove slowly past a dense thicket of trees into the warehouse parking lot, we saw the black car parked near the building and no one in it or near the front door. Yamato pulled off into some grass beside the trees, where we couldn't be seen from the warehouse, which evidently was closed on the weekend because there were no other cars in the parking lot.

"Don't they have night watchmen?" Yamato said.

"It's not night," I said.

"Well, good God, a warehouse this huge must have some kind of security."

"Dogs," I said. "Maybe they have dogs inside."

"What should we do?"

"I don't know. Do you think they're breaking in?"

"Maybe. You know what would be ironic? If these animal rights people broke in and then dogs attacked them."

"I don't think dogs understand irony."

"Should we go look for them?" Yamato said, squinting toward the warehouse.

"I guess," I said reluctantly. "I hate it when people do suspicious shit and we have to go look for them."

"Should we draw our guns?" Yamato said while we walked toward the warehouse.

"Now you're making it sound dangerous, goddamn it. These are animal rights activists. These are supposed to be cheerful, gentle, harmless people who help turtles cross the street."

"Turtles, maybe. Not us," Yamato said. "Some animal rights activists blow up buildings, you know."

"I guess you don't want to date her anymore," I said.

"I'm not sure I could date an herbivore. So should we draw our guns?"

"God, I'd hate to shoot an herbivore."

"Just because they're herbivores doesn't mean they don't have bombs or something."

"All right, all right. We'll take our fucking guns out. But she really won't like you now."

"I think, you know, if you arrest someone, you shouldn't ask them out," Yamato said.

"That's what Miss Manners says."

With our guns dangling in our hands, we snuck up to the corner of the warehouse and peeked around the building, which stretched back about three hundred yards. No one was there. We walked around the other corner and peeked around it, seeing no one.

"Shit," Yamato said. "Now we have to go look for them."

This was distressingly true, and we walked along the side of the warehouse, looking for opened doors or windows, through which we'd enter into a vast and probably dark warehouse filled with unknown things and unseen people. The window at the first office we came to was broken out. Yamato and I looked at each other for an explanation.

"Herbivores," I said.

"I don't want to crawl in there. There's broken glass," Yamato said.

"Well, let's go look for a broom," I said, crawling through the window and into the office. Yamato crawled in behind me, whispering "Ow. Ow. Ow," as if he were being cut by everything he touched.

"Shut up," I whispered.

"I don't like this," Yamato whispered.

"I don't think we're supposed to," I whispered, as I slowly opened the office door slightly and looked out into the immense darkness of the warehouse. It was filled with gigantic looming things stacked fifteen or twenty feet high. The only light in the building was pale and sickly, coming in from skylights about every fifty feet in the ceiling, producing hazy columns of light surrounded everywhere by darkness.

"This is too gothic for me," Yamato whispered. "Darkness and shadows. Unknown, ominous shapes outlined by an unearthly light."

I looked at Yamato and whispered, "That's very eloquent. Possibly you should become an art critic. Now shut up."

"What're we going to do?" Yamato whispered as we squinted into the upsetting darkness of a building the size of three football fields.

"I don't know," I whispered. "But I have a plan."

"What?"

"Let's walk around until we see them."

Quietly and slowly we began walking into the huge rows of stacked boxes and crates rising up everywhere around us.

"This reminds me of the Grand Canyon," I whispered.

"It does? I didn't know they had warehouses in the Grand Canyon," Yamato whispered. "What if they're planting a bomb?"

"I survived the Viet Cong. I don't want to be blown up by herbivores."

"That'd be embarrassing."

"Being dead isn't embarrassing. It's worse than that."

On and on we walked, noiselessly, on the rubber soles of our adidas shoes, squinting anxiously into the hot, humid darkness, holding out our guns, which I couldn't imagine us using. At that instant there was some noise, some odd, indistinct sound ahead of us in the dark. We stopped and listened. Maybe they'd heard us and were hiding, waiting. As stupid as it seemed for them to have guns, maybe they did. There was nothing intrinsically peaceful about people who believed everyone should abide by their brand of morality, and suddenly, there in the dark, the harmless herbivores seemed like predators. There was noise again, echoing lightly from some of the tall stacks of boxes and crates about fifty feet in front of us. It seemed like I heard whispering. Yamato and I stared at each other. He held up his index finger and shook it twice toward the sound. This was maddening. It didn't mean anything. I held up my finger and did the same thing, then leaned toward his ear and whispered, "What the fuck does that mean?"

"I don't know. I saw it in a movie," Yamato whispered. "What should we do—sneak up on them?"

"Sneaking seems appropriate," I whispered.

"Okay. You go first."

"No. You go."

"But you're older than I am," Yamato whispered.

"And I intend to stay that way. That's why I want *you* to go first," I whispered, pushing Yamato. He pushed me back.

"What if they have a bomb?" he whispered.

"I doubt if they have a bomb. They probably have tofu," I whispered, walking more quietly and deliberately than before toward the spot where the noise came from. We walked about two feet apart, holding our guns in front of us as we advanced through the gloom, and there were voices, soft, muted voices, a woman's and then a man's. The voices seemed to be about thirty feet in front of us, behind one of the huge stacks of metal drums, or barrels, and almost directly beneath the pale and ominous light from one of the skylights, as if they'd chosen that eerily lighted spot to do their unknown work. Yamato and I approached the corner of the big stack of metal drums behind which were the voices. There was enough darkness where we were going to risk looking around the corner without being seen. Holding my gun directly in front of my chest, ready to drop my arm in an instant and fire if they had weapons and saw me, I poked my head around the corner far enough for one eye, my left eye, to see L. D. Krite and Skip standing in front of a life-size deformed pig with a caved-in back and head and a black tube running from its anus. I ducked my head back and looked at Yamato.

"*What?*" he whispered.

"I can't tell. It looks like they've got an inflatable pig."

"What?"

I peeked around the corner again, with both eyes, and saw the deformed pig changing shape, becoming fuller, less deformed. I realized the black tube in its anus was an air hose connected to a bicycle tire pump that Skip was using to inflate the pink pig. Yamato got onto his hands and knees beside me to peek around the corner as the pig became fully inflated, and L. D. Krite pulled the hose from its anus.

Skip picked up a flashlight from the floor and turned it on to help L. D. Krite look into a silver briefcase she opened on the floor beside the pig. She pulled out a bundle of something that looked like five or six sticks of dynamite taped together. Yamato tugged at my pant's leg. I didn't know what to do, didn't know if it was really dynamite or not, didn't know if it was a fully operable bomb that could be set off instantly or accidentally, or if it was just a dummy bomb, which would explain why they had an inflatable pig. It wouldn't make sense to have an inflatable pig if they were going to blow up the warehouse. But it would make sense to have one if they weren't, assuming the pig and a fake bomb were part of a grotesque protest against canned animals, which would mean they were merely setting up a threatening display to be discovered later. Yamato tugged on my pants leg again. I wished he'd quit it.

L. D. Krite took a small box from the briefcase. It had a dial on it, like an oven timer. Electrical wires came out of the box. She began fastening the wires to the bundle of dynamite, or the bundle of something. Neither of them said anything now, as if this ritual were too somber to be violated by words. After connecting the wires to the bundle, L. D. Krite placed them both under the inflated pig. She took a big, rectangular piece of white paper, maybe poster paper, from the briefcase. A loop of something was fastened to the back of the paper, and L. D. Krite put the loop over the pig's head so the poster hung around the pig's neck. There were words on the poster. By squinting, I could read them. They said: "I have a right to be here."

It seemed as if I'd heard those words in an old song from the early 1970s, some tedious, metaphysical song about everyone—not necessarily pigs—having a right to exist. I was trying to think of the melody when Yamato stood up beside me and whispered, "What should we do?"

"Arrest them."

"What about the bomb?" he whispered anxiously. "What if it blows up?"

"Then we won't have to arrest them."

Yamato sighed quietly and whispered, "Now?"

"Now," I whispered.

Yamato made the sign of the cross on his forehead, even though he wasn't Catholic. Together we stepped forward into the edge of the hazy, sickly light from the skylight, pointing our guns at L. D. Krite and Skip. They didn't see us. Although we were only fifteen feet away, we were still so quiet in our running shoes and still so obscured in the dark that they didn't know we were there. They stood sideways from us, staring down at the pig and the dynamite, possibly admiring it.

"They won't ignore us now," L. D. Krite said.

Yamato took another step forward into the light with his gun in front of him and said, "Room Service. Don't move. You're under arrest."

That was an old idea of his, that he'd like to arrest somebody by saying Room Service instead of Secret Service. I never thought he'd really do it.

"He means *Secret* Service," I said, stepping into the light beside Yamato as L. D. Krite screamed and fell backward onto the floor. This made me realize she'd never go out with Yamato.

29

In the *Post* the next day it was announced that the Secret Service had thwarted a terrorist attack against luncheon meat. We were heroes, even though no one knew who we were, even though the bomb turned out to be fake dynamite, and even though the only danger of an explosion would have been if too much air had been forced into the pig's anus. We were told the pig was being held as evidence for a federal trial. But most importantly, and also most curiously, the president wanted to thank us personally for arresting L. D. Krite. The president asked to see us in the Oval Office, and when Yamato and I got to the door, it was being guarded by two agents we didn't know. They stared at us suspiciously. One of them stepped in front of Yamato and said, "May I see some ID?"

Yamato smiled politely and took out his wallet and showed the agent a card.

"That's a Western Auto charge card," the agent said in a mildly displeased tone.

"Do you take Visa?" Yamato asked, then took out his ID and showed it to the agent, who smiled and said, "Oh. You're one of us."

I showed the agent my Safeway check-cashing card and my library card, as well as my Secret Service ID, and then Yamato and I opened the door to see the president, who was seated at his desk watching television.

"Hey, Andy."

"Hey, Barn."

It was "The Andy Griffith Show." I wanted to say, "Hey, president."

The president turned off the television and looked at Yamato and me with what almost was a smile. It was as if he almost had an emotion.

"You're the two agents, aren't you?" the president said, which was strange, since he'd been with us dozens of times but seemed not to recognize us.

"Yes, sir," I said.

"Do you have a few minutes?" the president asked.

"We have as many minutes as you want us to," Yamato said.

This made the president smile, and he stood up and said, "Would you like a drink? Bourbon? Gin? Cognac?"

"Bourbon," Yamato said.

"Cognac," I said, since it was more expensive.

"I used to think cognac was a sissy drink," the president said amiably as he walked to an ornate liquor table and began hoisting glasses and decanters.

"Blackbeard drank cognac," I said, although I had no idea if he did.

"So you've studied pirates?" the president said as he poured the liquor.

"Mainly the Pittsburgh Pirates," I said.

"Ah. Baseball," the president said in a friendly tone as Yamato and I walked over to get our drinks. "Are you two baseball fans?"

"Yes, sir," Yamato said cheerfully as we stood next to the President of the United States of America and drank liquor. "We have our own team."

"Really?" the president said, and I thought how odd it was that Yamato and I, who never liked the president, were now so jovial and polite with him. You really had to be, or he could nail you.

"Yes, sir," I said. "We have a team, and the CIA has a team. At least, they're supposed to. We're scheduled to play them in a covert game on Bastille Day, if we can ever find out where the game is. The location is secret."

"You're shitting me," the president said with astonished amusement. I'd never heard a president say "shit" before. I was trying to imagine Thomas Jefferson saying it.

"Nope," Yamato said. "We really *are* playing the CIA. I think. I mean, we intend to play them, if either side can find out where the game is. The rule is, neither side knows the covert location. It's the spooks versus the spooks."

"Is that what the teams are called—the Spooks?" the president asked.

"We have no idea what the CIA is calling their team," I said. "But our team is called the Avenging Blowfish."

The president squinted at me. "Avenging," he said, as if studying that word by itself, and then he added the other word: "Blowfish."

"We wanted a dignified name," Yamato said.

"And then we changed our minds," I said.

"Well, it's a distinctly memorable name," the president said. "When did you say the game was going to be played?"

"Bastille Day," Yamato said.

"I don't see the relationship between baseball and the French Revolution," the president said.

"Well, we'll be playing the game at night, so I don't think we'll be able to see the relationship between anything," I said. Yamato and I were probably being too strange for the dignity and seriousness of the presidency, but what allowed us to do so was that we didn't care.

"A night game," the president said. "So you found a field with lights?"

"We thought we'd just use phosphorous grenades," Yamato said.

The president blinked.

"I think he's employing humor," I said.

"Baseball's supposed to be hard, but not fatal," the president said, and we all smiled. "Anyway, I just want to thank you two for your work in arresting those two animal-rights loonies."

"You're welcome," I said.

"They're not really loonies, sir," Yamato said.

Oh no. Here it comes, I thought, watching the curious look on the president's face.

Yamato said, "Unquestionably, they did break the law and deserve to be punished. But, speaking for the leader, L. D. Krite, whom we interviewed and whose phone we tapped for a few days, she's not a loony. She's a zealous and passionate woman who seems to me to be quite faithful to her ideals. And while she did break a few laws, she's probably more sane and rational than most people you'll meet."

The president didn't know what to say. He scratched his nose and looked at me for help. I held my palms up in front of me and said, "I think what he means is that even though she broke federal, state, and local laws, he'd like to have dinner with her."

"What?" the president asked, frowning and smiling at the same time.

Yamato blushed and stared down at the floor. He said, "But of course I haven't asked her out."

"You mean you want to date a woman you just arrested?" the president said.

"Well," Yamato said. "Yes."

The president downed his bourbon, wiped a drop of bourbon from his lip with his finger, and said, "I've never heard of a successful marriage that began with an arrest. But what can I say? Love, like a wildflower, can grow in even the most arid soil."

"That's an interesting quote," Yamato said happily. "Who said that? Wordsworth? Emily Dickinson?"

"Aunt Bee," the president said. "On 'The Andy Griffith Show.'"

"WHY'D YOU do that?" Yamato asked as we left the White House.

"Do what?" I said.

"Tell the president I wanted to date L. D. Krite."

"Well, you're the one who started it. You defended her when the president called her a loony."

"She's not a loony," Yamato said.

"See? You're doing it again."

"I can't help it. Something, I don't know what, just fundamentally attracts me to her. I don't care if we arrested her. I want to get to know her."

I looked at Yamato as we walked and said, "You could send her some flowers in jail."

"Shut up," Yamato said.

"You could send her a greeting card with bond money in it."

"I'll kick your ass," Yamato said.

"You can't kick my ass," I said.

"I know karate."

"So do I."

Just as Yamato turned toward me as if he were going to spin his body and kick me in the face, we heard someone across the street with a bullhorn in Lafayette Park. It looked like a few dozen people were having a demonstration.

"What the hell's that?" Yamato said, staring at someone wearing some big blue box over their head and torso. As we got closer, we could read the letters on the box: SPAM.

"Uh-oh," I said. "It's the pig people."

A man with a bullhorn aimed it toward the White House and said, "The sleeping giant of vegetarianism has awakened, Mr. President!"

"Maybe they mean the Sullen Green Giant," I said.

"And maybe they mean your ass," Yamato said. "You started all this Spam stuff."

"I did not start it, you son of a bitch. Abbas started it."

"Maybe so. But you got blamed for it. And look," Yamato said, pointing toward the demonstration. "It's still alive."

"I wouldn't be too goddamn smug about that. One of your darling pig people is in jail."

Yamato closed his eyes and put his fingers over his face. "I know," he said sadly. "I don't know if she'll want to go to a movie with me now."

"Dutch," I said quietly. "You arrested her. Like the president said, this probably won't lead to marriage."

Yamato nervously tapped his finger against his lower lip and said, "Maybe if I send her some Godiva chocolates along with a referral for a lawyer."

30

Wearing only a pair of black panties, Natelle crawled above me on her hands and knees in bed. The soft flesh along the insides of her knees pressed against my legs as her breasts swayed lightly above me. Her face was directly over mine, and in her eyes, which never moved from mine, was a look of peace, or adoration, or love, or wonderment, some secret look I'd never seen before in her eyes and which seemed to swell peacefully in her as she searched in my eyes for exactly the same look. She leaned her head down to kiss me, to wet my lips with her own, and my stomach tingled and felt ticklish and hot, like electricity going through me, but it was Natelle, passing into me. I put my fingers on her stomach, and she moaned and shuddered and pressed her lips harder onto mine. I felt light. I felt like I was going to cry from the grace of her. She kissed my chin and my neck, and traced her tongue along my skin from my neck and my chest and onto my nipple, and held my nipple with her lips. I held in my hand the warm fullness of her breast, and touched my fingers along the smooth front of her panties where it was soft and moist. She began moving there, slowly raising and lowering herself in a rhythm as she kissed my neck and tingled me and took my hand with hers and put it inside her panties, and my fingers were wet in the softness of her. Her hand was warm when she put it inside my underwear, and the tips of her fingers were wet and sticky from me as we kissed again and she lay fully on me now and moved her panties aside and still held onto me with her fingers as she put me inside of her, and we were the same two different people looking inside each other's eyes as if to find the last concealed part of us finally given away.

I lay still for a while in the dark, wondering where Natelle was. I'd just given my love again to her ghost. Her ghost didn't even know. It was terrible, giving yourself away to someone who didn't even know you'd done that. To someone who, if she ever found out, might find a need to give you back. That was why Natelle was so sad and I had to hold her, when we pretended to be giving her an annulment and I said we were going to give her back to herself. You want to give yourself away, and be kept.

I hadn't seen Natelle in four or five days now, since that night, and I missed her like a lover, like waiting for the world to resume, and every ordinary pleasure seemed tedious. I just wanted to see her eyes again. There was an anxious, manic, aching emptiness in me that most Americans were taught should be filled by Jesus. It wasn't Jesus I wanted to marry. I knew what Dr. Boulan would say. "If this isn't working, love someone else." Like you could go pick someone else.

"I'll take *her*. No. That other one. Wait. I mean someone else. Just give me a Sears catalog and I'll pick someone from there."

I got out of bed and took a bottle of beer from the refrigerator, then remembered I hadn't eaten much dinner, so I took a few big swallows of milk and then orange juice, which I figured took care of nutrition, then took my beer to the living room and turned on the TV. There was a show about little predatory birds called kites.

"I made a kite once," I said to the TV.

On TV, a kite caught a field mouse and flew with it in its talons to the side of a thorny tree, where it impaled the mouse on a big thorn.

"Look. He's putting his groceries away," I said, trying to amuse myself and pretend I wasn't depressed.

The phone rang. I ran over to it as if the only person it could be was Natelle. It was a man who said, "May I speak with the woman of the house?"

"If there's a woman here, she's hiding from me," I said, and hung up. My head hurt, as if it was simultaneously full and empty; full of memories I wished I never had, empty of the ones I wanted and never did have. The phone rang again, as if the stupid son of a bitch was calling me back. I picked it up instantly, in case it was Natelle, and it was. She said, "Doyle, I just called to let you know I've decided to leave for a while. In the morning I'm going to a retreat center in the mountains for a week."

"You are?" I asked. We hadn't seen each other or even spoken for days, and now she was going away.

"I need time to be alone and think," she said.

She was leaving me, and she wasn't even mine.

"You mean about your marriage?" I asked.

"Yes. The remains of it. I just wanted to tell you this so you wouldn't think I was abandoning you. I'm sorry I haven't called. I've just been terribly depressed, and maybe I just need to go away, to get so far away from everything that . . . I don't know. I don't know what at all," she said quietly.

Anything I said would hurt me, so I didn't say anything.

"Don't think I'm leaving you," she said, explaining why she was leaving me.

"I do love you, Doyle. I do. But you're coming into my life right when everything else is leaving me. Everything hurts too much, and I don't know what to do about it. So I'm going to go away for a while and escape from everything, in order to confront it."

She didn't say anything else, as if it were my turn to talk, but I was too confused and sad to say anything.

"I'm leaving in the morning," she said, even though she'd already said that.

"What will you do on the retreat?" I asked, because otherwise my silence would hurt us too much.

"Just be alone and think."

"Can I go on the retreat with you? I won't bring any guns."

"It's a retreat center for women only."

"I could wear a dress," I said.

"I've never seen you in a dress," she said quietly, as if wondering what I'd look like in one.

"I think I'd probably look lovely."

"I think you would, too. But you still can't go. I'll be back in a week. That's not so long. And we can find time to talk then. Will you please wish me well?"

"I wish you better than well. I just wish I could help you."

"I know. And you can help me by being here when I get back," she said with something that sounded like hope.

"I'll be here. Do you mean here, in my apartment, or there, in your apartment?"

"I mean just here to see me. That reminds me. I know this is an awful thing to ask, since you can't see me now and I'm going away, but could you water my plants while I'm gone?"

"Sure I will. That's not awful. Maybe I can't see you, but I can at least see your furniture."

"Are you mad at me?" she said anxiously.

"No. I just miss you."

She was silent for a few seconds. I heard her sigh. She said, "You're one of the dearest men I've ever known. But this is a dangerous time for me, Doyle, so I have to be careful how our emotions get mixed together right now. We can talk about that when I get back. Okay?"

"Okay."

"And also, the key to my apartment will be under a loose brick above the front door."

"A loose brick," I said. "Reminds me of my head."

She laughed and said, "And I also remembered that your spookball game is this coming week. Bastille Day? I'll be on the retreat, but I thought that, on that day, at noon, I could wave to you from the mountains, as a sort of encouragement. Do you want to do that, wave to me at noon on your game day? Or is that too childish?"

"I'll wave to you at noon, on Bastille Day. Which mountain will you be on?"

"I don't know the name of it. Just wave toward all the mountains. You'll get the right one."

31

Natelle's letter was dated July 11th. It was handwritten in black ink on one page of gray paper. She said:

Dear Doyle,

Some of the women I've met here talk about coming here to get their heads on straight. I keep expecting to see women with their heads on sideways.

The sanctuary is lovely, but like a resort where no one has any fun. Every day, I sleep late, as if sleeping late were my goal. It seems like I've built up a lot of emotional tension, some toxins, over the last year or so, and I think they're bleeding out of me now, leaking from me like poison from a wound. There's a certain amount of bitterness and sadness still lodged in me, like a glowing rock.

I've taken a few long walks on mountain trails, looking for solitude, and keep running into a dozen or more other women looking for the solitude we keep denying each other. Pain has its comedy.

I feel lonely up here. But then, I felt lonely down there. I wish I knew who I was lonely for. Sometimes I think it's you. But don't take that as an offer. It's a confession. I'm not sure what's true or what *should* be true. Sometimes I can't help wishing I could think of a way to reclaim my marriage, but that would be like picking up a handful of shattered glass. My hands are still bleeding from all the attempts. I give up.

But, now, it's like I'm trying to remember the years before I was married, to think of what I was doing then, as if I should resume my life at that point. I don't even remember what that point was. So it's like I'm trying to learn how to live again, and I can't remember how. To lose something as profound as love seems like a death, only no one dresses you for the funeral. You have to dress yourself. And you can't mourn the one who left you. You can only mourn yourself. Maybe that's what I'm doing. I'm having my funeral. But I hope this death gets over fairly soon, and I will be back.

Remember to wave to me on Bastille Day.

Love,

Natelle

I read the letter three times and was reading it again, pretending she was talking to me and smiling. I put the letter up to my nose to try breathing some faint fragrance of Natelle, and I held the letter over my face, because her hands had touched the letter where it now touched me. And in this sanctuary of paper and hope, in my childlike trance of love, there was a voice.

"Coldiron. Take that goddamn paper off your face."

It was Doltmeer. We were in a briefing about some visiting politicians from Azerbaijan. I lifted the letter up over my eyes to see Doltmeer and about a dozen agents staring at me in the back of the room.

"Would it be possible for you to pay attention?" Doltmeer said. "Do you even know what country we're talking about?"

"Arizona?" I said. "It's one of those Russian places with a 'z' in it. I can't pronounce it. Azer-ba-jam. Apple butter. I forget."

I talked with Dr. Boulan on my lunch break, sitting in a chair next to her and showing her the folded-up letter I carried with me in my pocket like the latest mystical proof that Natelle existed, and I couldn't let the proof go.

"Well, I think you want me to tell you that perhaps you're a little bit crazy," Dr. Boulan said, calmly rubbing the tips of her fingers together and smiling lightly. "You have this almost comical need to be told you're a little bit crazy, and that isn't so bad."

"You mean I'm *not* crazy?" I said, absentmindedly holding Natelle's letter against my cheek.

"It's not 'crazy' of you to look at a letter from a woman you love and be thoroughly transfixed by it, and keep it with you. Possibly it could interfere with work, yes. And possibly it could be regarded by some people as wrong or inappropriate for a grown man to sit in a serious meeting with a love letter over his face."

"I don't care."

"Yes, you do, or you wouldn't have asked me about it. You do, like everyone else in the world, have a few things wrong with you, but being in love isn't *per se* one of them, unless you elevate that love to the status of the only possible good in the world, which I suspect you sometimes do."

"Well, I don't think I *quite* do that," I said, because she was right.

"No? Well then, what else in the world would you put on an equal level with Natelle?"

I couldn't think of anything.

"So," I said. "What's wrong with loving her more than anything else?"

"Possibly nothing, unless one of the things you think Natelle is going to do for you is save you."

"Save me? She hasn't done that so far. Nothing has."

"Do you think you need to be saved?"

"We all need to be saved from something."

"And what would you like to be saved from?"

"Being alone."

I held the letter in the fingers of both hands, to be able to touch it the most.

"So even with Natelle, you still feel alone?"

"I'm not *with* her," I said quietly. "I don't have her. I never do. You know, maybe when you grow up, if you grow up right, and I don't think I did, you're supposed to be able to go out into the world every day with the feeling, maybe some natural or intuitive or subconscious feeling, that regardless of what might be wrong in your life, there's always something you can go back to that will make you feel safe. I just have me. So I think what I need to be saved from is being the only one I have. And I don't expect or hope that Natelle could *save* me in some profound and final instance that can't be undone. Everything can be undone. Nothing is final, except certain purchases at department stores. But you know what I'd like? I'd like to be saved maybe just once or twice a week. And by 'saved,' I mean . . . I don't know. But

I'd like to be able to make love with someone who loves me, even if it was just a fiction, a stupid, convincing lie that I was telling myself. This is supposed to be ordinary, isn't it? This is supposed to be a common part of daily life. Not for me. For me, it's like fantasy. For me, it's like a myth from ten thousand years ago. For me, it's like the goddamn afterlife. Maybe when you die, someone holds you. They don't do it now. It won't happen.

"And you see? You see why I do stupid things like keeping this letter in my hands? Because it came from her. It came from her and it's all I have. I have this piece of paper with part of her heart written down on it, and she names *me* in her heart, and I don't want to let it go. I just want to hold it," I said, and I closed my eyes and sighed.

"It's perfectly healthy for people to keep relics or objects of their loved ones with them," Dr. Boulan said encouragingly. "And what does it mean? It means you love them. I've known women who mailed their panties to their husbands or lovers."

I looked up at Dr. Boulan. "Maybe I should go check the mail again," I said.

At Natelle's apartment that evening, when I went to water her plants and look at her furniture and think, "There's her chair. She sits in it," "There's her light. She turns it on," "There's her bed. She sleeps in it," I opened her dresser and looked at all the panties and brassieres and slips folded and piled together in their blues and blacks and whites and pinks and lavenders, like a garden of lingerie, and I rested my face in the middle of their softness, like resting my face in Natelle. I said, "Come home," knowing she was two hundred miles away, maybe trying to decide if she had a home, or if I belonged in it. I picked up a pair of black silky panties and held them to my face and breathed in, hoping they'd smell like Natelle. I tried to breathe in the tiniest remaining scent of Natelle, but all I could breathe in was maybe the scent of laundry detergent.

> Far away, beyond your reach,
> I detect your scent;
> It's Tide with bleach.

32

At the Nevermore Bar & Grill, where Yamato and Widdiker and I had gone to do what men without women did together, which was get reasonably drunk and distract each other with amusing and usually pointless remarks, we spent another evening patiently wasting our lives. One serious subject I could have mentioned and wasn't about to was Natelle's black panties folded in my pants pocket. A lot of people, maybe even Yamato and Widdiker, would've regarded that as inexcusably weird. Maybe even depraved. I didn't. The panties were like an icon; an article of religious devotion. Usually an icon was a picture of some religious figure with a burning candle in front of it. I didn't want any burning candles in my pants. The panties, along with the letter in the same pocket, were how I felt closer to Natelle. It was my attempt at magic. Or primitive religion. Being devoted to someone who, I knew, might never be devoted to me. So having her panties in my pocket was really an expression of faith. Actually, I wasn't sure whether it was faith or idiocy. I felt like I'd mastered both.

We were just sitting at the bar because the bar was there; Widdiker said, "Do you think every moment of life is precious?"

Yamato looked perplexed. I was.

"I was just thinking that," Widdiker said. "People say every moment of life is precious."

"Not this one," Yamato said.

"I had a precious moment a few days ago," I said. "I forget why."

A few moments passed and we were silent, each of us staring off at different people we didn't know. And so we sat there and drank. Alcohol was a good drug. It made you feel serene when there was no natural cause for that emotion. It made you seem happy without any memory of why you should be, because there *was* no memory. Alcohol was a bad drug, and we liked it.

"What's this I hear about you and L. D. Krite?" Widdiker said abruptly, glancing at Yamato.

Yamato looked defensive and a little bit anguished, although he smiled. "I don't know. What'd you hear?"

"I hear you have a crush on her," Widdiker said.

"A crush," Yamato said contemplatively, and sipped some beer. "That's one of the strangest words in the English language. You 'crush' fruit. You 'crush' your enemy. Why would 'crush' have anything to do with affection?"

"Irrelevant," Widdiker said. "Strike that from the record. You don't want to answer my question, do you?"

"No," Yamato said.

"She's pretty," Widdiker said. "I saw her picture in the

paper, when she was being taken to police headquarters in handcuffs. I could understand being attracted to her. Are you going to ask her out?"

"Shut up," Yamato said, smiling with embarrassment.

"I think if you testify against her, she won't go to the movies with you," Widdiker said.

"I know. I'm thinking about having amnesia," Yamato said.

"In court?"

"I don't want to testify against her. I *like* her," Yamato said, and sighed. He looked at me and said, "Will you testify against her, so she'll hate you and not me?"

"Sure. I don't mind being hated," I said.

"She still won't like you," Widdiker said. "You arrested her."

"But it was just a formality. It wasn't personal," Yamato said with a remorseful look, and it seemed more and more certain that Yamato genuinely was infatuated with L. D. Krite. I felt sympathy for him. We both had romances that involved ourselves and women who didn't particularly want us.

"Have you sent her flowers?" Widdiker said.

"No."

"Chocolates?"

"No."

"Lingerie?"

"No."

"Bail?"

"I'm getting tired of you. Why don't I pull your intestines out and choke you with them?"

"That'd be a felony," Widdiker said. "Then you could go to jail and see L. D. Krite."

"Well, I guess your death is worth one date," Yamato said.

"Whose death?" someone said, and we all turned to see Lou Benador and Ricky Kee behind us.

"Uh-oh. Spooks," I said. Benador and Kee stepped to the bar beside Widdiker and ordered scotch.

"Have you found out where the game is?" Yamato said.

"What game?" Benador said.

"Don't feign ignorance," Yamato said.

"He's not. He really *is* ignorant," Widdiker said, repeating his favorite line.

"What's the name of your team?" Yamato said.

"What makes you think we have a team?" Kee said.

"Well, if you don't, we'll kick your ass," I said.

"That's the *only* way you'd kick our ass," Benador said.

"What's the name of your team?" Yamato said.

"The Assassins?" Widdiker said.

"Spooks-R-Us?" Yamato said.

"The Buttfuckers?" Widdiker suggested.

"Your vulgarity shocks me," Benador said indifferently.

"The CIA's incapable of shock, unless it's an electrical charge you're applying to someone during an interview," I said.

Benador smiled at us dramatically and said, "But after I tell you, you have to tell us the name of *your* team."

"Sure. Go on."

"All right," Benador said, taking a drink of scotch and staring at each of us with a cold and intimidating look. "We've named ourselves the Raging Tree Frogs."

"The Raging *Tree* Frogs?" Widdiker said. "What a stupid name."

"Yeah. Ours is better," Yamato said.

"It's more dignified," I said.

"Well, what is it?"

"The Avenging Blowfish," Yamato said.

"See? We told you it was more dignified," I said.

"You guys are the Avenging Blowfish? What a stupid name," Kee said.

"It's not any stupider than your name," Widdiker said.

"Why don't you call yourselves the Avenging Blowjob?" Benador asked.

"We wanted to name ourselves after an animal. A blowjob's not an animal," I said.

"By the way . . . where's the game being played?" Yamato said.

"Outdoors," Benador said.

"Oh. I know where that is," I said.

"So you don't *know* where it's being played?" Widdiker said, sneering at them.

"As if you do?" Benador said, sneering back.

"It doesn't matter if we don't know where the game is," Widdiker said. "We'll play one wherever we want to."

"That's a violation of the rules," Kee said.

"Violation *is* our rule," Widdiker said.

33

On top of the pool table in the back room of Papa Doc's, the fashionably tasteless bar where we went when we didn't want to be middle-class, Widdiker arranged a large stack of black-and-white aerial photos of the metropolitan Washington, D.C., area, which all of us in the Avenging Blowfish looked at curiously as we stood around the pool table with bottles of beer, like members of the Allied Supreme Command preparing for a final strike against Nazi Germany.

"Gentlemen, look," Widdiker said in an imperious tone as he gestured at the glossy photos of the whole city. "These are the latest Air Force satellite photos of Washington and its surrounding areas. Thanks to NASA and the Air Force, we can use these spy satellite photos to locate every baseball field in the area."

"Jesus Christ," Deek said. "You got NASA to take pictures of *baseball* fields?"

"No. I got the Pentagon to do it. I don't think NASA has any interest in baseball."

"Isn't that illegal?" Oxler asked.

"You're talking about using a two-hundred-million-dollar military satellite or something just to take pictures of baseball fields," Pascal said.

"That's why these are such good pictures," Widdiker said cheerfully.

"Couldn't we go to prison for that?" Horner wondered.

"Well, I suppose if this information got into the wrong hands—that is, the American government—yes, we could get in trouble. Now will everyone just shut up and look at the pictures?" Widdiker said irritably.

For a few seconds, everyone shut up and looked at the pictures. Then DeMarco said, "Hey! There's my house!"

"And look," Yamato said. "There's my dog!"

"We're not supposed to be looking for your dog. We're supposed to be looking for baseball fields," Widdiker said.

"Here's a baseball field," I said, pointing to one.

"And here's one," Horner said.

"Here's one. And another one," Deek said.

"There's where I do my laundry," Yamato said.

"Why does it matter," DeMarco said, "if we use high-resolution satellite photos to find ten dozen baseball fields if we don't know which one's the right one?"

"Well, that's a good point, DeMarco. Shut up," Widdiker said.

"You know there's not really a game," Pascal said.

"Of course there is," I said.

"It's all bullshit. It's just a farce."

"It's just a joke. There's no proof that anyone really planned a game. It doesn't exist."

"Heathens," I said. "Sometimes things only exist when you want them to."

Everyone stared at me curiously.

"Who said that—Kierkegaard?" Widdiker asked.

"Who's Kierkegaard?"

"What position does he play?"

"Kierkegaard didn't say that. It's just true," I said. "Sometimes things only exist when you want them to. So if you want the game to exist, it will."

"You mean, even if there's not really a game, we could play it anyway?" Deek asked.

"Isn't that our plan?" I said.

"Well, it is now," Widdiker said.

"But," Oxler said, "what if the CIA goes to a different baseball field than we do?"

"Then they'll play their game, and we'll play ours," Widdiker said with apparent satisfaction.

"Then how do you know who wins?" Deek said.

"I'm tired of all these whining, trivial questions," Widdiker said.

"I don't think it's trivial to ask how you decide who wins a baseball game played by two teams at different locations," Yamato said.

Widdiker sighed impatiently and said to me, "What'd Kierkegaard say about baseball?"

"Nothing that I'm aware of," I said. "He was a Danish religious philosopher."

"Really? We could use a Danish religious philosopher in the outfield," Deek said.

"Yeah. Someone with vision," Yamato said.

"Night vision," DeMarco said.

"Everyone shut up and study these satellite photos," Wid-diker said.

"There it is," Horner said exuberantly, tapping his finger on the map.

"The baseball field?" several people asked.

"My car," Horner said. "I have a satellite photo of my car!"

34

On July 14, Bastille Day, the day of the Big Wave to Natelle in the mountains—Natelle, who made my heart flutter and twitter and oscillate in the blessed pathology of love—the day of our fantastic and mythological baseball game at a location still unknown to us, Doltmeer called a meeting and said, "You're going to Indizal."

Panic and sadness rushed through me, and I was slightly dizzy, realizing that a trip of any nature to Indizal would probably last at least four or five days and I'd be gone when Natelle came home; gone when she arrived to tell me what she'd decided about her life, and possibly about me, although I wasn't necessarily in her life, and wasn't obviously out of it, either. This hurt even more, to realize again as I'd always known and tried to deny, that the one person in the world who mattered to me could come home refreshed and sane and ready to bravely go on without me, unaware she was doing that. She couldn't even leave me. You had to have someone before you left them, and she had never had me.

Suddenly nothing made sense. Life was normal. It seemed like I was dying of something I couldn't report, because no one was supposed to know I had it.

Doltmeer pulled a world map down from the blackboard and pointed his finger at the North Atlantic off the African coast.

"Here's Indizal," he said.

You couldn't see anything. Indizal wasn't on our map. Doltmeer took a pen from his coat pocket and drew a dot in the ocean.

"*There*," he said. "As you're somewhat familiar with Indizalian politics already, you'll be leaving tomorrow to assist with advance security for the president and his staff for an economic conference of small and inconsequential countries that . . ."

I was too depressed to care or listen. All I could do was sit still and hurt. I thought of all my prayers, the dozens and dozens of prayers asking that Natelle and I would love each other, and it was like my prayers had risen up out of my heart and into the sky and up past God and far out into the immense waste of the universe.

Still, we had our covenant at noon. The Big Wave. That was sacred. That was like a prayer. I could at least do that. One more prayer. Despite all the failure, all the fragility, all the fresh sadness swarming through me like blood, there could always be one more prayer.

I had to do it from federal court. Yamato and I were required to appear at L. D. Krite's pretrial proceedings to answer questions from the attorneys. Yamato got a haircut. He also wore a new suit, a pale blue suit with white stripes that didn't look as much like a Secret Service suit as it looked like a lover's suit. He wanted to look nice for L. D. Krite. It was pathetic and stupid and reminded me of the immense waste of the universe, where all my prayers were swirling. My heart went out to Yamato. He was as pathetic and stupid as I was. So I didn't say anything to him about his haircut or his new suit.

Yamato and I sat with federal prosecutors on the opposite side of the courtroom aisle from the defense attorney and L. D. Krite, who wore a simple black pantsuit that, despite her remarkable prettiness, made her look to me like a Ninja warrior. Yamato kept trying to inconspicuously and subtly glance over at L. D. Krite, to see if perhaps she'd smile at him, but she wouldn't look at us. She had a stoic look, an expression of dignity and defiance. Yamato leaned his head toward me and whispered, "Remember, *you* answer all the questions, so she'll concentrate all her anger and contempt on you."

"Oh boy," I whispered.

I kept looking at my watch, and one of the prosecutors was still asking me to verify key parts of my written report when noon arrived, and I just couldn't care then that three lawyers and L. D. Krite and a federal judge and Yamato were looking at me when one of the prosecutors said to me, "So you couldn't have known if it was a real bomb or not?" and I turned toward the mountains and imagined Natelle smiling at me and I waved at her.

"What was that?" the judge said.

Of course I couldn't tell him. You couldn't dare tell anyone what it was really like to be alive. They'd think you were crazy.

"It was a signal," I said, hoping Natelle waved back.

"A signal of *what*?" the judge said, looking toward the wall where I'd waved. "Are you expecting someone?"

"Not expecting, your honor. Merely hoping."

FROM SOME primitive or subconscious urge to try to rationalize myself into spontaneously feeling better, I thought of Meher Baba, this popular occultist from the 1960s who said, "Don't worry. Be happy." I wanted to find Meher Baba, throw him through a plate glass window, and say, "Happy?"

Pain was real. You couldn't happy it away. Which were my brooding thoughts on Bastille Night when I realized in my aching loneliness for Natelle that, not only would I be thousands of miles away when she came home from her retreat, she might not even have wanted to see me if I was there. At her apartment, where I went to water her plants and put her panties back, I decided to leave her a note to explain where I'd be.

Dear Natelle, to whom my heart is an open and unread book . . .

I threw that away.

Dear Natelle, I put your panties back.

I threw that away.

Dear Natelle, Sometimes it feels like I'm already married to you and I'm the only one who knows it.

That was thrown away.

Dear Natelle, I'm in love with you, but I'm told this can be managed through drugs and neurosurgery.

I wadded that one up and heaved it.

Dear Natelle, I'm really sorry I won't be here when you get back, but we have to go to Indizal for a few days or longer for some stupid international crap that the president will attend. I hope your retreat went well.

I hope you feel better about your life. I'd like to help you. I'll be gone.

I miss you a lot. Is it wrong for me to say that? Sometimes I think it's wrong for me to say *anything*. Maybe if a surgeon removed the front part of my brain, I wouldn't miss you. Bye.

I had to go to the Nevermore Bar & Grill to meet everyone for our final game plans, and I felt awful, as if depression and anxiety and sadness were having a fair in my head. I thought of Meher Baba, and I wanted to crush his jaw with my elbow and say, "You look like I feel, Mr. Baba." I was the only one who could help myself, and I didn't know how to do it. That was why we had psychiatrists, so they could listen to our problems and say, "You really *do* feel awful. I'm glad I'm not you."

Somebody had to be me. I accepted that responsibility and went to the bar, where everyone was drinking beer and being stared at in our jerseys with the names Beowulf, Cervantes, Bovary, Smerdyakov, Caulfield, Miss Ophelia St. Clare, Dilsey, Earwicker, and K.

Cervantes raised his beer bottle above the table and said, "A toast!"

Miss Ophelia St. Clare immediately raised his bottle also and said, "Some toast!"

"French toast!" Beowulf said.

"Muffins!" Dilsey said.

"Bagels!" Caulfield said, and we all raised our beer bottles together in a jubilant ritual that couldn't possibly have any

meaning; which, when you considered the nature of spookball, was appropriate.

After nine-thirty, when it was dark, Widdiker walked up to
the bartender and said to her, "If a group of men calling
themselves the Raging Tree Frogs comes in here looking for
the Avenging Blowfish, would you please tell them we didn't
go to Georgetown?"

"I guess so," the bartender said.

"It's important," Widdiker said. "Tell them that it's Georgetown that we didn't go to."

"All right. And where else aren't you going, in case they
ask?"

"Georgetown is sufficient," Widdiker said. We picked
Georgetown, not because we found subtle clues that that's
where the game would be played. We picked Georgetown
because we knew where it was.

It was time. We drove in two cars and parked about five
blocks from the baseball field, where we assembled around
the trunk of Yamato's car to get our equipment.

"Bats," Yamato said.

"Bats," Deek replied.

"Glow-in-the-dark balls," Yamato said.

"Glow-in-the-dark balls," Deek said.

"Flashlights," Yamato said.

"I thought we were supposed to play in the dark," Deek
said.

"We're also supposed to cheat," Yamato said.

"Oh. That's right. Never mind."

"Gloves," Yamato said.

"Gloves," Deek said.

"Infrared night-vision scope," Yamato said.

"Where'd you get those?" Deek said.

"Machine guns," Yamato said.

"Won't that be too loud?" Deek asked.

"And beer," Yamato said. "All the equipment's here."

"Gimme those night goggles. I'm the manager," Widdiker said, grabbing a device that I think was used primarily by attack helicopter pilots for blowing up tanks at night. Widdiker put the device on his head and looked like a rhinoceros, with a bulging, ominous snout.

"Do I look like Yogi Berra?" Widdiker said.

"You look like a mutant," Horner said.

"Can you see anything?" Pascal asked.

Widdiker moved his head around for a few seconds, then said, "I can see the Grand Canyon."

"Really?" DeMarco said. "Can you see the Northern Lights?"

Widdiker pointed his finger upward and said, "I can see that streetlight."

A woman and a man walked by us on the sidewalk, staring at us apprehensively.

"Act normal," I said quietly. "No. Wait. That'd be too disturbing."

"Good evening," Widdiker said pleasantly, nodding his scope at the couple. "We're the Avenging Blowfish."

They walked away without saying anything, and Pascal said, "What if they call the police?"

"Well, if enough cops come, they can be the other team," Widdiker said, grabbing a bat and a glove and saying, "Let's go. But everyone be quiet. Shhh!"

"Shhh," someone went, and then all of us started going, "Shhh. Shhh. Shhh," as we walked along the sidewalk and down the street toward the darkened baseball field under a starry sky with no moon. Instead of just walking onto the field, we pretended that the CIA might be spying on us from somewhere around the field, so we stood behind some thick bushes and trees to see if anyone else was out there.

"Can you see anything?" Yamato whispered to Widdiker.

Widdiker looked over the bushes with his night scope, then whispered, "I can see the Great Pyramids of Egypt."

"Oh, God. We're not going to get anything done, are we?" someone complained.

"Aside from the pyramids, do you see anything?"

"Everything's green," Widdiker said. "These are giving me a headache. Someone else put 'em on."

He took the goggles off and gave them to Yamato, who put them on and peeked through the bushes.

"Do you see anything?" Pascal whispered.

"Yes. Yes I do," Yamato whispered, and then didn't say what.

"Well, what the fuck do you *see*?" I whispered.

"Out in the outfield, there'a a man and a woman having sexual intercourse," Yamato whispered.

"They're screwing?"

"I've seen it before. I know what it is," Yamato whispered.

The rest of us peeked over and through the bushes to see them, but we couldn't see anything.

"How do we know you're not just making that up?" DeMarco whispered. Yamato gave him the goggles and he looked over the bushes.

"My God," DeMarco whispered. "There's two people screwing."

"What position are they in?" Oxler whispered.

"Left field," DeMarco whispered.

"I didn't mean that. I mean are they in the missionary position?"

"Missionaries don't have sex," DeMarco whispered.

"I guess we'll have to wait until they're through," Pascal whispered.

"I had sex outside one time," DeMarco whispered.

"Yeah, I know. I saw you," Horner whispered.

Everyone started giggling, and Widdiker whispered, "Shut up. They might hear us."

"And what're they gonna do—say, 'Hey, what're you guys doing with all your clothes on?'" Deek whispered.

Everyone began giggling again, clamping our mouths shut and holding our noses to keep quiet, but we were at least fifty yards from the intercoursing couple, so they probably couldn't hear us.

"I had sex in a swimming pool one time," Deek whispered.

"I had sex in a bed one time," I whispered.

"One time I had sex in a hammock," Oxler whispered.

"With a ham hock?" Yamato whispered.

"Have you ever had cunnilingus?" Deek whispered.

"No, but I've had linguini," DeMarco whispered.

"I wish you guys would shut up. I haven't had sex in a *year*," Widdiker whispered.

"I haven't had sex in so long I donated my penis to the Smithsonian," I whispered. "They have it in a display along with dinosaur teeth. It's called 'Things You Can't Use.'"

"They're leaving," DeMarco whispered. "She's putting her bra on."

Everyone tried to see, but there was just darkness. As soon as the couple walked away, we all stood up and walked down to the baseball diamond. Widdiker looked around in the darkness and said, "Are there any Raging Tree Frogs out there?"

There was no answer from the outfield or the trees or the dark.

"I guess they're not here," Oxler said. "So do we go ahead and play ourselves?"

"That's right. Let's get out there and kick our asses," I said.

I volunteered to be the batter, since, like at every other gathering, if we put everyone in the field, we wouldn't have a batter.

I couldn't see anything except a slightly dark form where Widdiker's voice was. Beyond that, all I could see were the upper outlines of trees beyond the outfield. No one else was visible.

"I can't see anything," I said.

"Do you think that has something to do with it being night?" Widdiker said.

"This is stupid," someone in the outfield said.

"Well, then, why're you here?"

"Because he's stupid."

"Okay. Everyone turn on their flashlights," Widdiker said, and we did, shining them on each other so that here and there in the dark were long, yellow beams of light crisscrossing each other for no reason except screwing around. Someone started singing, "Yooouuu light up my life."

"Okay," Widdiker said. I waited for him to do something.

"Okay," he said again.

"Okay *what*?" I said.

"Okay," he repeated, as if all he was going to do was stand at the pitcher's mound and keep saying "Okay."

"Okay. Let me get the ball ready," Widdiker said. He turned on his flashlight and shined it on the ball for a few seconds, then turned off the flashlight and held a faintly glowing, orange baseball. It looked like glowing debris from a volcano.

"Are you ready?" he asked.

"Not really."

"Where are you?" he said.

"Here," I said.

"Well, should I pitch toward the sound of your voice, thus striking you in the head?"

"Should I throw a phosphorous grenade?" DeMarco said. "You could see him then."

"Yeah. If my clothes were on fire, you could see me," I said.

"Just use your flashlight," Widdiker said.

"You mean you want me to throw my flashlight at him?" DeMarco said.

"Turn on your flashlight," Widdiker said.

"How can I hold a flashlight and a bat at the same time?" I said.

"I could turn mine on," Oxler said from behind home plate. It was so dark, I'd forgotten we had a catcher. Oxler turned his flashlight on and put it on the ground behind home plate.

"Don't throw very hard," I said. "If you hit me with the ball, I'm throwing this bat at you."

"Whiner," Widdiker said.

Widdiker shined some more light on the ball to make it glow again.

"Are you ready?" he said.

"No."

I saw the ball rise up in the dark over Widdiker's head and I clenched the bat tightly. The orange ball whizzed toward me, right at me, and I jumped back and heard the ball bounce off the wire backstop.

"Strike one," Widdiker said happily.

"That wasn't a strike. You almost hit me," I said as Oxler picked up the ball and tossed it back to where he imagined Widdiker was.

"Okay. We'll say it was a ball," Widdiker said, turning his flashlight on to shine it on the ball. "Are you ready?"

"No."

This time, the glowing ball came relatively close to the strike zone, and I swung at it and missed. But no one could have seen me swing.

"Ball two," I said.

"You swung at it. I heard you," Widdiker said.

"Did you *see* me swing at it?"

"He swung," Oxler said.

"You didn't have to tell him," I said.

"Okay, strike two," Widdiker said, shining his light on the ball. "This is going to be a split-fingered fastball."

"You don't even know what a split-fingered fastball *is*," Deek called out.

Okay," Widdiker said. "This is going to be a spitball."

"Don't spit on the ball," I said. I could hear Widdiker clearing his throat, as if trying to accumulate all of the saliva and phlegm he had.

"He's going to throw a phlegm-ball," Yamato said.

"Don't put phlegm on the ball," I said.

Widdiker kept clearing his throat as loudly as possible, then started making spitting noises.

"Everyone back up," Deek said. "If Coldiron hits that ball, there'll be phlegm all over everyone."

Widdiker shined some more light on the ball and said, "Wow. This is really sticky."

"And it's going right back in your groin, too," I said. "I'm aiming a line drive at your balls."

"Ready?" Widdiker said.

"Unfortunately for you, I am."

The glowing ball came toward me in a blurred, orange arc, and when I realized that this one was going to be well within the strike zone, a little burst of exuberance and adrenalin raced through me as I swung as smoothly and violently as I could. It was a solid smash, and everyone yelled and screamed in glee or awe as the glowing ball rose far, far up into the immense night, still going upward and away, this faint blur of orange looking like a comet leaving the Earth while I ran slowly to first base; slowly, because I wanted to watch the ball; slowly, because in the dark I didn't know where first base was.

Several people were yelling, "Home run! Home run!" and right when the ball had passed its highest stage in the dark, and began its descent that would give us a one-to-nothing lead over ourselves, there was a gunshot and a flash in the outfield, where Deek was, and then two more shots from the same gun.

Boom! B-Boom! And the ball actually went backward, my God—at least one of the bullets hit the ball pretty squarely—and the ball rose up a few feet and went backward and then down into the infield, its pale, orange glow beginning to diminish, like it was dying.

Everyone was completely silent, as if realizing that when you shoot a gun in the city, police might come. Squinting in the dark, I walked over to the barely glowing ball and picked it up and felt a bullet hole in it. Everyone from the infield and the outfield ran silently up to me and stood around me in a circle, and I could smell the gunpowder from Deek's gun.

"Deek?" Widdiker said. "Why'd you shoot the fucking ball?"

"Well, I just felt it was my responsibility as an outfielder," Deek said.

I walked up to Deek with the ball and said, "You *shot* my home run."

"I think we should go," Yamato said. "Someone might call the police."

Oxler shined his flashlight on the ball and we all looked at the bullet hole.

"It was going to be a home run," I said wistfully. "I never hit a home run before. Do you understand that?"

"I'm sorry," Deek said.

"We better go," Pascal said impatiently.

"I think I hear a siren," Horner said, and it sounded like there was a siren somewhere.

"I mean, damn it," I said, looking at the wounded ball. "I'll never be anybody's hero, like Roger Maris or Reggie Jackson. I'll never be famous, or particularly well-liked, and maybe no one even misses me, you know? Maybe right now in the world there's not a single person who wonders where I am or when they'll see me. And maybe everything I do is so ordinary it'll be forgotten almost the instant after I do it. And when I die, they'll misspell my name on the tombstone, and the inscription will say 'Like Everyone Else, He Died.' And I'll be completely forgotten, like a withered old artifact that isn't even as valuable as a petrified dinosaur bone. But I at least thought, for a few seconds tonight, that if I'm going to be denied everything else, I could at least have a home run. That's all. No wealth. No fame. No wife. No lover. But as a trivial consolation, an accomplishment of no real meaning, I thought I could at least have the harmless glee of hitting a baseball so far that no one could *catch* it. But you shot it. You shot my home run."

"I'm sorry," Deek said gloomily.

"The siren's getting louder," Widdiker said. "We better evacuate."

Everyone started running off the field except me. I shined a flashlight on the ball and made it glow again, except for the bullet hole. I looked out into the dark where my home run had been going when it was shot and I ran a few steps forward and then *threwwwwwww* the ball as high and hard as I could, and watched the little orange streak go forward with my life. It went into the trees and I heard it hit something, and it was gone.

"Home run," I said, and I imagined Natelle smiling at me. Then a police car drove up to the edge of the baseball field with its flashing lights on, and I used my Secret Service training to run off into the dark, welcoming trees.

35

There was a thunderhead off the coast of Indizal as our jet approached the island, and Widdiker looked out the window in front of Yamato and me and said, "Look. That *cloud* is bigger than Indizal."

It almost was. From the air, Indizal looked like an inflatable island, like one of those random geographical features produced by a volcano, that stuck pathetically out of the ocean for no clear reason. The island was surrounded by a dozen or more smaller islands that looked as if they were dropped out of the sky and just hadn't floated away yet. When we landed on what appeared to be a dangerously short runway, I couldn't tell if the pilot had the front of the jet tilted upward or if the weight of the jet made the island tilt. The worst thing was when one of the crew members opened the door and a wave of heat and humidity raced in

with the overpowering odor of unknown plants and flowers, as if the island were attacking us. Just a few seconds
after I'd stepped onto the runway and started sweating, a
giant flying bug landed on my forehead. Despite the fact
that several government and military officials were standing there to greet us, I yelled, "God*damn* it!" and slapped the
bug off my forehead.

All of the government and military officials looked at me
and laughed. One of them, an officer in a gray uniform,
walked up to me with a cheerful smile and said, "God*damn*
it!" then lightly slapped himself on the forehead. I think the
only English he knew was what I had just taught him. He
bent over and picked up the giant flying bug, which was
slightly twisted and mutilated now, and held the bug in front
of me and said something in Spanish, which of course I didn't
understand. Another officer walked over to us and said, "I
am speak English. He is say this is a gravedigger beetle. Has
poison bite, but usually only bite bugs. Maybe he mistake
you for bug."

"God*damn* it!" the first officer said, laughing again as he
slapped himself on the forehead.

"It's good that you're teaching him English," Deek said as
he walked by.

For two days we simply attended security meetings, studied
the official schedules of the president and other politicians,
studied maps of the city and the surrounding countryside—as
little of it as there was—and staked out our spots in the
Hotel Grenadier, where the president and everyone else
would be staying. A grenadier, I found out in a dictionary,
was a soldier in a special regiment, or a soldier equipped
with grenades. This meant that Indizal's most elegant hotel
was named after grenades. Widdiker said that after the
maids made your bed each day they put fresh shrapnel

under your pillow. That's when I started calling it the Hotel Shrapnel.

It wasn't a good sign. Nothing was. Natelle was on her retreat, trying to reassemble her ruined life, possibly deciding whether I should be a part of it and unable to tell me so because I was gone, against my will. My home run, the only home run in my life, was shot down during our victory over ourselves, and the police came. Then we flew to an island that was essentially a volcano that hadn't recently blown up and didn't need to, because politics were so volatile on the island that there were plenty of mortars and rocket-propelled grenades and automatic rifles for everyone. Even though the PDF had ostensibly been defeated in the recent civil war, there were dozens or even hundreds of PDF fighters and mercenaries on Indizal and its nearby islands, hiding out in the jungles that no one cared to search because of such things as gravedigger bugs, vipers, mosquitos with lethal bacteria, and a virtual absence of roads to go on to look for them. Plus the hotel was named after grenades. Everything was a bad sign. I didn't really believe in omens, but I believed in reality, and this was bad reality, crawling all over us like the first tingling sensations of a panic. And I was lonely. I didn't want any of this. I just wanted to love Natelle and be loved back. But the world didn't work that way. As far as I could tell, the world didn't work at all. That was why we had hundreds of armed men on a volcano with trees. That was why Natelle had a ruined life with no instructions on how to fix it. That was why I was always on the verge of giving myself to her, with no obvious proof that she wanted me.

On the evening of the second day there, when Natelle would come home and I couldn't see her, and we had the night off before the president arrived in the morning, I snuck down the street from the Hotel Shrapnel to a little bar to get pleasantly drunk. I ordered a gin and tonic without any tonic, just the way Aramilo drank them, and I held the gin up to my nose and breathed it in, and it made me tingle with the promise of peace; I needed peace and there wasn't any in me, and I knew I wasn't just about to drink. It was worse than that. I was about to annihilate myself. This wasn't gin. It was anesthesia. I drank to feel human. Or probably to *stop* feeling human. And I wanted that gin badly, wanted it to come into me and race through me like the peace I didn't have. And it would do that. It would cover me like a layer of blessed numbness, through which no sadness could enter and none could leave. And when the layer wore off, all I'd have to do would be drink again and drink again and again, until I wasn't *any*body anymore, until I was a blob of pain fighting itself.

My face and my hands were sweating, either from having no gin or from wanting it, and I realized, or it seemed like I did, that even if Natelle might never want me, at least I better want me. Maybe I'd be alone all my life, but I'd be alone with me, and I'd better be nicer to *me*.

I picked up the glass and tossed the gin behind me, listening to it splash on the floor.

"God*damn* it!" a man yelled. I looked behind me and it was the same officer I'd seen at the airport, sitting now at a table with a dark trail of gin across his pant leg. The officer slapped his forehead and smiled at me, as if even though I'd just thrown gin on him, he was willing to think it was some bizarre American bar ritual and there was no reason to be mad at me. Still smiling, he picked up his glass of beer and tossed the beer behind him onto another officer, who began laughing and slapped his forehead and said, "God*damn* it!" and then threw his beer on the first officer. It worried me that I was teaching them how to be Americans.

WITHIN MINUTES after Air Force One landed at the airport and the president and his gang of middle-aged white men in expensive suits stepped off the jet and into the vast crowd of Secret Service agents, reporters, camera crews, and Indizalian politicians and military officers wearing elegant white suits, I recognized on the tarmac an inconceivably frail and tiny figure: Ambassador Hobar Aramilo, who waved a conductor's baton as he directed an orchestra playing "Begin the Beguine."

Over my earphone I heard someone say, "Isn't that a dance song? Do they expect the president to *dance*?"

I was supposed to be looking for shooters, snipers, and madmen, and I was, but the music made me think of Natelle, an urgently loved woman as distant as a faintly twinkling star. I didn't feel well. I couldn't imagine that I ever had. I kept looking for madmen and wondering where Natelle was, but I was distracted when the orchestra stopped playing its instruments and everyone began whistling the theme song from "The Andy Griffith Show." Evidently, Aramilo had found out that it was one of the president's favorite shows.

A voice in my earphone said, "What're they going to play next—the theme song from 'Petticoat Junction'?"

The president held both of his hands above his head and waved to the orchestra as agents herded him and part of his gang into some old 1960s black Cadillacs to take them to the Hotel Shrapnel for the first meetings of the Economic Summit of Small and Inconsequential Nations. The summit had a real name, but I never used it.

The bad thing about this trip, aside from the fact that I was about four thousand miles from Natelle, was that Indizal still had armed insurgents, some of whom might want to shoot at us. Presumably, they were in hiding and were either so fearful or demoralized from their drubbing in their little civil war that they weren't a danger to anyone. This was bullshit. Anyone with a gun was a danger, including us. As we were taught in our earliest days of training, anyone could be a threat to the president: Busboys, bellmen, barbers. Dishwashers, dancers, doormen. Waiters, wine stewards, winos. Reporters, receptionists, ranchers. Generals, gardeners, gumbo. Well, maybe not gumbo.

"Everybody is a suspect," Doltmeer liked to say. "The only way to make the world completely safe for the president is to kill everyone else on the planet. Clearly we don't have the budget for that."

In Indizal, though, the most ominous people weren't the hidden members of the PDF, but some of the very politicians the president was to talk with at the summit; the ill-tempered and envious leaders of struggling little nations who were understandably indignant about the dominance of the Western World, meaning, in my opinion, Matt Dillon and Miss Kitty. And in a way, the city of Rio D'Iguana did resemble Dodge City, Kansas, in the sense that, back in the late 1800s, Dodge City was swarming with armed civilians who freely roamed the streets and hotels. And so it was here, with each leader from each country bringing with him or her a dozen or more bodyguards carrying machine pistols and machine guns and automatic pistols—everyone protecting their leaders as though they were queen bees. Including ourselves, there were at least two hundred armed men at the summit, ready to shoot anyone who looked suspicious, and of course everyone looked suspicious. If, as we were told, one of the goals of the summit was to help disintegrate the cultural and economic barriers that sustained nationalism and war, then it was pretty obvious that we were the most heavily armed pacifists in the world.

Before the state dinner at the Hotel Shrapnel that evening, I was one of the agents assigned to hang out in the hotel kitchen and make sure none of the kitchen staff put bombs or poison in the food.

"Why would they want *you* in the kitchen?" Yamato wondered as we walked to the kitchen.

"It must be my extensive experience with Spam," I said.

"Don't do anything you'll regret."

"You know, usually you don't know what you'll regret until you've already done it."

"Just don't do anything stupid," Yamato said.

"Fine. We'll assign that to someone else."

"I don't see why you always have to be so cranky," Yamato said soothingly.

"I'm not cranky. I'm sullen."

"Maybe you should try yoga. Have you ever tried yoga?"

"You mean inner calm? I'm too turbulent for inner calm."

"Never mind. Let's go in the kitchen and check for exploding entrées."

The kitchen staff was outnumbered two-to-one by bodyguards. Each of the thirteen nations represented at the conference (thirteen, another bad sign) put two of their bodyguards in the kitchen. The food was going to behave itself. But not the chef.

"I cannot *kook* like this," a middle-aged man in a chef's outfit said peevishly when Yamato and I walked in. He carried himself with the dignity and impatience of a head chef, and I walked up to him and said, "I'm Doyle Coldiron, with the

United States Secret Service. Do you have any Fritos, or Ruffles with ridges?"

"Stay out of my way, unless you want scalding, sautéed mushrooms in your face," the chef said.

"I prefer *my* mushrooms on a plate, thank you," I said, smiling at the other bodyguards. They didn't say anything, and stared impassively at Yamato and me as we stepped cautiously away from the chef. I whispered to Yamato: "Watch that man. He has knives."

In a way, it was comically pointless to have bodyguards spying on the kitchen staff, since any of them at any time could easily sprinkle into the food some exotic herb or powder that none of us could identify and which could kill everyone at the dinner. You merely had to hope they wouldn't do it. Of course, the presence of twenty-six men with guns was intimidating.

Yamato and I stood near the two swinging doors separating the kitchen from the main dining room, and one of our jobs was to prevent anyone without the proper photo identification badges from going through the door.

"We should have a secret password," Yamato said.

"Like what?" I said.

"Something hard to say. Like 'Worcestershire sauce.'"

"Oh, that's *good*. That's good. Let's try it."

We smiled and peeked through the windows of the swinging doors at all of the presidents and premiers and emirs and eminences in the dining room, and we finally saw someone coming toward us. It was a man in a tuxedo who had the proper photo ID—a hotel employee—but we wanted our fun, so when he walked through the door, Yamato said, "What's the password?"

He looked at us with uncertainty and said, "Password? I wasn't told there was a password."

"It's just a minor deal. Here," Yamato said, and wrote the password on a piece of note paper and showed it to the man. "Can you say that?"

The man read the password and said, "I've never been able to say that right."

"Try," Yamato encouraged him.

The man looked at the word and said, "Wor-ses-ter-shire?"

"No," I said. "Try again."

He said, "Wor-sister-cester?"

"Ohhh, I *like* that, but it's wrong," I said.

"It's a good password, isn't it?" Yamato said. "No one can say it."

"Well, may I come in anyway?" the man asked.

"Just for a few minutes," I said. "And don't tell anyone the password."

"I can't," he said.

"We should use that password more often," Yamato said. "What's another good password?"

I thought for a few seconds and said, "Martina Navratilova."

"Excellent," Yamato said. "How can you even *say* that?"

"I'm not sure that I did," I said. "But we can use both passwords for the rest of the summit. You know, walk up to some sub-assistant emir from Yemen and say, 'Excuse me. You can't be in here unless you say the password,' and then show him the passwords and see if he can say 'Worcestershire sauce' or 'Martina Navratilova.'"

"They'll hate us," Yamato said.

"That's fine."

"I know."

Aside from being watchful, there was nothing to do, and Yamato and I walked over to one of the big wooden tables near the door to watch two of the chefs, or whatever the hell their titles were, butchering a freshly killed pig, slicing through flesh and bone with astonishingly sharp knives.

"What part does the Spam come from?" I said.

One of the chefs said something to me in French.

"I'm from Kansas," I said. "That's west of France."

"Leave him *alone*, Doyle," Yamato said, picking up a stick of celery. "I know what we need. We need some cheese for this celery. See if you can find any Cheez Whiz."

I was looking along the table for any evidence of cheese, when there were some smashing, crashing noises and violent screaming from the back of the kitchen. I had pulled out my gun and had it aimed toward the source of all the smashing and yelling, when there was an explosion, like a gun being fired; then came the sound of machine guns, automatic weapons, and something slammed fiercely into me, burning and stinging my left thigh. I saw whirling, vague colors, and felt the odd sensation of falling, of dizziness twisting through my head, and everything turned bright yellow and white as I lay curiously on the floor, knowing I'd been shot. I wondered if I should stop the bleeding or if I should shoot somebody. My job was to shoot somebody. I couldn't tell if my eyes were open or closed, if the shooting and screaming I heard came from my recent memory or if it was still going on. It occurred to me that I was dying, that the reason everything looked yellow and white was that this was what you saw right before you died, and I didn't *want* to pass into the afterlife. I wanted to feel Natelle breathing on me.

"No!" I yelled, as if I could simply refuse death, and someone fell across my legs, a heavy man. It was the head chef. He'd tripped over my legs and was crawling under a table, while automatic weapons kept smashing and splattering things in the room. Far away, at the back door, where sunlight came through, I saw two men leaning in and out of the door to fire machine guns into the room. People were shooting back, and some of the doorway was completely torn away by bullets. I heard Yamato yelling, "Doyle! Doyle! Get out of the way!" I couldn't crawl. I decided to shoot somebody.

Lying on my back, I raised my gun up toward the back door, and when a man leaned in with his machine gun, I shot him. He spun backward and out of view, and my gun flew backward over my head from the recoil, so now my gun was gone. No one shot me in Vietnam, and now, in a hotel kitchen, someone had shot me. I didn't *do* anything. Everything was so loud and frightening, and I was sweating, and very cold. I almost couldn't hear anyone screaming anymore, as if they were screaming more quietly, now, and going away, and Natelle had a kite. It was transparent, and we couldn't see it in the sky, but you could tell from the pressure on the kite string that we were flying it. I stood behind her with my arms around her, and with one hand on hers as she flew the kite, and I was drifting into her, and she into me.

"Don't let go," she said. She wasn't talking about the kite.

Everything grew darker until there was nothing left to see but a wavering field of darkness. It sounded like someone was yelling. I wondered who it was. I wondered if I'd died, and gotten lost, and instead of going toward the light, I'd wandered into the dark, and God was yelling at me.

"Over here! Over *here*, stupid!"

I wondered why God would call me stupid. I thought God was nicer than that.

"Stop the bleeding. Tie something around his leg," someone said frantically. I knew this wasn't the afterlife. I could smell gunpowder and spices. I started to fall asleep again.

"Don't pass out, Doyle. Try and stay awake. We'll get you to a hospital right away. Don't pass out," Yamato said as he squatted beside me and someone tied something onto my leg.

"Someone shot me," I said. "And then Natelle and I were flying a kite."

"Well, that's good, Doyle. That's exactly the way the world should be. And don't pass out."

But I did.

36

A gigantic animal with the black body of a scorpion and the head of a snapping turtle was chasing me across a school playground. There were no other people there, no one to help me, and I desperately climbed the metal steps of a big slide to get away from the snapping scorpion, whose stinger was aimed right at me as I slid headfirst down the slide into the roaring vortex of a luminous, orange tornado that sucked me violently and instantly through an almost airless darkness where I couldn't breathe, and my lungs hurt as the tornado shot me far above every visible cloud and into the bluest calm so high above the Earth that I could see the curve of the planet, and the infinite darkness beyond, where I thought God lived. And I thought God was looking at me, suspended there between rising and falling, like God was curious about me, like God was amazed that I'd gotten that far without a plane or wings or any magic, like God was wondering if I could endure this, like I was an interesting peculiarity. There was no one to catch me in that dizzying, unbalanced, frantic instant when I was weightless, and just now beginning to fall every one of those miles back onto the only place in the entire universe where all my life I'd searched and waited for someone who, even as I fell, I kept hoping at last to see. The wind closed my eyes, and it felt like someone was reaching for me. I didn't know who it was. All my life, I never knew. The wind stopped, and when I opened my eyes to see what it would look like when I was dead, Yamato was sitting beside me in a chair, and I was in a bed I didn't remember. I was trying to recall who I was, and who was reaching for me, and why they didn't touch me, like a hand just out of sight. I didn't know whose it was. Yamato smiled at me with what looked like gratitude. I didn't do anything. I didn't remember ever doing anything, as if I had a past but it wasn't mine anymore. I was supposed to remember something, but I couldn't remember what it was. I remembered waving to Natelle. I missed her. She didn't know that. She was supposed to know that. Maybe Natelle was reaching for me. Maybe God was. Maybe I was reaching for myself. Yamato was still smiling at me, so I looked at him.

"Can you hear me?" he said.

"Yes." I didn't know why he asked that. I could always hear.

"Do you feel better?"

"Better than what?" I said, trying to remember something.

"You were shot," Yamato said. "Do you remember that?"

"Oh," I said, trying to think, trying to let dark, tangled slivers of things race through my head. I remembered part of it.

"Yes. I remember that."

"You're pretty doped up on morphine, now. I'm sure none of this is very clear to you, so I'll tell you what happened, and then you can remember it if you want to. We were in the kitchen in the hotel and somebody started shooting into the kitchen with automatic rifles and machine guns, and you were shot in the leg, in your left thigh. The bullet went completely through your muscle, so you were bleeding like hell. You passed out, but before that, you took the time to shoot someone. You were lying on the floor and shot someone. We were having a goddamn firefight in a hotel kitchen, Doyle. It still scares me, like it isn't even over, but it is. And we won. We nailed their asses. We killed six of them. They killed two chefs. I think it was the PDF. I don't know."

Yamato sighed very loudly, like he was still being scared. I looked at him and said, "Now I remember. I was looking for cheese."

"Yeah. You walked around the table to look for cheese, and then the shooting started."

"I won't look for cheese anymore."

Yamato laughed. He looked better now. "I don't think that's why the shooting started, Doyle. But I can understand why you'd never want to look for cheese again."

"I guess they never had the dinner," I said, looking for the first time at the IV tube in my arm.

"No. Nobody ate."

"Are they mad at us?"

"Fuck 'em if they are."

"Okay."

I raised my arm with the needle in it and said, "I don't like this. Needles make me pass out."

"You can do that in a hospital. No one minds," Yamato said. "How do you feel?"

"I'm not sure. I can't tell how I feel."

"It's probably the morphine. Morphine gives you a high on top of pain. I'm sure that feels strange. Speaking of strange, right after the shooting stopped and you were lying on the floor looking all pale and woozy, you said you and Natelle were flying a kite. I think you were delirious."

"Delirious?" I said wonderingly, and I remembered the dream. "I don't think that was delirium. I think it was hope."

"I'm sorry," Yamato said, shaking his head apologetically. "Of course it was hope."

"Should I call Natelle?" I wondered. "No. Never mind. I think she wants me to leave her alone."

"Why would she want *that*?" Yamato said cautiously.

I wasn't sure. I said, "I'm not really in her life. I'm on the edge of it."

"That's bullshit," Yamato said. "You might not be her lover, but you know she loves you. And you've been shot. You're in a goddamn hospital. Of course she'd want to talk to you. I'm going to go get you a phone, or a walkie-talkie, or some kind of goddamn radio, and you're going to call Natelle."

"What'll I say to her?"

"What kind of stupid question is that? You'll say 'Hi, Natelle. This is Doyle. I've been shot. And how was *your* day?' Say whatever the hell you feel. And stay here. I'll be right back," Yamato said, and left the room.

I loved him for that, for trying to help me find Natelle. I just didn't know if she wanted to be found. Maybe when she came back from her retreat, she'd want to stay away from all men with penises. All men had penises. It seemed like I wasn't used to thinking. Thoughts came to me, and I wondered whose they were. I reached down between my legs to make sure my penis was still there. It was. Not that I anticipated much of a future for it.

Yamato walked back into the room with a phone and said,

"Here's a portable phone. This is only for serious national emergencies, like calling your girlfriend. I'll dial the White House for you. Here. And you just ask for Natelle and talk to her for a while, and I'll go and leave you alone. I'll be back in half an hour or something." Yamato handed me the phone and walked out of the room. The phone was already making its peculiar long-distance noises, and a panic went through me; a rushing, dizzying flow of panic that Natelle might not be there, or she might be too busy to talk, or, as soon as she recognized my voice, she'd withdraw from me resentfully, mad that I'd violated her solitude, mad that I'd committed the sin of needing her.

One of the operators answered the phone and I told her who I was and who I wanted to talk with, and she put me on hold. I heard the phone switch.

"This is Natelle," she said, sounding remote and busy and unwilling to be bothered, as if she didn't know it was me. Or maybe she did.

"Hi. This is Doyle. I just thought I'd call you from a foreign country. If you're busy, I can call you later."

"Doyle," she said in a suddenly serious and wondering tone, and I was afraid she was going to say she couldn't see me anymore because she didn't want me to be in love with her, and she'd decided that in the mountains, and would I graciously go away?

"Doyle," she said. "We were told there was some kind of attack last night on the hotel where the president's staying. They said several people were killed and a Secret Service agent was shot. Who was shot?"

"Me. They shot me in the leg. It doesn't hurt. I think that's because they gave me morphine. It feels like I'm floating inside my own body. It's like . . ." I was going to say it was like the feeling I had when I held her one time, but that might've scared her, to know I'd kept that a secret, so I kept it again. My whole life was squashed inside of me. It could only come out for the one person who maybe didn't want it to.

Natelle was quiet. I couldn't even hear her breathing. Maybe she was crying.

"Please tell me you're all right," she said sadly.

"I'm all right."

"Are you in a hospital?"

"Yes. I don't know which one. I think I passed out or slept. I don't even know what day it is. What day is it?"

She was crying. I started crying with her, because I wanted to hold her and I couldn't.

"I wish I could hold you," I said.

"I know," she said, either as if she knew I loved her or as if she knew she loved me.

"What do you know?" I asked.

"Where were you shot?"

"In the left thigh. It hurt pretty badly at the time, but not now."

"I'm so sorry, Doyle. I'm so sorry I can't hold you now. I miss you."

Something stirred beneath all the morphine, an emotion that not even drugs could overpower. At first I didn't know what it was, it was so unusual. It barely spread into me, barely advanced. Then I knew what it was. I felt happy. It didn't even seem like my emotion, but it was in me, so it was probably mine.

"I want you to come home, I need to see you," Natelle said, like a thought was bumped up out of her heart by everything else she couldn't quite say, like everything was storming in her and swirling and needing passage out, and the one thought that made it out was *I need to see you*.

Just for a second or two, we were both silent, maybe each of us surprised by what she'd just said, as if we were suddenly closer than we ever were before, like every secret finally spoken made us more real to each other.

Maybe that was mystical blather. Maybe it was a morphine dream. One other possibility was that it was true.

"I want you to come home," she said again.

"Home?"

"I need to *see* you. It doesn't mean I'm in love with you, and it doesn't mean that can't happen. Don't trap me into saying something."

"I won't."

"The Italians have a saying," she said.

I waited for her to say it, this saying that had something to do with the outcomes of our lives.

"Oh, I can't remember it," she said sadly.

"Well, maybe that's because you're not Italian. You're French. Do the French have a saying? Say one of those," I said, trying to amuse her so she wouldn't be so anxious.

"But I'm not thinking of one of those," she objected.

"You're not thinking of the Italian one, either. How about the Belgians? Do they have a saying?"

"I think I've forgotten all the sayings of Europe," she said.

"Well, then, say something from yourself."

"All right," she said. "I want you to come home. I'm not sure what I mean by 'home.' I think I mean somewhere near me. Because I miss you, and I'm scared for you. And last night. Last night . . ." She stopped, and was crying.

"Natelle? What is it? Did something happen to you?" I asked, wondering if she'd been attacked. "What happened?"

"I'm sorry," she said, and was sniffling and catching her breath. "Nothing happened to me. It was *you*, Doyle. They told us there'd been shooting in the hotel in Indizal. They said several people were killed and injured, and they didn't give any names and I didn't know *who* was killed, or who was injured. And for a second, I imagined you were dead, because I didn't know, and I started crying, and just put my face down on my desk and cried, because I thought you might be dead. And Theresa, who'd just gotten the report from a radio news bulletin, said no, no one from the Secret Service had been killed, but one of them was shot. And suddenly you weren't dead, thank God, but maybe you were shot. And I didn't *know*. And I kept seeing your face, smiling at me, and I imagined blood all over you and I was panicked. And no one in the Secret Service would tell us anything. I called and asked about you and they wouldn't tell us *anything*. I didn't know if you were shot or not, until you called. And it hurt me, Doyle. It really hurt me, like I hadn't realized how important, how godawful important you are, until I imagined you lying somewhere with blood all over you. I'm so sorry. I'm so sorry," she said, and was crying again.

"I'm fine, Natelle. I'm fine. I'm right here. I'll be in the hospital for a few days and then I'll be home to see you. I promise. I've missed you, too. I always do. And . . . I don't know if I should tell you this."

"What? Tell me what?"

"Well, it might be upsetting. It's about something that happened after I was shot."

"What happened? You can't upset me. I already am upset."

"Okay. I thought of you. I think. Or I dreamed. I don't know which. It was when I was lying on the floor in the hotel kitchen, and I was bleeding and real dizzy, and my mind seemed to switch away from all the shooting, because that was too horrifying, and suddenly I was with you. We were flying my Stealth kite. Yamato called it a delusion. If it was, it was just the delusion I needed. I was in the middle of all this shooting, and I didn't even hear it anymore. It was like I had to go to the safest place I could find, and the safest place was you. We were flying the kite, and I was holding you, and you told me not to let go. I wouldn't do that. I'd never do that."

That was too honest. It was an announcement of love to someone who'd just crawled from the wreckage of love. She was quiet, like everything I'd just said to her was piercing her. I waited for her to say something, and all I heard was her breathing.

"I don't know if I'm the safest place to be," she said finally. "But I'm glad you didn't let go."

"Of you?" I asked.

"I'm not talking about the kite."

37

I asked immediately to go home, and they sent me to Dakar, the capital of Senegal, Africa. Agent-in-Charge Hamsted said my wounds were too severe to ship me off thousands of miles to a hospital in Washington, and they had no faith in the hospital in Indizal, so they sent me, along with Yamato to watch out for me, to the nearest reasonably decent hospital, which was in Dakar. I tried to be depressed, but they gave me morphine and antibiotics.

"Why won't you bastards let me be depressed?" I said as the nurse, a man, shot me up with morphine.

"And why does he want to be depressed?" the nurse said to Yamato.

"I think he feels it's his right," Yamato said.

The nurse shook his head and handed me a paper cup

with water and a big blue and white pill. "This is a sedative. Take this, and you'll feel better."

"I don't want to feel better. I want to go home," I said.

"You can't go home until your wound is stabilized and you don't have a fever like you do. Take your pill."

"It's not fair to make me feel good against my will," I said.

"Take the pill, or I'll simply inject a sedative into you."

I took the pill, but I kept trying to be depressed because I couldn't go home and be with Natelle, who I thought would hold me and love me, although maybe she wouldn't. Natelle herself might still be so depressed about her life that she might barely be able to smile for me; especially since I'd just been shot and now she had that knowledge to hurt her. Everything was wrong, which would have depressed me, except for the morphine and sedatives. Unwillingly, I felt good.

"How do you feel?" Yamato said after the nurse left.

"Wonderful, goddamn it."

"I'm sorry you feel wonderful. It'll go away," Yamato said.

"It better," I tried to say peevishly, but I was incapable of being peevish.

We were there for four days. Gardenaul called me from the White House and told me how sorry he was that I'd been shot. He described my actions as heroic and admirable.

"Someone shot me. That's heroic?" I asked.

"But you had enough wherewithal to shoot someone back. That's heroic," Gardenaul said.

"It wasn't heroic. I was terrified that he'd shoot me again. So I shot him."

Gardenaul insisted that was heroic. Heroes weren't born. They were assigned. And Gardenaul said my slate was wiped clean. The previous "incident" involving the canned luncheon meat no one was going to name was now forgotten.

"Thank God," I said.

"Or me," Gardenaul said, reminding me that he was an accomplished son of a bitch.

Yamato stayed in a hotel near the hospital and visited me several times a day, always bringing me a French newspaper I couldn't read so he could hold it in front of me and say, "And the top story of the day . . . is something *else* we can't understand.'" Plus he brought me chocolate and croissants that I wasn't supposed to eat, but I ate them anyway. The nurse kept giving me morphine and sedatives, so I felt ecstatic for no reason. Still, I missed Natelle. It was the one sadness that narcotics couldn't quite obliterate.

One afternoon when Yamato and I were looking out the window at some seagulls trying to steal a fish from a pelican in flight, Yamato said he missed L. D. Krite. I said, "How can you miss her? You've never had her."

He smiled and said, "You've never had Natelle, and you miss her."

"True," I said.

Yamato took the lid from a little brown box he'd carried in with him and said, "Look." He held up a pale white carving and said, "I bought this for L. D. Krite."

"What is it?"

"It's a dolphin carved out of whalebone."

"It's pretty," I said. "But . . ."

"I know," Yamato said, sighing and then grinning morosely. "I don't think an animal rights activist would like a dolphin carved out of whalebone."

"But it *is* pretty," I said, trying to cheer him up. "Maybe you could tell her it's a dolphin carved out of a poacher."

"No. I saw some jade earrings she might like."

"Are you going to ask her out?" I said.

Yamato opened the bottle of warm beer he'd smuggled

into the room and took a big drink. He said, "It'll probably fail. I know. But, you see . . . I'm just *attracted* to her. I'm sorry I arrested her."

"You shouldn't talk about that on, like, your first date."

"Don't make fun of me."

"I'm sorry. I didn't mean it."

"I have to try," Yamato said. "I'm just spontaneously, naturally *attracted* to her. I like her. It's not my fault. I don't care if she committed a felony. And if I send her some earrings and she tells me to go to hell, well, I can't help it. But I have to find out if it's possible for her to like *me*. She did when we were interviewing her. Remember?"

"Yes. She liked you."

Yamato looked at me seriously and said, "Do you think I'm stupid?"

I tried to think of the right answer. Unable to think of that, I spoke anyway.

"Anyone who feels as strongly as you do would be stupid if they didn't try," I said.

Yamato breathed in deeply and sighed. "Then you don't think I'm stupid?"

"Oh, I *know* you are. But so am I."

He smiled at me and said, "I'll go buy the earrings now."

And I was stupid, too. I lied to Dr. Boulan when I told her I didn't think Natelle could save me. That *was* what I hoped for. It was painless to admit, now, in my cocoon of narcotics, that I didn't just see Natelle as a wonderful woman who I could love and who might love me. I saw her as the center of the universe, the one being to whom I could look for all love and all hope, as if none of that was in me or in anyone else. I knew it was. But I'd turned Natelle into a religion. She was just a woman, not a church. And I didn't even know what she was going to save me from. Being alone? Being me?

I was trying to have an insight, and all I could think of was that I'd backed myself into a corner, and the corner was me.

I was all I had. Was that so bad?

Yes.

No.

I was willing to accept both answers.

I wanted a revelation from God. I waited a few seconds. I didn't get one.

My arm itched. That wasn't a revelation. It was the needle in my arm, taped onto my flesh, where the antibiotic dripped in from the big plastic bag. It made me look like an experiment. I felt like one. I got very slowly out of bed, because I was dizzy and floating, and stood up next to the metal pole with wheels on it that connected me to the plastic bag, and I took a walk down the hall. It was like I was taking the metal pole for a walk. Some visitors in the hall stared at me limping along with my hand on the metal pole.

"We're taking a walk, my pole and I," I said, and almost smiled in my narcotic, mystical state. We went outside, my pole and I, onto the big sun deck, where visitors and casualties like myself could smell the ocean and watch seagulls try to steal fish from pelicans. I sat down in a white metal chair with my pole right next to me, like a friend, and the pole and I looked at the ocean. Somewhere over there was Natelle. She wasn't going to save me. And I wasn't going to save her. Up out of the buoyant serenity of my narcotics came a little flow of sadness, and I cried. I didn't know who was going to save anybody, and it seemed like I should pray. I prayed, *Please help us do whatever we should do, even if we don't know what that is. Please let Natelle and I always love each other and always be friends. Please give Natelle peace, and maybe me, too. And if I have to get used to being backed into a corner that's me, could you please put someone in the corner with me? You know who I'm talking about, too.*

It wasn't a very good prayer, but it was what I thought of.

My pole and I were still looking across the ocean when Yamato walked up with some jade earrings held out to me. He had at least as much pathetic hope as I did. That's probably why I liked him.

38

On our long flight back to Washington, I was still a little bit feverish and my forehead felt as warm as a dinner roll. Although the jet was filled with dozens of people, I had the sense that the only reason the pilot was in the air was to get me back to Natelle. Yamato sat next to me, most of the time holding the little gift box with the earrings in it, like a mystical artifact from his heart. I had a gift box, too, with an onyx cameo showing a smiling woman, who I hoped would be Natelle. I opened the box and took out the cameo on its silver chain and said to Yamato, "This is prettier than yours."

Yamato shook his head no and said, "My earrings are lovelier."

"Oh, they're lovely, all right. But my cameo's more endearing."

"Endearing, maybe, but not as enchanting as my earrings."

We were two men hoping like boys that a woman would like us—would want to keep us. Like so many other people in the world, we'd always been given back. That was part of what hurt Natelle so much now, the horror of being given back. I imagined her climbing a ladder, and then the ladder vanishing.

I was struggling through that metaphor, wondering if I was supposed to catch Natelle, or just hold her after she hit, and rock her in my arms until she caught her breath, when Yamato showed me the dinner menu.

"Meat," he said.

"Yes," I said. "They have meat."

"L. D. Krite's a herbivore. Should I just eat vegetables?"

"I don't care."

"She's not my girlfriend yet. And might never be," he said, reading the menu and pointing his finger at Beef Tips with Noodles. "Beef," he said. "A cow's an herbivore. Maybe if I eat an herbivore, that'd be the first step toward becoming one."

"Oh, yeah. You tell that to L. D. Krite: 'Maybe I'm not a vegetarian, but I *eat* them every day.'"

"Better not," Yamato said, looking at the gift box again. "And when I send this to her, what should I say?"

"Well, you better not say anything. You better *write* something."

"I know that," Yamato said, as if he'd just realized it. "But what should I write?"

"This is a tough one. I don't know how you express affection to someone you arrested."

"I was thinking of apologizing," Yamato said wistfully.

"That would be a good start."

"This is all pretty stupid, isn't it?" Yamato said.

"Stupid?" I wondered. "Strange, yes. But stupid? I don't

think so. Romance isn't particularly rational to begin with. And it's not supposed to be. It's not like you're supposed to have a list of thoroughly rational, defensible reasons why you like somebody. It's what you feel. That's all. And you merely hope they feel the same way. And that's all you can do. Hope."

"I know," Yamato said, and he was quiet, as if absorbed in hope. I looked at him in my peripheral vision and felt bad for him, because he was so much like me. We were two men halfway through our lives, still operating on the unreasoning hope of the children we once were. We were bigger, now, and had suits and guns. But still we were boys, wishing someone would find us. You always thought, even without proof, that someone was looking.

I was going to cry, but I didn't want Yamato to see me. I rubbed my hands over my eyes to keep from crying, and found out when my fingers touched the skin above my eyes that I was still very warm.

"I think I still have a fever," I said.

"Remember what the doctor said?" Yamato asked.

"No. He didn't speak English."

"Well, the nurse said the doctor said you should see a doctor when you get home, in case you still have a fever. Do you want me to take you to a doctor when we get back?"

"No. I want to see Natelle."

"She'll just give you a different fever."

"She did that a long time ago."

IN THE cab on the way to Natelle's apartment, I felt dizzy and lightheaded and hot and cold, which, in the traditional fashion of my peculiar thinking, reminded me of the symptoms of menopause. The cab driver kept glancing at me in her mirror, and finally said, "Are you all right?"

"I feel a little hot and cold at the same time. Could be menopause," I said.

"You're the wrong sex," she said.

"I was male at birth. There was nothing to be done about it."

I stared out of the car. Everything seemed unreal, as if everything around me had suddenly started moving in slow motion, as if my fever had gotten so bad that my perception was distorted. I squinted my eyes to look clearly at everything, then realized everything was moving in slow motion because we were in a traffic jam.

"Can't you drive on the sidewalk?" I said.

"That's illegal," the cab driver said indifferently.

"Not if you're on official government business," I said, taking out my wallet with my picture ID and holding it over the back seat so the driver could see it. "I'm with the Secret Service and I have urgent business. I want you to drive on the sidewalk and get around these cars."

"Really?" she asked in an anxious voice.

"Really."

"Does this have something to do with national security?"

"It always does. Now please drive on the sidewalk, being careful not to hit any more pedestrians than necessary."

She drove slowly up onto the curb, honking at pedestrians, who lurched out of our way as we drove along the sidewalk and up to the intersection, where the road was clear enough for us to get back onto the street.

"That was a highly competent job. You can expect a letter of commendation from the White House," I said, looking around for police cars, since the police wouldn't commend us.

It was dusk when the cab driver left me standing with my crutches in front of Natelle's apartment, and, looking up at her second-story windows, I was in a cold sweat, either from blood poisoning or love. I knew blood poisoning could be cured by antibiotics. Love was untreatable.

Hobbling quietly up the steps, I felt a constant surge of apprehension and dizziness and hope, trying to think of what I'd say when Natelle opened the door. She'd see how pale and sweaty I was.

"I'm having menopause," I'd say. I wished that I wasn't so dizzy. Natelle would see me and get worried and be gentle with me, and I didn't want her to be gentle. I wanted her to knock me to the floor and hold her mouth against mine until her breath came out my ears. I wanted her to kiss my lips and my neck and my chest, and put her hand between my legs.

Maybe I just wanted her to hold me, so we could feel the softness of each other's flesh, like there really was something good in the world, and it was each other, and we'd look into each other's eyes as if we couldn't possibly see enough.

And maybe she wouldn't even be home. I didn't call her to find out. Maybe she'd be on a date. She wouldn't do that. Maybe she'd be out with a lawyer. Women getting divorces often saw lawyers. Maybe she'd be out with some of her girl-friends, having dinner and getting drunk and defacing their memories of men and wondering if they should become lesbians because all men were assholes, except for a few million of us you never heard about.

I was at her door, breathing in deeply to calm myself, wishing I could tell her every affectionate thing I'd ever felt about her, every true and astonishing secret she ever gave birth to in me, wishing, if there were things I'd forgotten or been afraid to tell her that could sustain the slight and wavering magic I had that kept me in her life, that all of those things would rush to me in a single insight and I'd *tell her*, as if there were some torturous and cruel spiritual maze you had to pass through without error, and if you missed a step or turned wrong even once, the punishment was that no one would love you, and you'd be alone and lie awake at night like I did sometimes, realizing in a tingling panic that of all the millions of people in the world, not one of them wondered where you were, or would ever want to hold you.

This was the maze I was in when I knocked on the door and Natelle opened it. After everything I'd just thought about, I couldn't think of what to say to her.

"I'm back," I said.

She stared at me silently, with pain and fear, looking at my crutches, looking hard into my eyes, as I looked into hers.

"You're so pretty," I said, not caring anymore if I scared her, since *I* was scared. We might as well be scared together.

"My God, you're so pale. Have you got a fever?" she said, walking up to me to put her hands on my cheeks and forehead.

"Your hands feel good," I said.

"You're sweating," she said, rubbing her finger across my forehead.

"I feel anointed when you do that. Would you do that again . . . rub your finger across my forehead?"

She leaned into me and put her arms around me and squeezed me to her with her cheek against mine. I felt the softness of her breasts on my chest, and she breathed deeply and sighed on my neck, and I felt her shudder.

"Are you scared?" I said.

"Please don't get shot again. Please don't," she said quietly. She kissed my neck, and I tingled. Not like we were going to make love, but as if she loved me. We held each other for a while and breathed together.

"I feel happy," I said. "*That* doesn't happen very often."

She pushed into me a little harder, and I pushed back. Something was going on, but I didn't give it a name. I just gave it room.

She stepped back from me, keeping one hand on my waist, and said, "Well, good Lord, let's go inside." She put her hand on my forehead again as we walked inside and said, "You've got a fever. Did they let you out of the hospital with a fever?"

"I don't know if I had a fever or not. I just left," I said.

"Did they give you any medicine?"

"Pain pills. Antibiotics."

"Sit here," she said, holding onto my arm as I sat on the couch and dropped the crutches to the floor. She sat beside me, looking anxious and gentle, and said, "How do you feel?"

"I don't know. I feel so much," I said, smiling at her face so close to mine. "How was your retreat?"

"The retreat?" she said. "You just got out of the hospital after being shot. I think we should talk about that."

"No. It's probably a little scarier than a retreat operated by Catholic nuns. Unless the nuns had guns. Did they?"

"Doyle, you don't look well," she said, leaning a little closer to me and putting her fingertips on my cheek. It was wonderful, being touched by her. I couldn't tell her that, because maybe she didn't want it to be wonderful. Maybe she did. I had to find out.

"Did you figure anything out on your retreat?" I said.

"Doyle. You've got a fever. You've been *shot*. I'm worried about you."

"Well, good. And I'm worried about you," I said, putting my hand lightly on her shoulder.

"We can worry about me later."

"Let's worry about you now."

"Maybe I should call a doctor?" she asked. "You're pale. You're sweating."

"We can call a doctor in a little while. I just need to be with you now. I've missed you. I worried about you. I prayed for you. I don't care about my stupid goddamn fever. Okay . . . I care a little. But I mean . . ."

She put her hand over my mouth and smiled at me in a sad way and said, "At least let me get you something cold to drink, for your fever. Do you want iced tea? Water? Coke?"

"Beer."

"You can't mix beer and painkillers."

"Coke," I said.

She got up and walked to the kitchen.

"Don't leave," I said.

"I'll be right back," she said, sniggering at me.

I watched her get a can of Coke from the refrigerator and get a glass from the cupboard and pour the Coke in the glass, because it was wonderful to watch her do anything, to see her at all.

"I like to look at you," I said.

She stared at me briefly, stared straight into my eyes, and didn't say anything, like I'd just given her a secret and she was wondering what to do with it. She brought me the glass of cold Coke and I drank some as she sat next to me again, with her knee slightly touching mine. She sat sideways, looking at my face, being quiet and simply looking at me. I was starting to get an erection. One more thing I couldn't tell her.

She put her hand on my shoulder, touching my flesh through my shirt, and she said, "I guess I should tell you a little about the retreat."

"Yes."

"But I feel so stupid talking about that when you were *shot.*"

"Yeah, but that's over with. I can tell you about that later. I mean, basically someone shot me and I shot him back, or I shot someone. I didn't get his name, and he didn't ask mine. But the shooting's over. What I want to hear about now is you. I want to find out how *you* are. So please tell me how you are."

"I'm better," she said in a weary voice. "I didn't really decide anything. I went to the mountain. I didn't come back with any commandments or anything. No revelations. No talks with God or angels or ghosts, although sometimes I felt like a ghost, haunting myself, trying to remember where I'm supposed to be, or who I'm supposed to be. I think, you know, when part of your identity comes from another person, and you become part of that other person, and then they betray you and they're gone, it's like an actual part of you is gone with them. Part of you is suddenly missing, and you want it back, and it never will come back. And do you remember what I said to you in the letter about how this was like a death? I had a funeral."

"A funeral?"

She nodded her head. "There was a bird, a dead bird near a tree when I was out walking on a trail by myself. It was a little bird with beautiful yellow and black feathers, just lying near a big pine tree with its wings folded up, dead. It didn't look injured. I didn't see any wounds. It just looked like it stopped flying, like it had flown all it could and it just couldn't fly anymore and it died in the air, and dropped to the Earth, where I found it. I looked at the bird's yellow and black feathers still so brilliant in the sun, and it reminded me of everything dead in *me*, of everything flying along in me and just instantly dying."

She closed her eyes and breathed deeply, and I touched her cheek while she tried not to cry.

"And so, I had a funeral for us," she said. "I know it's stupid, but I did."

"It's not stupid. Tell me about it."

She touched my hand on her cheek and said, "I found an old limb on the ground and used it to dig through all the rotting pine needles and the ground near the bird, and I dug out a hole, maybe six inches deep, maybe a little deeper. I cried while I was digging. It seemed like all my emotions were trying to escape from me at the same time, and they just knocked me over, and I fell forward on my face on the ground and just trembled and cried with my face in the pine needles and my hands grabbing whatever weeds or flowers or pieces of bark were there, like I had to hold something, some*body*, and no one was there, just weeds and dirt and the Earth. And I held that, and I cried for a long time. I cried for the death of my marriage. I cried for everything that was ripped from me and stolen forever, like I'd just fallen from the sky right there in the dirt. And finally I couldn't cry anymore. It just stopped. It was enough. And I wiped the dirt and twigs and pine needles from my face and remembered I was supposed to be having a funeral. I put the little bird into her grave and covered her with dirt. I put a rock on the grave. I can't remember what I said. I prayed something. I thought I'd remember it forever, but I don't. I think what I prayed or said was . . ."

She was silent, and looked at me, thinking, and she said, "'I fell from the sky, dead, and just had my funeral. I guess I'll go take a shower and have dinner.'"

It didn't seem possible that she could be so serious and then so silly.

"Did you really say that?" I asked.

"No. That's just what I thought of now," she said. "But I did think that. Everything was so serious and sad, and I thought of how dirty I must've been from lying on my face on the ground, and so I thought that, no matter how awful everything was, and even if I didn't know what to do about it, I still needed a shower. Plus I was hungry."

"So you prayed: 'I fell from the sky, dead, and just had my funeral. I guess I'll go take a shower and have dinner'?" I asked.

She smiled at me. "I'm trying to make it sound better than it really was. But I'm fine, mostly. I think I'm just going to have to be depressed for a few weeks or months. I don't think you solve sadness. I think you just feel it, and it goes away when it wants to. So I didn't make any big or startling decisions on the retreat. I decided I get to hurt for a long time."

"I'll help you," I said.

"You'll help me hurt?"

"Well, no. I think you know how to do that."

She smiled and leaned against me and kissed my cheek. She put her arms across my chest and my back and held me. I felt warm and light, like her affection was radiating into me. I had an erection, a separate being in my pants with no sense of reason or timing, and I was grateful to have Natelle's flesh against mine, which I didn't think I should tell her. I always couldn't tell her what I needed most to say. I was going to, though.

"I love you," I said, waiting for her to rise up and pull away, to ask me to stop it, to tell me I was mistaken, to persuade me forever of the idiocy of my heart. But she didn't move, except to breathe, one of her breasts softly pushed against me. And she didn't say anything, a silence in which I imagined she was wondering how to keep me. Or if. Long ago in a secret moment that even *I* didn't know about, I gave myself to her, and waited to be taken in, or told why I never could be. It was like waiting for the world to begin, or to be told again that it would not.

Her face was against my neck and my chest, and she breathed on my skin. I wondered which sentence that was.

"I love you," she said quietly, and my stomach tingled, like she moved into me. "Don't think that's an offer," she said. "It's only a truth."

"What does *that* mean?" I said.

"You don't know?" she said.

"I don't know anything, until you tell me."

"It means no one can have me, now. But still I love you," she said, and lightly rubbed the flesh between my neck and shoulder.

" 'Now,' as in forever?" I asked.

"Now, as in *now*," she said. "On the retreat, I was afraid of you. I was afraid you were in love with me."

"I am."

"You're not supposed to be," she said.

"I didn't choose to be. It just happened. It's like being born. One day, there you are."

It was strange that we were that close, holding each other like lovers, and wondering how far apart we were supposed to be.

"I could leave you alone," I said experimentally.

"No, you couldn't," she said. "I think you wanted me almost the first time you saw me."

"That's true. But how would you know?"

"I didn't. I just tricked you into confessing it. But, also, I could tell by the way you looked at me. Whenever we talked, you always looked at me a second or two longer than was necessary, like you were wondering what to do about me."

"I still wonder that."

"Sometimes you stared into my eyes a little harder than

necessary, almost like you were hoping to enter me through my eyes. I didn't like it at first. I thought you were lascivious. But you always looked sadly away and moved on, like you were lost and belonged to no one, and you just went away. Not to any particular place. Just away. Sometimes you broke my heart when I looked at you. It wasn't that I felt sorry for you. I felt something far stronger than that, almost like I wasn't *supposed* to let you walk away. It scared me, that maybe I wanted you to look at me again, to see if I could enter you through your eyes. This was infidelity. Adultery of the heart. People make fun of that, but it's true. No matter who you're with, a lover or a husband, you can always be attracted to someone else. You can always find another person you want to spend the rest of your life with, until your life is a series of selections and betrayals. Maybe they should have that in the marriage vows—'To have and to hold until either of you finds someone better, which could be this afternoon.' So I resisted that, and Gabriel didn't. And then you die in your heart, still conscious, and watch your own death."

I moved my hands along her back, to try to soothe her, and just to feel her.

"I'm not even sure why people try to be monogamous," she said. "It sounds like a medical condition anyway. You have monogamy. Here . . . rub this cream on it."

I had to laugh. As sad as she was, she was suddenly being funny, the same way I did it, as an anesthetic against the world.

"The other choice is polygamy," she said, "which sounds like a geometric shape, like a polygon. So if you're a poly-game-ist . . . what's that word?"

"Poltergeist?" I said.

She started laughing and shook against me.

"So those are the three categories of marital love," she said.

"Monogamy, which requires an ointment; polygamy, which means you have three or more sides; and poltergeists, for which you need an exorcist. Maybe *that's* what I should tell the church. I don't want a divorce. I want an exorcism. But I don't know if the church considers marriage a form of demonic possession. Oh well," she said, and sighed on my neck and chest, which made me tingle and want to make love with her. But practically anything she did made me tingle and want to make love with her.

She rested her face on me again, and moved her arm away from me to scratch her leg, and when she moved her arm back to me again, the palm of her hand accidentally brushed across my erection. Now she knew. I wondered what she was thinking, as if it might be an offense for me to have an erection.

"Uh-oh. One of those," she said in a slightly amused and embarrassed voice. "Does this mean you're not thinking Platonic thoughts about me?"

"Well, I'm sure Plato had erections, too," I said. "He just didn't write a book about them."

She laughed, but that didn't mean we were safe from the taboo subject of sexual love that was always submerged between us; and not submerged anymore. I wondered if Natelle was aroused, if there was any fragrant wetness between her legs that, in a way, she wanted me to know about, and in a way, she didn't. For a few seconds, we didn't say anything, but just held each other in our intimate secrecy. And maybe it was love, but you couldn't just dumbly say so, like a child or a teenager blurting out every impulse and passion like an emotional music box. And if we *did* have it, it moved impatiently through us like souls we kept hidden, wondering first if they were real, wondering then if we should release them.

She released hers not long ago and was crushed.

Or you could crush yourself, like I did. You could conceal so many emotions so densely within yourself that one day they all fly out in a horrifying swirl. Then you go see a psychiatrist.

I didn't know what to say to Natelle. The last thing we'd spoken about was my penis. Plato's, actually.

"What're you thinking about?" Natelle said.

"Plato's penis," I said.

She made a quiet, sniggering sound against my chest, sort of like a repressed snort.

"You sound like a pig," I said.

She snorted again. "Like that? she asked gleefully.

"I get excited by women who snort," I said.

"Do you mean by women in general, or just by me?"

"Just by you."

She snorted. "Doyle?" she said.

"Yes?"

"I like to hold you."

"Then keep holding me," I said, touching my fingertips to her cheek.

"Do you want to make love with me?" she asked in a quiet and curious tone, not as if she were offering that or requesting it, but as if she just wanted to know.

"Yes," I said.

Almost nothing was secret now. It seemed like whoever said anything next would take us forward, or apart. I waited, staring at one of her eyelashes blinking near my fingers.

"The truth is, I'm wet," she said.

A tiny flash of joy or gratitude or something I couldn't name flashed through me. It was odd how she could say that to me so cryptically, and I knew she was announcing the symptoms of love. I felt lighter and warmer than ever.

It could have been bacteria, but I had to assume it was love.

"I don't know why I told you that," she said. "Except, well, you know," she said, pointing her hand at the expansive arch in my pants. "I thought since it was happening to you, you might as well know it was happening to me."

"I'm glad," I said. "Are you thinking about Plato?"

"No. Just you."

Again I didn't know what to say or do, or how to move or if to move, if I should stay exactly as I was or tilt her face toward mine and kiss her or wait for her to kiss me. Everything seemed immediately possible, and all of it beyond control. I was paralyzed by the joy of it.

"I'd like to go to bed with you now, but we shouldn't," Natelle said. "And do you know why?"

"Well, in case I don't, I'm assuming you do," I said.

"Because I'm still married."

"That's one reason. Do you have any more?"

"Yes. I'm in between lives right now. I'm throwing away the old one, and beginning the new one. You don't want to get mixed in there now, and risk being thrown away."

I wasn't sure what she meant, but I said, "No."

"I don't have very much hope left," she said. "Most of it's missing. I think it leaked out of me."

I put my hand on her cheek and said, "There's hope in my fingers. Can you feel it?"

"Yes. But you need more fingers than that."

I put my other hand on her face and said, "There."

"I think you need more fingers than *that*," she said.

"But those are all the ones I was born with."

"And I like your fingers, too," she said, and put her hand on one of mine and guided it down to the top of her breasts.

She sighed very deeply and said, "But we can't do this now," and she put my hand back on her cheek.

"My life is still being ruined," she said. "If we made love now, you'd be a part of that ruin. I'm afraid I wouldn't be able to distinguish you anymore from everything I'm trying to get rid of. It's like you'd be contaminated with all the death in me, and I can't let that happen. Do you understand?"

"Do you mean the words, or the sentences?" I said. I was either dizzy from what we were talking about, or dizzy from my fever.

"Are you all right?" she said, leaning back to look at my face. "Doyle . . . you're *white*."

"Caucasian, actually," I said.

"Are you going to pass out?" she said anxiously.

"No. Or at least not until you know this . . . not until you know . . . can you hear me? It sounds like I'm pretty far away from myself."

"I can hear you," she said, and kissed my cheek.

"I like that," I said.

"Not until what?" she said into my ear.

"I'm not going to pass out until you know that I'm not going to be a part of your ruin. Okay? I promise. I'll wait outside, as close by as possible. And then when you come out of the ruins, I'll dust you off and hold you, if you want me to. Because you know . . . I waited for you when you didn't even know I was waiting. I could still do that. I know how."

"Oh, Doyle," she said, and sighed on me, like she was breathing her life onto me. "I don't know how much of me there's going to be left to wait for. And I can't promise you anything. We might never be lovers. We might only be friends."

"Isn't life a goddamn mystery? And still I wait to see what

happens next," I said, smiling at her. It looked like she was going to cry, and instead she smiled.

She put her lips lightly against mine and just held them there. Maybe nothing more than a tenuous fondness that she'd later withdraw, although I decided it was a consecration that swelled inside me and made me feel she'd entered me. We made a pact, and the pact was us. I felt lighter and dizzier. It was ecstasy, love, and also bacteria. I had to push her face away, I was so dizzy, and I said, "Do you want to make love with me before I pass out?"

"Should I take you to a doctor?" Natelle said.

"I'd rather make love with you here."

"Why do you want me so badly?" she wondered.

"That's how I've always wanted you. Badly."

"How do you know you'll love me tomorrow?"

"If I'm not dead, I'll love you tomorrow."

"Don't talk like that."

"English is the only language I know."

She unbuttoned her blouse and took it off, staring into my eyes as she unfastened her pastel blue bra and pulled it off.

"I guess we're not going to the doctor," I said.

"No," she said. "Although you might need one when I'm through with you."

"I hope you're never through with me," I said as she stood up and took her pants off and slid her panties down her legs and onto the floor. She untied my shoelaces and took my shoes off, and unbuckled my belt, saying, "Are you still with me?"

"Present," I said, as the dizziness of love and bacteria swirled in my head, and Natelle unbuttoned and unzipped my pants and pulled them from me, revealing both my urgent erection and the unhappy-looking bandage on my leg.

"Are you sure this won't hurt?" Natelle asked, lightly putting her fingers on the bandage.

I put her hand on the ridge in my underwear and said, "There . . . *that* won't hurt."

Being careful not to bump my wound, Natelle kneeled over me on the couch and straddled my legs. Using one hand on my shoulder to steady herself, she used her other hand to guide me into the luscious warmth of her. She gasped as I slid into her.

"I love it when you say that," I said.

"I feel like you're floating into me," she said.

"Maybe I am," I said, home within her where it was peaceful and warm and dark as she squeezed tighter against me while my head drooped weakly onto her breasts, and I was so grateful for her as I passed out again.

ABOUT THE AUTHOR

John Welter began his writing career as a newspaper copy boy, buying cigarettes for the city editor. Since then he has worked as a reporter for newspapers in the Midwest and the South and published humor sketches in *The Atlantic*. His first book, *Begin to Exit Here: A Novel of the Wayward Press*, was widely praised and was selected by *Library Journal* as a "Word of Mouth" recommendation for 1991. He lives in North Carolina, where he writes a humor column for *The Chapel Hill Herald* and is a manager for a mail-order company. He has never been a Secret Service agent, but sometimes wears dark glasses.